# Follow the Rainbow

**R.R. Jaruhar** is the author of the critically acclaimed memoir *Railwayman* (Rupa Publications, 2020). Born in 1947 in Bihar, Jaruhar joined the elite Indian Railway Service of Engineers in 1968 and received numerous awards during a distinguished career of thirty-nine years. After retirement, he has been advising organizations like the World Bank and has chaired many expert committees constituted by the Indian government.

Jaruhar's perspective on life and relationships shines through in his writings. He lives in Gurugram with his wife Anubha.

Also by the same author

*Railwayman*

# Follow the Rainbow

R.R. Jaruhar

Published by
Rupa Publications India Pvt. Ltd 2022
7/16, Ansari Road, Daryaganj
New Delhi 110002

*Sales centres:*
Allahabad Bengaluru Chennai
Hyderabad Jaipur Kathmandu
Kolkata Mumbai

Copyright © R.R. Jaruhar 2022

All rights reserved.

No part of this publication may be reproduced, transmitted,
or stored in a retrieval system, in any form or by any means,
electronic, mechanical, photocopying, recording or otherwise,
without the prior permission of the publisher.

This is a work of fiction. Names, characters, places and incidents are
either the product of the author's imagination or are used fictitiously and
any resemblance to any actual person, living or dead,
events or locales is entirely coincidental.

ISBN: 978-93-5520-414-1

First impression 2022

10 9 8 7 6 5 4 3 2 1

The moral right of the author has been asserted.

Printed at HT Media Ltd, Greater Noida

This book is sold subject to the condition that it shall not, by way
of trade or otherwise, be lent, resold, hired out, or otherwise circulated,
without the publisher's prior consent, in any form of binding or
cover other than that in which it is published.

This book is dedicated to Shiv Baba,
who scripted it in its entirety.

# Contents

1. Maya's Daughter — 1
2. Transformation into Sahiba — 10
3. Great Gandak and Maya — 36
4. Sahiba — 86
5. Sahiba, the Princess — 119
6. Recuperation Abroad — 163
7. Sahiba Follows the Rainbow — 191
8. Sahiba Weds — 211
9. Sahiba, Bahu Ma — 224
10. Adieu — 231

*Climb every mountain,*
*Ford every stream,*
*Follow every rainbow,*
*Till you reach your dream.*

—'Sound of Music'

## One

## Maya's Daughter

January to March is the period of festivity in India. People from far-flung countries visit since the weather is amicable for hosting conferences and seminars with great pomp. Delhi, as usual, is a favourite locale and has the infrastructure to support it. Besides, it is the capital. All the government offices are located in the city, and so are some of the big institutions and research centres as well. So, getting a good number of participants is relatively easy.

With this purpose, I travelled from Washington, USA, in February to attend and participate in a seminar on Heavy Haul (HH) Railways, organized by the International Heavy Haul Association in Delhi. The Indian Railways had joined the International Heavy Haul Club recently with the introduction of heavy hauls in its system. This exercise had assumed greater significance because heavy hauls were introduced on a mixed traffic route, which carried both passengers and freight traffic. In other systems globally, heavy haul has always been introduced on dedicated freight routes. As a recognition of this feat, the two–yearly seminar of the association was being held in India. And rightly so, the Indian Railways was also a co-organizer of the event.

I had travelled with Nick—Nicholas Carlton—my Swedish colleague and project director at the World Bank in Washington. He was responsible for picking me for this

World Bank assignment as a Technical Consultant for the Heavy Haul project. At the time, I was lying loose, and had little to do. I remember I was in Jaipur in December for a holiday and wanted to visit the sand dunes. I don't remember the reason or understand my excitement.

I got a call from a friend of mine who said that the World Bank was keen to have me in their team. A representative, Nick, was in Delhi, and wanted a chat before he left for Washington. I agreed to drop my plan and I returned to Delhi the very next day. We met at the office.

At the end of a long chat, Nick asked me, 'Can you change the IR (Indian Railways) or help us change it?'

I answered carefully. 'Nobody can change anyone, not unless they want to change by themselves. That is for sure. But I believe I can present a mechanism or a scene that might make the change irresistible to them.'

'What do you mean?' Nick said.

'Suppose, I tell them that by reducing the weight of their freight wagon by simply two tonnes, their pay load capacity goes up by that much? They would certainly be interested, right? I can then tell them how it could be done. They would be compelled.'

'That sounds wonderful. We'd be interested in having you join us, Barun,' he said warmly. Nick has always been very fond of me. Although he is younger than me, we have always bonded well.

Soon after, he asked me to come for the HH seminar in Delhi. I had some other work and did not want to go, but he insisted, saying that I was the pioneer of their success in the heavy haul segment. I must go. Frankly speaking, I have never been fond of attending seminars. Apart from meeting old friends at the venue, I found nothing of interest. But this seminar was different; the World Bank was funding a project in India!

I knew that Nick sincerely wanted me to take a break and visit my country. His concern was subtle but it could not go unnoticed. So, I agreed to come.

## II

I didn't like cross-Atlantic flights; they were long, boring and tiring. But with Nick keeping me company, I was engaged. He was a wonderful conversationalist. After dinner, he started to talk about work.

'You were the pioneer of HH (heavy haul operations) in the Indian Railways. Why was it so important?'

'Look, Nick,' I said, 'we had to increase the train load in terms of the tonnage it carried. From 3,600 tonnes to 5,400 tonnes meant going up to 1.5 times the existing train load. So instead of running three trains, you could do with two! That saves line capacity, rolling stocks and manpower. The productivity improves by more than 35 per cent.'

'But other countries have introduced it much earlier.'

'Yes, they have. First thing, you want to have something when you need it the most. Necessity is the mother of invention, you know.'

Nick laughed and said, 'Many do say that what the Indian Railways achieved was like picking a hanging fruit, already placed to eat.'

'I too have heard this quip from friends at the World Bank. Their team has studied this project. They had interviewed me also, but I do not know why the World Bank did not produce a report. Otherwise, I would have replied to it suitably.'

Nick laughed and said, 'I too do not know why the World Bank did not produce a report. I find that Harvard, the IIMs and even the Indian School of Business (ISB) did produce a report on it. But anyway, what would have been your reply?'

'Have you heard the story of the Pandavas who were lost in exile and thirsty? They saw a beautiful lake. They wanted to have their fill to quench the thirst but they couldn't.'

'I have heard of the Mahabharata. Five brothers, right? Yudhishthira was the eldest and wisest among them.'

'That's it. As soon as one of the brothers reached the lake to take some water, a deity arose and told them that unless they answered his question, they could not drink from his lake. If they insisted, they would die. None listened, and all four of them—except Yudhishthira—lost their lives trying to drink the water without bothering to answer the question of the deity.'

'What happened then?'

'Yudhishthira arrived and the deity asked his question. "Tell me, what is the greatest wonder?" the deity said. Yudhishthira said that if he replied, the deity would have to restore the lives of his brothers again. The deity agreed.'

'And his answer?'

'Yudhishthira said, "Everyday people see that the one who is born must die, and still people desire to live longer—isn't that the greatest wonder?" The deity smiled and bestowed life to his dead brothers.

So, you see. Water was available aplenty, but none could touch the water unless he answered the riddle. The fruits were low hanging, weren't they? But for the last twenty-five years, no one could pluck it simply because they did not know the answer to the question.'

Nick smiled warmly. 'What was the question?'

I answered with a smirk. 'The question: why is it that the HH was on existing tracks everywhere, but not in India?

This nobody could answer. In sheer frustration, one wrote that not an ounce could be added to the existing axle load. The answer was that they were pursuing a wrong formula, a flawed understanding of a simple fact and the fruits remained on the branch.'

'That is very interesting indeed. So, what was the answer?'

'Very simple. I dared to ask what others did not. The design fellow was using an outdated formula. He was asked to change to a modern formula. We decided to conduct tests to determine the correct value.'

'Oh!'

'Same for the bridges. The existing calculation showed the bridges were overstressed by 200 per cent. If HH loading was added it could go up to 260 per cent. I asked that with 200 per cent overstressing, bridges should have broken down by now. No bridge had shown any distress signal. So, I said that bridges do not lie. If they are fine there were only two possibilities—one either so much of loading was not coming actually on them or there were some incorrect assumptions in the design or calculation, or both.

So, the answer was to discard the old formula and go for actual load testing and revise our calculations based on the actual results.'

Nick laughed and said, 'It is a real breakthrough and I wonder why the World Bank could not catch the story. But Barun, no doubt you are only one of your kind.'

Having said this, Nick had turned—perhaps to sleep. I was looking out of the window and wondering how big a turnaround had come for the Indian Railways. But there was no time to dwell upon that. So, I followed Nick and went to sleep.

## III
## The Seminar: Meeting Sahiba

The seminar was held at the Le Meridian Hotel in Delhi, which has wonderful seminar facilities. Luckily, the organizers had put me up in the same hotel. So, it was all very convenient.

I had been requested to help with this seminar in many ways. I had to go through the papers submitted for the seminar, selecting the ones to be included, considering papers from different regions and countries. I had to ensure that all the regions and sub-continents were represented. It was a tall order. I tried to do justice to it. In the end, I was satisfied because the selected papers were relevant to the theme. I was also asked to chair two of the sessions besides being in a team that would select the best presentation, which would be awarded during the valedictory ceremony. Reno, or Reynold Cooper from the Canadian Railways, was my teammate for this purpose. Reno was a wonderful person.

As the session continued, it got very hectic. I tried my best as Reno regaled me with his never-ending anecdotes. On the second day, I had two sessions and a paper selection meeting with the officials of the association.

Lunch at these seminars is always a treat, providing a sumptuous fill for all palates. I finished the main course and eagerly headed towards the dessert section. There was a splendid display of all kinds of sweet treats. I searched for something purely Indian, perhaps if I were lucky, of Bengali origin. As I stood watching, a young lady walked towards me with a vivacious look and a captivating smile. She seemed to be from the event management team.

Politely, she said, 'Sir, come with me. I know you like the kesar payas.'

I agreed. I did indeed enjoy kheer.

'I knew you would like it. In fact, I was waiting for you to come here.'

I was a little surprised. 'That is kind of you. But I don't know you. How did you know that I like this particular dish? And how do you know me?'

She didn't answer, and guided me to the dessert. She kept smiling softly, with a glint of mischief in her eyes. But I was not sure of it.

'I am Barun De from the World Bank,' I said, introducing myself.

'Dr Barun De. I closely followed your seminar. I was swept off my feet by your incisive treatment and command of the subject.'

'Well, thank you so much. I am very impressed that you followed a technical session like this. You are a member of the event management team, I suppose?'

'Yes, Sir. Your name was familiar to me, so once I learned that you were here, I followed the session keenly. Sir, why don't you sit down and enjoy the dish?'

I was pleasantly surprised. As I moved towards the empty chair indicated by her, I asked again how she knew of me.

'Sir, you know Maya?'

'Maya? Which Maya?'

'Maya, Sir. Do you remember meeting her in Bagaha, while doing the Gandak Bridge?'

She was still smiling, but I felt as if I was hit by a thunderbolt. Bending halfway to sit, I stood up and looked straight into her eyes and said, 'Maya from Tharu village? Of course, I know her. So, well. How could I not? I remember everything about her. But...'

I was almost shaking. But the lady elegantly looked on with a smile on her face, as if she were the quiz master with all the answers.

'Maya,' she finally said, 'used to talk about you, but I did not know you. I remembered your name though. So, as an event team manager, I was going through the schedule of this seminar. I was struck by your name, Dr Barun De. I knew you as Barun De, you did not have the doctorate title then. It also mentioned that you were coming from America... so, I was not very sure. But I took a chance. I am so glad that I did.'

She was right. I had obtained the doctoral degree later on. I did not like to be addressed as Dr Barun De. But some people still addressed me with the title, it was unavoidable. But suddenly, a realization struck me like a bolt of lightning. I had not taken my eyes off her for a moment.

I slowly said, 'I never knew that Maya would talk about me, but I am happy that she did... Now, don't tell me you are her daughter?'

She took a step and came closer to me, her smile still intact. Then came the final blow, almost in a whisper.

'Yes sir. Of course, I am her daughter.'

I felt as if I had lost my senses. I sat down in the chair, holding her hand, wanting her to sit by my side.

'Oh my god! You are Maya's daughter? How are you here? What are you doing here in Delhi?'

For the first time, there was a quiver in her voice, and her eyes suddenly grew moist. She sat down beside me. 'Yes, I am indeed Maya's daughter. I am a qualified team event official and I cover many seminars. That is what I am doing here'.

'Tell me your name dear.'

'I am Sahiba, Sahiba Deb.'

My memories were blurry. I asked, 'If I remember correctly, Maya had once introduced a small girl to me as her daughter. Her name, if I recollect, was Payoli. Are you her?'

'I am her only daughter. I was called Payoli then, I was maybe five or six years old. I do not have a very clear memory of you. But your name is so familiar in our household. My name has been changed to Sahiba now.'

This was astonishing. For a while, I was dumbfounded, struck by utter disbelief.

'Look, Payoli—Sahiba, you were a small girl when I had met you. You used to follow your mother around, holding her sari at the worksite in Gandak. You were a village girl who had never left the village.

I see you today with a different name. You've become a modern, elegant woman from a girl wearing a frock. You speak in English with confidence in your eyes. My dear, it is too much for me ... but the look in your eyes certainly reminds me of the mischievous, shy gaze of the child Payoli. It is a great transformation. I cannot believe I am holding the hands of Maya's daughter. You know I have to chair the next session. It starts in fifteen minutes. I must leave to regain my composure ... then chair ... the session.'

I added quickly, 'The seminar ends at about 4.30 p.m. I am going back to the US tomorrow. So, I will find you after 5 p.m. I'm staying here, in this hotel. I shall pick you up from here and we can talk. We could sit down in the lounge, but too many people here know me. So, if you have no objection we can go to my room and talk with ease.'

She laughed easily. Her joy was difficult to miss and my confounded disbelief was written all over my face.

'No worry, Sir.'

There was still that quaint mischief in her eyes.

*Two*

# Transformation into Sahiba

The next session was to start in ten minutes. I had to compose myself. I needed to think about the topic of the session. There were four papers: one from China, one from Brazil, one from Australia and, of course, one from India. The Chinese presentations are usually difficult without an interpreter, but as the session started I was soon in command. The session lasted till 4.05 p.m. Then, there was the valedictory function. As usual, it was a session for thanksgiving and to welcome everyone (in advance) to the next biannual session in Sydney. That was the end.

The seminar officially lasted three days, but the last day was meant for tours and sightseeing. So, for most of us, the valedictory function marked the conclusion.

I took some time to meet and bid farewell to many of my friends. Some young participants also wanted to meet me. But all said and done, I was ultimately free within twenty minutes. I then headed straight towards the reception counter, where Sahiba was supposed to be waiting for me.

I found her chatting with a young lady, with her back turned towards me. As I approached her, the other lady gestured to Sahiba. She instantly turned towards me with a beaming smile.

'Sahiba, I am sorry I kept you waiting. I had to meet many people after the seminar. It was very difficult to get away. It is criminal to keep such a comely lady waiting, I know.'

'No, Sir. I saw that you were busy. I can understand that. But Sir, meet my friend, colleague and flatmate, Shruti—Shruti Shirodkar from Nagpur.'

Shruti was a tall, slim and elegant lady with beautiful eyes. As she looked towards me, I could see that she had a warm smile as well.

I met her warmly. 'Shruti, it is nice to meet you. All of you have done a wonderful job holding the seminar,' I said.

'It is my pleasure and honour to meet a celebrity like you. I thank Sahiba for that. She has been continuously talking about you. She says that the way you held her hand, she felt paternal protection and affection. I thank you, Sir.' Shruti said.

Shruti told me that her parents were in Bhopal, although she belonged to Nagpur. I saw Sahiba blushing as Shruti talked about her. There was that same spark—an unmistakable spark of Payoli—as I gathered my memories.

As I was talking, I felt a faint tap on my shoulders. I turned to find Nick looking very benevolently at me. 'Sorry if I have disturbed you, Barun. I just wanted to tell you what a fabulous job you did at the seminar. You know I am leaving tonight for Paris. I will join you in the office in Washington on Monday.'

'Come, Nick. Just see whom I have met. This is Sahiba. I knew her mother, Maya, so well. She was a young girl then. I am meeting her after twenty years. The best part is that she found me! Nick, you know, I nearly fainted. And that is Shruti, her friend and colleague. Ladies, meet Nick. Nicholas Carlton is my boss at the World Bank and a Project Director.'

Nick spoke with them in his usual jovial manner and with great warmth. 'I am so glad to meet you, Sahiba, now that

I know you can make Barun loose his senses. But, whatever, he showed no sign of it while conducting the session. My God, twenty years.'

Soon, Nick remembered that he had to hurry and left.

Shruti picked up the conversation again. She wanted to know how Sahiba would get back home later, as she was leaving for Bhopal. I told the girls not to worry. My office car would drop her home.

After that, we walked towards our room. She walked so gracefully. I wondered how a village girl had transformed into such an accomplished lady. Maya had told me that no woman from her community had ever left their village. Even after their marriages, they stayed on. Only the men folk moved, and that too only sometimes. So, I was curious about the transformation. On reaching the room, I signalled towards a sofa and told Sahiba to sit down. I took a seat opposite to Sahiba.

'Sahiba, so here we are. We will order dinner from the hotel's room service, and something to drink, if you wish? We can relax and talk. I am going away tomorrow by an afternoon flight. Actually, I have to come back to Delhi after a couple of months and perhaps, I may have to stay in Delhi for a couple of years. They have fixed an apartment for my stay. I was supposed to see it this evening. But I have already cancelled it. I can get out early tomorrow morning and have a look at the place before going to the airport.'

She was listening in rapt attention and nodded in agreement. We ordered for some light dinner to be served at 8.30 p.m. and some soft drinks, and then we gave the staff instructions not to disturb us. It was almost 6 p.m.

Then, I settled down to hear what Sahiba had to say.

## II
## Sahiba's tale

Sahiba spoke very softly and clearly. 'You know, Sir. I was only five or six years old when I met you, with my mother. Maya has always been far-sighted in the village—she had to be as the undisputed leader of the clan. It was a matriarchal society after all.

Maya told me that "Barun Sir" had left for a new post, and he had left without meeting her. I thought she was saddened by it but I didn't pay much attention back then. Then one day, she told me that you had asked her to educate Payoli, her daughter. She also told me that this was impossible in that village. "I have to find a way to do this. Barun Sir is an angel and if he said these things about you, it must be with purpose. I have no definite vision of what that could be like—maybe you'll turn out to be a real princess after proper education."

I had, of course, told Maya once about the power and virtue of proper education. I wanted the so-called socio-economic changes due to the Gandak Project to continue, especially by influencing the young kids. It was desirable, if not essential. And that meant proper and good education, which was the key to change. I had said this with conviction, but had been unable to provide a ladder to achieve this goal. So, it was a mere wish at that time. But I was surprised to learn that Maya had taken such serious note of it.

Sahiba continued with a faraway look in her eyes. From my hotel room, the light of Lutyens Delhi's lit her face. It reflected her childhood days. 'Look Sir, I don't know but this idea had seized Maya a great deal.

Once, we had finished our dinner, my father spoke to her. His voice was always low and respectful when he spoke to my mother. "You have earned some good money now, Debi. Save it now for Payoli's wedding," he had said. Maya had rebuked him sharply, "Payoli's wedding? Are you crazy? She is so young, you know. How has the thought of her wedding come to your mind?"

Any other time, my father would have said no more. He usually kept silent when Maya raised her voice. It was a sign of acknowledging her authority, perhaps. But on this occasion he continued, "Villagers are saying that Payoli is coming of age fast. You remember, Payoli had performed at the function to felicitate Barun Babu. She looked like a woman. That makes people talk."

Maya gave him a stunned look and said nothing. That encouraged him. He said, "The blacksmith's son looks good, we might keep him in mind."

My mother got angry and said: "And what will the good blacksmith's son do? Run the hearth and make some iron utensils and sell them at the Friday Market in Bagaha? Look, stop talking of such things. Don't listen to useless things."

I said that I had never heard her talk about her husband. And I did not know if Maya addressed her husband that way.

'Yes, in our village no woman would talk of their husband. The husband was always addressed as the Adami, never by their name. I do not know my father's name, but he certainly loved me. He looked after me with a lot of care. I don't remember playing with him. But I think he said all this out of concern for me. I do not remember him talking so much to my mother until then. Sir, do you remember the function that was held in our village to honour you?'

'Yes, of course I do. I thought it was your mother's idea. I was hesitant at first, but I went there with Giri and Himangshu, our Deputy Chief Engineers. I saw you in a typical tribal attire, dancing in peacock plumes. You looked very smart.

Maya seemed particularly proud of you.'

'Yes, she used to pride herself on whatever I did. We rehearsed a lot for the performance. It was there I learnt how much you liked kesar payas.'

'How?'

'Maya told me that she had to prepare kesar payas for you because it was your favourite dish. She prepared it with a lot of care. She was so happy when you liked it. You had said that you hadn't tasted such a delicious dish before.'

'Oh, the cat is finally out of the bag. So, you remembered it for twenty long years! Even without knowing me well! You are great, Sahiba.'

She just grinned and continued, 'But from that day onwards, my mother would look very serious indeed. I never realized it at that time.'

One day, she said, "Payoli, we have to think about it seriously. Better it is done sooner. People talking like this can't be stopped. They might force our hand because it concerns the community. But don't worry. We will succeed." I did not know what she had in mind. She had warned me sternly never to say a word about it to anyone. But I never worried, because I knew how resourceful and determined she was.'

Sahiba suddenly asked, 'Sir, did you know, Maya could speak good Bangla?'

'Yes, I came to know about it accidentally. Maya used to come to our guest house whenever I was there for work. She would often walk into the kitchen. It was here she saw the payas being cooked. Our cook told her that I liked it very much. She learnt the recipe from him and must have improved upon it. When I had finished eating the sweet, she had suddenly said in Bangla—how was the preparation? I was astonished.

I asked her where she had learnt to speak the language.

Bagaha was never a Bengali area. I wondered if any Bengali family had resided there. She had smiled and said that she had learnt it from her mother. "Our great grandmother had learnt it from her governess—who was a Bengali lady from a royal family in Cooch Behar. She had advised our great grandmother to learn a foreign language and soon it was settled that Bangla would be the ideal option. And since then, this trait has been running in our family. Every mother has taught her daughter this language." I remember her sharing about her family history with me.'

Adding to what Barun had just said, Sahiba then shared her version. 'Maya said that she had learnt it that way and that she wanted to surprise you, Sir.'

I asked Sahiba whether she had learnt Bangla.

'Yes, I did. But it was not very good at that time. Of course, I became quite fluent later on. My mother has never told me about our ancestors, except once when she briefly mentioned that we belonged to a royal family from Rajasthan. So, I don't know how she had picked up the language.'

'Well, well that is another heart-stopping story. Maya had told us. That is how our respect for her rose so high. If she has not told you, I can. But for now, tell me about your story.'

She said, 'I have also no particular memory of any marriages in the village because I was very small then. I had seen some simple ones. The bride was usually young—not more than ten or twelve years old; her husband was always much older. This used to be a simple affair with some dances and feasts. The husband was older, but he was always subservient to the wife. But anyway, my mother was definitely scared. She was also apprehensive.

'One day, she told me, "Come, Payoli. We are going to the Friday Market in Bagaha. I shall also buy you a new dress." The thought of a new dress elated me. Maya packed something in a small bundle and so we were off on a bicycle. Maya riding and I on the pillion. She bought a good frock for me.

Then her rakhi brother, Suraj, met her. He asked her to follow him. Suraj, with his men, would often come to Maya. She tied rakhis on their wrists and called them her brothers. She would often say that her rakhi brothers had promised to help her, whenever she needed it.

'So, we followed him and reached a small bungalow outside the town. Sister Jane was waiting for us. Suraj introduced us to her. Then he pleaded. Maya was her sister and he had pledged all help to her.

Sister Jane smiled and welcomed us warmly. She said that Mother Grace had asked her to reach out and help us. She said we need not worry at all and that they would take Payoli under their care.'

'I remember that Maya kneeled down and told her in Bangla, "Didimoni, Payoli is a piece of my heart. It is so difficult to part with her. But her future here is bleak. I want her to be a worthy person, a princess." Then she held my hands and put them in Sister Jane's hands. She told me, "My child you go with her. A bright future awaits you. Remember the words of Barun Sir: never cry." Mother had told me never to cry, come what may. Then she gave a small bundle to Sister Jane and whispered something in her ears. She smiled and nodded. Suraj said that he had made all the arrangements for them to travel by train that night. So there was nothing to worry at all.

'My mother sat down by my side. She took my face in her hands and kissed me on the forehead. I put my small arms around her and nodded. It meant that I would follow her instructions. Then my mother got up quickly, held her brother's hand and swiftly walked out of the room. She never looked back at me. That was the last time I saw Maya.'

## III
## Sahiba travels to Darjeeling

'Suraj had made all the arrangements. I learnt much later that Maya had approached him for help. Suraj was an influential person with political connections. Maya had convinced him that I must be taken out secretly from the village to a faraway place to receive proper education. Maya had convinced him that I was doomed in the village. I would be married off to the blacksmith's son. She said it was my last chance to get away. I had to go to a distant place, where no one was likely to trace me.

'Suraj had found Christian missionaries in Darjeeling. They were willing to accommodate a tribal girl. He had persuaded them, citing special circumstances to the authorities and they had agreed to send someone to take charge of the girl from Bagaha and bring her to Darjeeling. Suraj was devoted to Maya, but he was also in awe of your words, Sir. He had spoken highly of you at the function and was keen to help.

'Moving out secretly from Bagaha was key. The train was scheduled to depart around 7.30 p.m. Suraj wanted to ensure that nobody saw me travelling to the station. So, he took us two stations beyond Bagaha and helped us board the train. He had given us enough food and fruits for our journey. Sister Jane embraced and comforted me. Although I was not crying, I did feel a strange void. Nobody other than Maya had until then held me in embrace. But it was warm and comforting.

'I had never been on a train before. The bicycle was the only transport I was used to. So, it was strange how the train moved, rattling and whistling as it moved during the night. Soon, I fell asleep in Sister Jane's arms. I did not know where we were going back then. But somehow, it never worried me as well. I just slept in the comforting arms of Sister Jane.'

'It was about 11 p.m. when Sister Jane gently woke me up. She said that we had to get down at Muzaffarpur and change trains. I had never heard of the station. She took us to the ladies' waiting room where we met two other sisters who had come to see us. They had also brought some food. They looked at me lovingly.

The train arrived and we boarded it. Reservations were made in the train, so we got a berth to sleep. This train was a fast one and did not rattle badly. Sister Jane made me lie down and then she seated herself beside me till the time I fell asleep again. When I woke up in the morning, I found Sister Jane still sitting by my side. I asked her, "Sister, why didn't you sleep? Did you keep on sitting like this?" She smiled and held my face in both her hands. "No, I slept for some time, but I kept checking if you were safe. I was worried because it was your first train journey. You should not get scared for some reason in your sleep." I felt her loving warmth surround me and moved into her arms again.

'She said that we would reach New Jalpaiguri in about an hour. I was to freshen up in the train. She took me to the washroom; back then I did not know how to use it. I was amused by the facilities. And soon, we arrived at the station where a car had been sent by the missionaries to take us to the convent.

I still did not know where I was going. As we sat in the car, Sister Jane said she was feeling relieved and relaxed as we had almost reached our final destination. "I am sure you will like the place Payoli. So, enjoy the ride to Darjeeling, take in the breathtaking views as we climb high up the mountain. It will be cold. But I have brought a shawl for you."

This was the first that I heard that we were going to Darjeeling. And it must have been far away from our village because it had taken so much travel.'

'The road journey was indeed breathtaking. I loved the sights: the misty heights of the mountains as we winded up the hilly road. Sister Jane slept through it. I thought she must have been tired because she had stayed awake to keep watch over me. After a good five-hour drive, we reached the church building. Sister Jane also woke with a start. She seemed delighted.'

'We had reached St. Joseph's Convent, where they lived. The imposing gothic style structure of the church was in front of me with its steep spires. A huge gate opened for us. We entered it, passing under the portal, where I was destined to spend many years of my life.'

## IV
## Sahiba in St. Joseph's Convent

'The car dropped us inside the premises of St. Joseph's Convent. Then, we walked down to the main entrance. I was in awe. We were met at the entrance by another Sister, Georgia, who told us that Mother was waiting for us in her room. Soon, we were there in front of her door.

Sister Jane knocked and we entered. Mother Grace was a tall person. She rose from her chair to welcome us with open arms. Sister Jane bent to greet her. I did not know what to do. I sort of folded my hands in the form of a namaste. Nobody had taught me how to greet or pay respect to a person from a religious order. But I did give her a broad smile. The Mother came up to me and patted on my head, showing great affection.

She said, "Sister Jane, you have done a wonderful job bringing this little one from such a faraway place. I was a bit worried, but thank God, you have accomplished a difficult mission. I understand the mother was worried. I pray to the

## Transformation into Sahiba

Lord that he gives us the power to look after such a cute little girl. Now, Sister Jane, you must be tired after this long, arduous journey. Sister Georgia will surely take care of this girl now. She will surely make her comfortable. Did Payoli have any problem on the way?"

Sister Jane said, "No, Mother. She is such a fine and cute girl. She never cried. She never asked me where we were going. She felt very cozy in my arms and soon fell asleep. There was no bother at all Mother."

"It is so good to hear about such a brave little girl. Now you must go. We will see her tomorrow morning around 10 a.m. okay?"

Sister Jane again bent to greet the Mother; she came forward to kiss her fingers. Seeing Sister Jane, I also bent to greet the Reverend Mother. She smiled warmly and kissed my forehead. Then we left slowly, closing the door behind us.

Sister Georgia was waiting outside. She held my hand. Sister Jane again kissed me. She told me to go with Sister Georgia, who would provide me with all the help I would need to settle down. She told me that she would also come down at night to see me.

Sister Georgia then took me to a big room. Three girls were already there and they said meek hellos. Sister took me to the washroom and helped me again, washing me down. Then she gave me a new dress and a sweater. I remember feeling refreshed.

'She brought me to my bed, which was already made. There was a blanket. She said that the table and chair was for my use. She said they would provide me with other essentials. The dinner bell would ring in forty-five minutes or so, and these friends and roommates would bring me to the dining hall. Then, she left.

My three companions came over and started talking to me

in Bangla. My Bangla was poor but I managed. I learnt their names. Reema, Poonam and Mary. They had already been there for about six months and all of them were orphans. They were very surprised to learn that my parents were alive and that my mother had sent me to the convent. They were also surprised that I had not cried or wailed at all. They said they would cry a lot in the beginning.

'I did not ask their age, but they were my peers. Mary had come from Siliguri. Poonam had come from Malda and Reema from Jalpaiguri. I did not recognize the names of all these places. When I told them that I had come from Bagaha, a faraway place, they had no idea either. We were soon comfortable with each other and they reassured me about the place.

'As the bell rang for dinner, they took me out to the dining hall, where other Sisters were seated. They told us to sit down. They said we would have to say grace before the dinner. All of them bowed down in some kind of a prayer, which I was not aware of. So, I followed the others and bowed my head. The dinner was good, but everyone ate in silence that night. After dinner ended, everyone thanked god for the food again.

'I must have slept soundly that night. As far as I can remember, it was Poonam who woke me up in the morning. Sister Georgia was there too. I got up. Sister told me to say good morning to all; this was my first lesson. She helped me to the washroom and gave me a toothbrush. I hadn't used a toothbrush before. But I was a quick learner. Sister Georgia told me to get dressed for the breakfast, after which we would head to an assembly. Thereafter, I would have to meet Mother Grace in her office. She helped me dress, combed my hair and made me put on my sweater. I did not have any shoes. Sister Jane had provided me with some old slippers. Although they were ill-fitting, they served the purpose for the time being.

After breakfast, we were taken for the assembly in the central courtyard. A parable was narrated and we were told to be good children. Frankly speaking, I had not heard much of "god" in our village. Now I was being told about Christianity and Christ. Totally unheard of. It was quite mystical for me. We did not have regular prayers. There was no concept of dressing for an occasion like this. It was very solemn. But it did fill me with a lot reverence for that someone named god.'

'Sister Jane was also at Mother Grace's office. There, the Mother greeted me again with warmth and asked both of us to sit down. Then, she looked towards me lovingly and said, "My child, Sister Jane has told me everything about you and your mother, Maya. Your mother's wish is for you to become an accomplished, well-educated person, so you may live a purposeful life. She has made a lot of sacrifices by sending you away to Darjeeling, fearing that her community might not allow you to have a proper education. I also learnt that your ancestors belonged to a royal family. The princess—your great grandmother—had to run away to this faraway place to save her honour." The Mother paused. I nodded because this was what Maya had told me as well.

After the pause, Mother Grace said, "My child, do not worry. You have come to the House of the Lord. He will take good care of you. There is a convent school where you will begin your learning. The Sisters will help you with your classes and teach you manners. Be obedient and follow them. Your mother has given me a bundle to give to you later, which we will keep safe till you are ready.

The Mother resumed, "This place follows the religious order of Christianity. You do not seem to belong to any religion. I do not insist ... but you can choose to accept Christianity as your religion. It will provide you with emotional stability."

I nodded. Religion had so far meant nothing to me. But perhaps, by being of the same religion as others in the convent, I would be more comfortable. The Mother was happy. She said that the priest would formally induct me in a simple ceremony. She said that she was sure I would be very happy in life.

Then she looked towards Sister Jane, "You know we have to change your name here. It is first for your safety, so that nobody can trace you. Secondly, as you start a new life in the Christian order, it is good to have a new name. So, we will christen you Sahiba. Is that good, Sister Jane?" Sister Jane nodded and said, "So, Payoli now we call you Sahiba. Isn't it a lovely name?"

Mother Grace smiled and said, "And it is a royal name too."

'Everybody laughed. I also started smiling. A new religion and a new name! The Mother said that Sister Georgia would take me to the market for shoes and other essentials. "Please enjoy. The Lord has ordained you a new life of promise," she said. She then rose from her chair and came around me to kiss on my forehead again.

'We left Mother's room excited. Sister Jane told me that vacations were on at the school. Regular sessions would begin in a fortnight. This free time would help me prepare for the session. She said that Sister Georgia would take me to the market after lunch and help me with the stuff I needed. Actually, I did not know what I would need. For example, in our village, a comb was something to be shared by all. But here, everyone was supposed to have her own comb. But I persevered.

'Sister Georgia took me to the market after lunch. Darjeeling had a good market. Lots of merchandise on display. I got a pair of leather shoes for class, sports shoes for games, socks, stockings, school uniforms and a jacket with St. Joseph's Convent School monogrammed on the pocket. I was so happy to have so many clothes. I had never seen such things being bought for my personal use before.

'We came back home—I had to call the church my new home now—and I had a new religion, a new name and a range of new outfits. Everything was new. In the rush of novelty, I soon forgot about my past. I did think of my mother. I missed her touch, her admiration. There was a void, which I was unable to describe as a child. But it all went by in a rush.

During the next fifteen days, before the school reopened after the vacation, I was taught about numbers and alphabets in English. I was given lessons in correct conduct and prayer. I acquired habits. I soon found myself transformed. I still used Bangla for conversation but was soon initiated to speak in English as well. I also realized that I enjoyed playing sports.

'The school reopened as scheduled. For the first time, I sat in a classroom. There were other students from the city as well. Not all were from the church. I was easy-going, and quickly had many friends. I paid attention and did well in my classes. Days and years passed, and soon, I was a senior student.

'I cannot imagine how much I would have missed out on if Maya had not taken your advice so seriously. Sister Jane was very proud of me, but scared. She would say that I had blossomed and I needed to be careful. I never understood what she meant until I passed the Senior School Certificate Exam with good grades.

'Sister Jane had told me to join the local college for graduation. It was a co-educational institution. Once I was there, boys started paying attention to me. I then realized the import of Sister Jane's observations. I was very careful. I was determined to fulfil my mother's desires and acquire a good education first. Maya had sacrificed so much. I, therefore, was determined that I had no time for such affairs. I remember my graduation. Sister gave me a beautiful sari to wear for the convocation function. Sister Jane, who loved me like a friend, told me I looked gorgeous.

'Yes, I realized that I was working to become a princess, just as Maya had said before our parting. I learnt music. I played the piano rather well. I joined the choir in the church and learnt Rabindra Sangeet. In the college, I participated in all extra-curricular activities, even theatre. My portrayal of Desdemona from *Othello* was often talked about. They said that it was a portrayal with extreme passion. The entire audience had been spellbound.

'The church kept me busy. There were a lot of things to be done. I was always a willing participant. They really loved me and I, them. I owed my change to them. I volunteered to teach in school and I really enjoyed it.

I had, by all means, blossomed and grown into a comely woman. But I still thought there was more to be achieved. St. Joseph's Convent had put me on a pedestal, but I still had to launch myself. It meant that I should move outside Darjeeling. I never thought that leaving this home would ever be necessary. But my future beckoned me.

We discussed it in the church. The view was that I should go to obtain a Business Management degree, which would be the most befitting. The thought of leaving was really unnerving, but the Lord solved this problem too in a masterstroke. The mother used to say, "Lord always opens a window when the door is closed."

## V
## Sahiba moves out of the Convent

Mother Grace called me to her office one day. Sister Jane was also with us. I had, by then, learnt all the protocol associated with meeting the Mother. I knocked and entered her room and bowed down to her in profound reverence. She rose from her chair and came up to me. She took me in her embrace. Then, she made me sit on the chair. She looked at me intently, without speaking a word.

Finally, she smiled and said softly, 'Sahiba, my child, I am so glad to see you come alive. I still look for the tiny girl. Now you have done so well. We are so proud of you. I thank the Lord who assigned us the task of developing and grooming you into a lady. You have done so well. I must congratulate you, my dear.'

'It was an emotional moment. I did not know what to say. But I gathered myself and thanked her. "I owe every bit of what I have achieved to you, the Lord and the entire family. I was a destitute whom you embraced. Apart from providing me with all material comforts, you have given me emotional support. My mother had taught me never to cry. But my heart is full and my eyes are full with tears today. Whatever I have done here was with a mission to push me forward. Mother, forgive me if I have erred. You taught us the virtue of purity in thought, deed and mind. I cannot thank you enough, Mother." I did not cry but my emotions welled up in my eyes. I choked. Mother came around and put her arms around me.

Mother said, "I realize that you have to climb higher still. Life is all mountains after mountains. Your goal is still higher. As much as I would have liked it, it is not possible to grow in Darjeeling. Sister Jane has told me that you wish to go for a

Business Management Programme. That seems good. There are two places—one is in Calcutta and another in Delhi. But as I understand, Delhi has much better opportunities. Delhi should be your next destination. That is what the Lord also seems to will. We will still provide you whatever material support we can. But it will be better to earn your way to the programme. This will also give you confidence."

Mother continued, "When you had come here and accepted Christianity eagerly, I thought you would become a nun. But seeing your accomplishments, we realize that you have greater heights to reach. Before you go out into this world, know that you may not find many things congenial. But have faith in Him and you will not take any wrong step. That is our belief. But be careful, and know that this place will always remain your home. Whenever you wish to return, its doors are always open for you, my child."

Then she rose from her chair and went to the almirah and opened it. She took out the small bundle Maya had given to Sister Jane. Mother placed it before me saying, "We have not opened it so far because your mother had told Sister Jane to give it to you when you had grown up. You are going to leave us in pursuit of higher education. So, it is time you have it. You can open it now." Then with a sigh, she added, "Bless her soul, my lord." I was so feeble that I could not understand what the Mother meant.

I opened the bundle with shaking hands. Inside it was an engraved silver necklace and a beaded chain with a small pendant at the centre. I immediately recognized them—they were royal pieces. The silver necklace was a royal insignia. I had seen it with Maya. The beaded chain was a piece for protection. Having come of age, I was going out into the world, alone, leaving the protection of the church behind. I would need this protection. The authority of the necklace granted me the sovereignty of the royal state. I did not know the meaning of all this when I had seen them with my mother. Now, with the knowledge I had, I could understand the significance.

My mother was very far-sighted. She had realized that I was the heir and had entrusted this to Mother Grace. But I remembered two beaded chains with my mother, but I couldn't be sure. Anyway, Mother was happy that the invaluable piece had been passed on to their rightful owner. Then, suddenly, it occurred to me. I asked her, "Mother tell me have you heard from or received any messages from my mother?"

'Mother looked far away and told me softly, "Suraj once sent a message through someone. Your mother Maya is no more. She died of a snake bite. That was five years ago. I, of course, never told you. There was nothing we could do."

'I was stunned. Blank. We had physically separated about fifteen years ago but there was an unknown bond. It appeared that the time had suddenly erased it.

'Then Mother Grace came towards me and held my hands. She told me, "My child, one last thing. Your mother gave you your name, Sahiba. She had told Sister Jane that you should be called by this name. It is our practice to change the name once someone becomes a resident of the convent, but we thought Sahiba was a good name and so we christened you."

'I did not know about this. I was stunned all over again. Mother told me that Sister Jane would take care of me. That signalled the end of meeting. I bowed down to her in reverence once again when we parted. I came out of her room, tightly holding on to the treasure handed over to me.

'Sister Jane was helpful. She gave me some useful references and arranged for my travel to Delhi. She also made arrangements for my accommodation at the Young

Women Christian Association (YWCA) in Delhi. Then she gave me ₹5,000. I remember, I cried then.'

## VI
### Sahiba in Delhi

I took a train from New Jalpaiguri. Someone had come to help me board the train. It was my second train journey and it would be a long one, all the way to Delhi. I reached Delhi in the morning after thirty-six hours of travel, and managed to make it to the YWCA located in central Delhi without any problem.

After settling down, my immediate job was to find some source of income so that I could sustain myself. Luckily, an event management agency took me. I had the reference provided by the St. Joseph's Convent. My accommodation for a month was also free of charge. I had obtained details of local business schools in Delhi. I applied and luckily, I was selected for a three-year course meant for working persons like me. I don't know, but everything kept rolling out fine. It was as if the Lord was himself taking care of everything.

My session was to start after six months. This gave me time to pick up the event management job. I had earned good credentials for it. I was trained for a month. I met Shruti and we soon grew close. She already had rented an apartment in Vasant Kunj. She very kindly invited me to join her. I couldn't have asked for more.

The event management job mostly required me to be in Delhi or around, so there was no problem handling it. Shruti was already working there and I was assigned to her team. She is a fine person. The business management course started, and I found it all so interesting. The first semester was hectic but thereafter, I settled down comfortably.

Like Mother Grace had wanted, I was able to sustain myself and carry on with the curriculum. I am in my last semester now. After that the institution will arrange a suitable placement for me. God willing, I should reach my goal.'

Sahiba had reached the end of her narration. She looked towards me with long lost affection, tired and glad that she was able to tell her tale.

I said, "I am sorry to know Maya is no more. In any case, you have conducted yourself in a splendid manner. I am totally overwhelmed, Sahiba, by the spirit and zeal with which you brought yourself to this position. Bravo!'

She just smiled and said, 'Barun, I am intrigued about Maya's death. A snake bite! I haven't ever heard of someone dying of a snake bite in the jungle. It's fishy.'

She again said, 'You know, Barun, I can imagine a bit of the furor she might have had to face after handing over me to Sister Jane. Everyone must have probably asked her where she had left her young daughter. Although she wielded a lot of authority in the clan, it couldn't have been easy on her. I can also imagine someone accusing her of selling me off!'

I told her, 'There is no use fretting about it now that she is no more. I have heard that she used to walk to the Narayani temple late in the evening. So, anything could have happened. Tell me, Sahiba, you often address her as Maya. Not as your mother. Any particular reason?'

She laughed and said, 'Right from my childhood, I used to call her Maya. Others called her Maya as well. And she liked that I called her by her name. She would often say that calling her Maa could make me feel dependent and weak. So, Maya is fine as an address. You cannot be dependent upon me.'

'Ah, that is why you call me Barun now, not Barun Sir,' I said mischievously.

'Oh! Barun! It wasn't on purpose. I'm just carried away. You now know how your advice to Maya became a mission for her. She ultimately left me with this, "Barun Sir is not an ordinary mortal." For us, you are like God. Have you heard anyone calling you God, Sir?' She said with utmost ease.

Dinner had arrived before I could answer. She dutifully said grace and then we ate in silence. Kesar payas had been ordered for dessert. Sahiba must have ordered it without my knowledge. She smiled encouragingly and I thanked her.

After the dinner, once the empty plates were cleared, I caught Sahiba by the shoulders and asked, 'Do you know the name of your great grandmother who escaped from her royal state?'

She looked blank and shook her head. 'No, I don't think Maya ever told me and I also never asked.'

I looked into her eyes and slowly said, 'It was Sahiba.'

Sahiba was taken aback. She sat down, holding her head, looking at me in disbelief. 'Oh my God! Is it true, Barun?'

'You see, Sahiba. Maya had known you'd escape captivity too. From the life of a poor girl to a life of liberty. That is why she christened you Sahiba, the name of your great grandmother, whose great escape was a success. Your escape was daring and courageous. So, it is very symbolic and apt.'

She looked in bewilderment and was unable to say anything. Then, I said, 'And the treasure handed over to you by Mother Grace when you stepped out into the outer world was again a symbol of royalty.'

Then from my bag I took out the beaded chain with the pendant. I placed it before her and said, 'Is this the second piece you were referring to?'

She snatched it from my hand and held it before the light. She jumped in joy and said, 'Yes, Barun. This is the one! Have you had it all this while? How did you get it?'

'Maya had once given me a small box. She told me to take it home and keep it with me. It would keep me safe. Apparently, it is what Sahiba had put on before she escaped from her castle.'

She was amazed. She looked at me in deep astonishment and said, 'Barun, is it possible that Maya wanted me to wear one chain while she gave you another for the same reason?'

'Maybe, Sahiba. Don't you see that one chain was worn by Sahiba, your great grandmother, while the other one was worn by Sham Sher Singh,' I said.

'Sham Sher Singh?'

'He was your great grandmother's companion, her manservant with whom she had escaped. It is a long story, which Maya had told us. Maybe she would have told you too once you'd grown up. I am sure. But I will tell you this story someday soon. Not today, but as soon as we meet again.'

Sahiba held my hands and asked, 'But tell me, what happened to Sham Sher Singh?'

'In the end, when they finally reached the forest of Bagaha, Sahiba married Sham Sher Singh.'

'Oh my god. Is that why women hold such authority? Because of my great grandmother? My head is reeling.'

She spoke with a queer smile, 'Barun, don't you see? God or Vidhata has sent us a clear message? It is a message that the two of us are here together now. We are inextricably united. Your advice to Maya became a mission for her. She set me on this course of escape, the same undertaken by my great grandmother. You too are, in a different incarnation, to lead me to my final destiny. I am sure of that. Otherwise, how could I have found you? Can you tell me that?'

'I don't know. I can tell you one thing. It is time for you to go to your apartment. Come, I shall drop you.'

'I can go with the driver. You have to leave early.'

'There will be no argument about this.'

I called the driver and I escorted Sahiba to the car. On the way to her apartment, I said, 'I am leaving tomorrow, but I have to see the apartment they have fixed for me before I leave. I don't know but if you do not have anything else to do, you can join me tomorrow. We can spend some time together before I depart. The car will drop you back to your apartment.'

'That would be wonderful. Tell me, what time will you come to pick me up?'

'Around 8.30 a.m. if it is convenient?' I said.

'That is fine,' she said.

I dropped her off and returned to the hotel. I quickly packed my things. I did not want to waste any time in the morning. I had told the reception desk that I would be checking out by 8 a.m. tomorrow.

It was very difficult to sleep. Sahiba's words kept me awake. I felt sucked into a vortex of events. She was perhaps correct. God was sending a message. Otherwise, it was very difficult to imagine how things so far apart moved towards each other in such a quick sequence. All trying to put two characters—Sahiba and Barun—in inseparable union. What was the purpose or meaning of this? Only God knew. All of us are actors in a grand drama. All have a unique role to play, a pre-ordained script to follow. Sleep under these circumstances was a difficult proposition.

After a night of broken sleep, I got up in time. I would try to make up for it during the long flight. I had breakfast, checked for my things and was in the car to pick up Sahiba. Traffic was mercifully light.

Sahiba was waiting for me. She looked gorgeous in a light blue sari. She joined me and we drove away. I couldn't stop myself from gazing at her. I could also locate a tinge of missing sleep in her eyes. But apart from that, she was as magnificent as she had been yesterday.

She smiled and said, 'Yesterday, I was wearing a uniform. This is my own sari. I like this blue. It reflects a flight through the blue sky.'

I smiled.

Upon reaching the location, we were showed the house with great enthusiasm. It was a newly built house and well located. The apartment was huge with three rooms. Sahiba was enthused by the apartment. She told me about décor in a giddy manner. Although it was well furnished, the broker told us that any change "madam" wanted could be made without any problem. We just smiled. Having agreed that the place was indeed ideal, we left for the airport. We held our hands on the way, saying nothing for some time.

I said, 'According to the current plan, I shall return here in two months. I'll let you know.'

'Barun, my semester too ends by March. Our event management company is organizing a show on Assamese textiles in Guwahati for the Bihu festival. It is a two- or three-day affair. I have plans to visit the Kaziranga National Park with a friend there. I too should be back by the end of April. Yes, in between all that, I also need to see about the placement...'

'Kaziranga is nice. You should not bother too much about your placements. Just see, and don't be in a hurry. When I am back, and I think Nick will also be there, we will try organize something good for you, okay?' I promised.

It was time for me to go into the airport. I held her hand again for the last time and turned away. She stood there for a long time. Her eyes were moist because I saw her gently wiping her face with her sari before she boarded the car.

*Three*

# Great Gandak and Maya

I was already late for my flight. Fortunately, there were no crowds. The business class counter was empty. I had only one piece of baggage to check in. With my UN passport, the immigration proceeding and the security check was speedily done. I decided against going to the business lounge and instead headed straight towards the designated boarding gate. Within half an hour, boarding was announced. I boarded and was given a comfortable seat. American Airlines did not boast of being a top-class service provider but I found that in business class, they had made some welcome arrangements to help passengers relax.

My intention was to settle down quickly, have lunch and sleep. They would be serving lunch soon; there was no question of sleeping before that. I cursed myself when Nick told me that he planned to return via Paris. Travelling alone in a long transatlantic flight was not very welcome. I wish Nick had listened when I'd said he should meet our Indian counterparts in Delhi itself. But Nick believed that every team member needed to be taken into account. He was very democratic about such things.

But my thoughts turned to Sahiba.

Everything had turned out for the good after all. Had a meeting been fixed in Delhi, I could not have found time for Sahiba. So, many heart-warming events had taken place in the past twenty-four hours. I needed the time to be alone. So far, I had just listened to her story; I had not had the time to reflect. But I had a long flight all to myself!

The Great Gandak came back into focus after so many years. Had I not taken this project, there would be no Maya, no Sahiba! I needed to go back in time. Think over the events of twenty years past. It was not going to be easy.

Sahiba was now at the centre stage. It was necessary for her to know this part of the story—my part. She did not know how I had come into their lives. Maya should have told her. She had said nothing about her great grandmother's escape from the princely state to Bagaha. But in all fairness, Sahiba could not be deprived of this tale. Maya was now no more. As it stood, only I could tell Sahiba about it. But... I was going to be away for about two months; Sahiba would be busy in Delhi trying to finish her last semester.

Sahiba was right. God was definitely trying to convey a message.

As I was trying to figure out how I could communicate with Sahiba, the air hostess arrived to enquire about my lunch preferences. I picked something vegetarian, hoping the airlines could deliver it. After a quiet meal, I started to feel sleepy. Mercifully, lunch had taken my mind away from Sahiba. I turned and finally closed my eyes.

It turned out to be a fairly good nap, and a sorely needed one as well. I had some papers to prepare for the meeting on Monday. I asked for some tea and was quite busy delving through them.

No thought of Sahiba came or haunted me. Whenever I was working, I could reasonably dispose of other distractions. It was a discipline I had learnt early in my life and I was really thankful for it.

The flight landed in the evening, almost in time. I was

back in my apartment in Washington DC for dinner.

Then Sahiba called. She wanted to enquire if I had reached safely. It was a pleasant call, full of warmth. She said, 'Barun, I already miss you. I think, I should have travelled with you. This would have lent our meeting some continuity.'

'You're crazy, Sahiba. You have an exam; how could you have travelled all the way?'

'Don't worry about my examination. In the worst case, I would have skipped it, and then taken it again in the next semester. You are right, Barun, I have become crazy. And I am not sorry for that.'

'If you are crazy, that is fine. But don't make me crazy, you know.'

'I can't help it Barun. Your arrival has been a whirlwind. Without you, I would have been comfortable grazing cows or being busy in the field. Without you I would not have set out to carve a lofty future for myself,' she said almost laughing.

'You'd have been happily married to the blacksmith's son,' I teased.

'Don't be mean, Barun. Getting married, after all, was not a bad idea. It may have been better than dying as an old dame.'

'I am sorry. But Sahiba, don't be disheartened. Wait for prince charming. He must be on the way,' I said.

We stopped after that. But it occurred to me that the question of marriage may be looming on her mind. I too thought about these things. God must have considered it as well.

## II
### Recalling the Gandak Project

I remained busy the entire week. But when alone, I often thought about what I could say if asked about the Gandak

Project. So far, what I had talked or written about Gandak was all technical or managerial. The construction of the bridge. That was the main theme. Writing about Maya in the context of Gandak was totally different. Remembering things after twenty years was not easy either. But after a lot of thought, I was able to conceive a canvas—the episode of Maya could be painted on it; and the landscape of Gandak could be on the background.

I had heard of the Great Gandak before I went there. But I did not have any particular idea about the river from the point of view of an engineer. The people of the area wanted a bridge to be constructed over the river Gandak. The government announced the construction of the bridge with immediate effect. Board members posted me there to work as the Chief Engineer of the project. I had protested against it. But I was told that I had to go. I was told that I was the only one who could handle a turbulent river like Gandak.

It left me fuming, but I soon realized that this was the price to pay for being an expert. After two days, I was in Gorakhpur to take charge of the project as its Chief Engineer.

## III
### The Great Gandak

I had not worked on this Zonal Railway. I did not know many people. And, I soon realized that I was not welcome here. I was given relatively junior and inexperienced staff as lieutenants. I welcomed them; it was easier to mould the newer people who accepted my leadership.

The Gandak River descended from the upper reaches of the Himalayas, bound by the Dhaulagiri mountain range in the west and the Manna range on the east. Seven streams, known as Sapt Gandaki, joined lower down to form the Great

Gandak. It entered through a deep gorge in Nepal, over which a barrage had been built as part of a cooperation policy between India and Nepal. It then moved into the plains of India. The river is known as Narayani or Saligrami in Nepal. The river, after hitting the plains, acquired a width of over 8 km near the bridge site. One could not see its other bank. On the right or west bank is the state of Uttar Pradesh (UP) and on the east is Bihar.

The river had to be tamed—its width had to be brought down to 3 km so that the bridge could be constructed. This was a great challenge which had defied solutions for more than fifty years.

## IV
## The Bridge the British had Built

The left bank of the Gandak is very fertile. It has a thick forest cover and is famous for its good agricultural produce. In order to harness the agricultural and forest wealth, the British constructed a railway line, connecting Chitauni in UP to Motihari in Bihar. Motihari was a district headquarter of the Champaran district of Bihar. The line had a bridge over the Gandak River. This proved to be a vital link between the two states. The British also had an eye towards military strategy, wanting to provide a rail link in the Terai region of the Himalayas, with Nepal in the north. It proved to be a very popular rail link.

Motihari is famously mentioned in the Indian history of freedom struggle. Mahatma Gandhi, after his successful campaign in South Africa, had just returned to India and visited Motihari in response to a distress call from the region's Indigo farmers. The British landlord, who owned an Indigo plantation, exploited the local farmers. The farmers were debt-ridden, and they had been conscripted into bonded labour. In Motihari, Mahatma Gandhi tried his experiment of non-violence for the first time in India. The local people rose against the atrocities committed by the British landlord.

The local government asked Mahatma Gandhi to leave the district, but he refused. He was arrested and produced in the district court the next day. A huge number of people gathered to peacefully protest against the arrest of Gandhi. The local government was shaken.

The judge asked Gandhi to furnish a bond of ₹100 before he could be released. Gandhi refused. He requested that the court take notice of the injustice and atrocities committed on the poor farmers instead of arresting him. He said that the court was in the wrong; they were shooting the messenger instead of taking cognizance of the crime. The judge was forced to release him without any bond.

The government also acted swiftly to discipline the Indigo landlords. They were forced to pay the farmers their legitimate dues. It was a sensational victory. Non-violent protest or Satyagraha had been implemented in the country. This started a new chapter in the struggle for Indian independence.

Gandak River had continued to drift westward, threatening the west bank. The rail bridge had ultimately washed down in 1924. The collapse of the bridge had disrupted the popular rail link between the two states. People of the area were also devasted by the frequent floods.

It was decided that a bridge would be constructed, which would also tame the river. But there was no technical solution available. It was presumed that a suitable person who had been entrusted with the construction efforts would be able to find a solution.

That is how I was sent in.

## V
## The Bridge Site and its Challenges

I had no real idea of the nature or the size of the problem. With my two deputies, Himangshu and Giri, I reached the west end of the river. Not able to see the other bank of the river, we crossed the channels by boat. We had to walk 9 km to reach the other end.

On that day, we traversed within the dense forests of Madanpur, a designated tiger reserve. This area was also infamous for dacoits who kidnapped people for ransom. The sun was setting and my deputies were growing quite nervous. They wanted us to get out of the area before sunset. Before getting out, we prayed to the goddess of Gandak at the Narayani temple. And by the time the sun started setting, we were already out of the forest area.

We returned to Valmikinagar. A barrage had been built over the Gandak River, half of it in Nepal and the rest in India. In a moonlit night, the river flowing through a deep gorge presented a wonderful and majestic view.

After spending the night there, we returned to Gorakhpur via the west bank of the river.

We now had a holistic view of the river. We also knew the problems and issues.

I had the experience to tackle the technical issues. But I also wanted my two deputies to understand and grow under me. Hence, we discussed all the plans in detail. There were several technical and administrative problems. But I was confident that they could be solved.

The most difficult issue was that of dacoits. There was a danger that people would be abducted, and its impact on the project was neither known nor appreciated. Additional police arrangement was no guarantee for safety; people could still be targeted. Even a single case of kidnapping could cause extreme panic, and each of the workers could flee and desert the working area. It was extremely necessary to prevent such an incident. We had to create an atmosphere of security and confidence so that people could work day and night without any fear. I spoke to every official in the district, and others at higher levels. I tried to explain all this to the authorities.

## VI
### The Project and its Stakeholders

We had several adversaries in the office itself. But despite that we were able to resolve all design and other technical issues. We had also fixed up a good agency to undertake the work. We were riding on a wave of success, well set to commence field work. The only problem, which had remained unresolved, was still the threat posed by the dacoits.

Steps to provide security in the area had been taken. The police of UP and Bihar had joined forces to lead a joint campaign. But I knew that was not enough to drive away the fears and apprehensions of the workers in the field.

We did not know how many dacoits were operating in the area.

Once, while we were trying to search the source and origin of a particular stream, we entered the deep forest. I was with Giri, and a few other locals who were helping us find the way. Enquiring, searching and moving along, we came across a hut. A few people were sitting outside, basking under the winter sun. We got down from the jeep. Without sparing a second thought, I walked towards them. They were perhaps alarmed by my khaki hat, as I saw them moving to stand up.

Without waiting for Giri to join me, I started asking them about the origin of the stream. One of them tried to say something but Giri gently pulled me away and thanked them. He hurried us back to the jeep. I was annoyed with Giri. I thought we should have questioned them further to gain information. But without saying anything, I sat down in the jeep. Giri drove back rather fast. I was perplexed and asked him what he was doing. He kept a finger on his lips, signalling for me to be silent. After driving for ten minutes, we were far from that place. Then, he stopped the jeep and turned to me. He said, 'Sir, we have narrowly escaped.'

I still did not realize what had actually happened and was rather annoyed with him.

'What happened?' I asked.

'Sir, perhaps you did not observe it. When you moved ahead to speak, I was suspicious. Why were there so many people sitting leisurely in the morning? Local men are generally busy with work at this time of the day. Some of them were drinking milk, which is quite strange. Then, I saw that you were talking to them. As I got closer to the hut, I glanced through the open door. I saw AK-47 rifles neatly lined against the wall. I'm quite sure that we had accidently reached the headquarters of a group of dacoits.'

'Oh my god! We had literally walked into their den!'

'Sir, upon seeing you in that khaki hat, and emerging from a government jeep, they too were alarmed. They did not expect to be disturbed. So, I pulled you out. I wanted to get out of that place as soon as possible.'

That had been a close encounter. I was lucky to have escaped. Had they known who we were, they would have taken us as hostages and demanded a hefty ransom in exchange. This brought the real problem to the front.

Contracts had been awarded. I had warned all the participating contractors about the reality of the problem posed by these dacoits. I had told them that I had made all possible police arrangements. It was still necessary to do something from our side to ward off the danger. I was not sure of a possible solution. When the contractor finally reported at the site, I renewed my earlier warning.

Then, it struck me. The real problem at the core was money for sustenance. We had seen the dacoits living in the jungle in a thatched roof hutment. It was, therefore, clear that they did not live a life of luxury or wealth. It was just enough money to keep their life going. I did not know if they had families to support. There were not many opportunities available in the area for them to earn an honest living. They must have resorted to violent ways to earn money. This was the socio-economic reality that no one had addressed. I was convinced that it was the real malady. If we could somehow address it, a breakthrough was possible.

But it was easier said than done.

A chief engineer of a project—a government officer—could not be involved in such an exercise. Any indiscretion, and it could turn out to be a booming scandal. Therefore, we had to tread very cautiously.

I first shared this with Giri.

He turned towards me with a broad grin. 'Sir, believe me. I too was thinking along the same lines.'

'Some telepathy Giri, I must say. It is now your idea and I have the honour to support or sponsor it. I think the correct role for me in this affair should simply be of one who says yes, or looks after the interest of both sides,' I said smiling.

'What do you mean by two sides, Sir? I thought there was only one side.'

'No, No. Look at it like this. These guys are to give up their present business under a promise of proper or adequate returns. The other guy is the contractor. He has the contract in his hand. He has to fulfil the promise made to them. It will be a service contract between the two of them. While the service contract is underway, there could be some differences. We don't know, but it is bound to happen. Who will resolve it? You are the first level adjudicator. And I shall be the ultimate and final adjudicator. Both the parties will have to respect the adjudicators. Higher the level, the greater the respect. It will work to douse or mitigate differences, if any.'

'Sir, you have thought through it all.'

'Now it is necessary to insulate yourself from the entire affair until it seems to be materializing. You have a local sub-contractor. He should be keen to have peace at the work site. It is for him to survey the area to find out the size and strength of the group. Secondly, I abhor hufta or periodical payments, or any kind of protection money. I am really interested if these people are ready to join as a stakeholder, as a genuine participant. They should understand that it would give them the much-needed honour from society. We want them to join as beneficiaries, reaping some of the benefits as a result of the economic development taking place in the area.'

'I agree with you, Sir.'

'After he has done the legwork, you can join as a good Samaritan. Your role is to bring some kind of sovereign guarantee for the scheme. We have to keep a low profile as far as possible. Keenness must be shown by the contractor. We should be seen as helping them along. You know, our detractors will see this as their final weapon to defeat us. So, if they get wind of it, they are sure to play spoilsport. You have to be very careful and cautious,' I asserted.

That was the general strategy. The local contractor was, of course, very keen. He had some local contacts in the area too. He moved very carefully. Word was sent to the local dacoits. This was a golden opportunity for them to get a share of the benefits accruing from the project. For this, they would have to eschew violence. They would have to sincerely help the project. Word also went around that the Chief Engineer of the project was honest, genuinely desirous of helping the local population. The message was simple: the project could prove to be a golden hen, which could yield them golden eggs. But if they used violence, the hen would be killed and nobody would get anything.

That evoked a lot of interest from the dacoits. The real issue was their compensation. If they could be compensated following honest means, then why would they refuse? From our side, we needed to know the size of the cake, and then try to make an offer that was irresistible. It was a tricky affair. We kept silent and waited for their response. We did not want to show that we were too eager or desperate for the deal.

Once they had realized that there was good money, it was for them to formulate their response. From our side, it was made crystal clear that unless all of them cooperated, the hen would go away. That was true as well, we were not posted here permanently after all. If the project could not be done for any reason, all of us would simply go away. So, it was in their interest to ensure the safety of the golden hen. This was clear to them.

We, therefore, waited patiently. Meanwhile, the local contractor was able to get some more information about them. It was found that the main group was led by Suraj. There were around ten or twelve men in his group, all of whom had control over the area. He also found that the abduction business had greatly declined. Firstly, there was greater vigilance by the police. Secondly, people in the area had become more cautious. That meant that their income from the abduction business was on the decline, which meant that our chances of success were better. Finally, word came. Suraj was ready to discuss terms. The local contractor first checked the genuineness of the people coming to meet. After that, Giri was prepared to hold a conference.

Their leader was a bit apprehensive. He came to meet around 5 p.m. along with two of his men. Giri was an easy person to talk to—he had a special quality of making people feel at ease. Giri listened to both the contractor and the dacoits. Suraj said that they did not have any skills for the work; they were only familiar with guns. He wanted to know what work they could do. Then, he seemed a bit afraid, noting the presence of a police post nearby. He said that they did not know any business or accounting, etc.

After listening to him, Giri asked, 'Can you organize trucks, supply them? Can you supply sand and gravel from the river bed upstream? Can you arrange and bring labour to do some work? No major accounting is needed to do this. You have your other members who can do the supervision.'

He replied that he could. These were simple jobs. Then he asked how much they would earn. Giri in turn asked Suraj how much he earned from their usual business.

The leader of the dacoits was visibly put off by that question. After all, it was no mystery that the core of the problem still lay in not being able to find a stable income. Suraj exaggerated their income. He said that they earned over ₹50,000 per month. The contractor, however, pointed out that the abduction business was declining and very few cases were being reported in the area. Given all this, ₹50,000 seemed to be wishful thinking.

Giri interjected and assured him. They could be earning up to ₹1 lakh per week. If they worked hard and did well, their compensation would rise.

Suraj was surprised. He started discussing the income with his men. Giri looked at the contractor and asked him if it was possible, and the contractor agreed.

Then Giri asked him, 'Can you pay them by cheque?' That too was agreed upon.

Then, Giri turned to Suraj, the leader of the group. He said that if Suraj and his men agreed, he would have to get an account opened in his name in Bagaha. That was the first step. Suraj nodded.

Then Giri said, 'Friends, all this is under one condition. There won't be any case of abduction in this entire area. There won't be any criminal activity either. No gun or any firearm will be allowed at the project site. You will work like any other common man. When I say there won't be any case of abduction, it means none whatsoever. You cannot say that it was a handiwork of someone else. For us, it is your collective responsibility to make sure of this.

In the course of work, if there is any difficulty or dispute with the contractor, you will not use force but will come to me. If you are not satisfied with me, you are free to appeal to the Chief Engineer. We all respect him a great deal for his kindness and fair play. Whatever he decides will be final and binding over both the parties.'

Suraj agreed loudly and said that he had heard about the Chief Engineer. He and his men would certainly abide by his decision, if it came to pass. He told Giri that with him in-charge, there would not be any occasion to complain. He went on to say that they had turned to a life of crime due to circumstances. Now god had given them a chance to mend their ways and return to the civilized society. On behalf of his men, he pledged their support and promised to abide by the agreed upon terms from that moment.

This was a breakthrough!

However, we were guarded. We ensured that nothing of the deal would ever be known to anyone else. We did not want someone to sabotage our efforts. I discussed it secretly, and also stressed that the men had to be given some latitude in the beginning because they did not know the work. However, quality had to be maintained as well.

We had to bear in mind that they were on the path of rehabilitation, and were doing so for our sake. Genuine mistakes were bound to happen. We had to be firm but tolerant. We also had to remember that we were not reformers. Our efforts could lead to their social transformation or rehabilitation, but we would not stand guarantee to that. Our exercise was limited to ensuring that they also gained from the socio-economic benefits accruing out of the project. And in return, they had agreed to participate in the project as a stakeholder in a civilized manner to avail those benefits. For this, it was essential that the project ran in an orderly manner. The distinction was very fine and subtle and I wanted my team members to appreciate it.

## VII
### Plunging in and a Bajrang Dal Special

We started work after the monsoons. We succeeded in commencing the efforts despite technical issues and my young team gained a great deal of experience in the process.

The news flew around that work was going on at a high speed. News also reached our bosses in Gorakhpur and they were taken by surprise. All of them wanted to come and witness the colossal operations on the field.

They were welcomed when they arrived. They were surprised that work went on round the clock, especially in such a dangerous area. Earlier, it had been unthinkable that one would set foot in the area after sunset. But instead, they found people working in the jungles without any qualms or police protection. They asked what had happened, where the dacoits were. Were we not afraid of them?

My response was simple: 'Our fellows are courageous. I too have often walked alone through the area. The dacoits, I am sure, they are just being very kind to us.' The bosses thought they were being snubbed, but they could do nothing but compliment the team. Our secret was well kept.

The most important job before the onset of monsoon was to undertake slope protection work. Since this was manual work, we could entrust it to the dacoits-turned-associates. We called them the Bajrang Dal—after all, they were a special force. I told my team that they had proved their worth. This work too could be entrusted to them and it would give them an opportunity to earn more and share a sense of responsibility.

The group was quite resourceful. Whenever a demand was made for urgent labour or local material, they were sure to arrange it. This aspect enhanced their reliability. Sometimes, there was an oversight or two. Once, they brought sand and gravel from the river bed upstream without proper forest challans. We explained that without official papers, this would be theft, which we could not allow. Soon after, they made sure to regularize the transactions on paper.

Our insistence on these formalities amused them initially. Suraj was used to breaking the law at will. He did not think it would be amiss if he procured something without paying any taxes. But he now had to tell the officials that they wanted supply with challans. He might have found it a bit embarrassing, but to his credit, he understood how to be law-abiding.

This incident was a small matter, but for him and his men, it was an important lesson requiring them to change their outlook and approach. Their old habits had to change. They willingly and dutifully did so. It spoke of their determination. I, for one, was very pleased. I considered it a good battle to win.

I rarely had the opportunity to interact with them. I left

it to the ingenious skills of the local contractor and to Giri, who closely supervised them. I was working at the site and they knew me. I had explained to Giri that I should be called to listen only as a third umpire or a final adjudicator.

In short, the Bajrang Dal had become a special force—very effective and valuable. This was what was expected of them. So, when additional reinforcement was required for pitching work or for turfing, they immediately responded.

Suraj told me that he could bring over Tharu tribal labourers—mostly women—as well; we then discussed it internally. The contractor said that he had heard about them. But the women would be inexperienced.

Experienced men were, however, not available, even at a higher wage. Under the circumstances, the locals had to be put to task. If the women were trained and guided in the beginning, they might pick up the work.

More importantly, these tribal women were conversant with the area. They deserved the benefits too. Besides imparting skills to the village people, we would provide an opportunity for them to gain from the project. They would become rightful stakeholders of the area, likely to be proud of their contributions.

From all these standpoints, it was a good idea. They had to be paid the prevalent daily wage, which was ₹80 per day. They would be transported to and from their village.

Bajrang Dal was told to bring about forty to fifty willing women from the Tharu tribes on a trial basis.

## VIII
### Maya enters

The first batch of Tharu laboures arrived from Tharu village, not very far from the site. They were divided into two groups.

The first was engaged in laying stone over a layer of sand and filter. They were trained. The second batch was engaged in putting grass in pods over the face of the embankment slopes. This needed some technical skill, but was simple to teach. Both the groups picked up the work in a short period of time and were industrious about it. Everyone was quite satisfied with their performance.

After about ten days of work or so, I was walking around the site to inspect their progress. As I walked along, a woman followed me. She reached out to me. I stopped to face her. Before me stood a woman of athletic built, not very tall but fair. She seemed elegant. She faced me and said apologetically, 'You are the Chief Engineer Sir?'

'Yes, I am. Tell me, how can I help you?'

'Sir, we are poor and ignorant. All the people here are from my village. My name is Maya. I represent all of them. Sir, for the first time, we have come out to work outside our village. Sir, we have heard you are very kind and helpful. Actually, we are not at all conversant with matters of money. I thought you could help and explain it to me.'

I was very impressed by her forthright statement, and surprised to hear that they were not conversant with money. So, I looked straight into her eyes. She looked at me without any fear.

I asked, 'What do you mean, you do not know about rupees? How can one do without money?'

In answer, she took out some money and carefully placed it on her palms. She told me, 'The contractor has paid us weekly wages. I don't know what to do with it. We don't have this in our village.'

I was totally taken aback by her matter-of-fact statement. I asked, 'What do you do if you have to buy something from the market?'

'We hardly buy anything from the market, except clothes, kerosene and salt. Everything else is locally produced. So, we exchange rice or other agricultural produce in exchange of these things.'

'Oh my god! You mean to say you are still bartering?' I said in surprise.

Then, I sat down on a parked roller. I asked her if she knew how to count. She nodded and said that she could count up to 100. 'That is wonderful. Now come here, and let me see what you have.'

She handed over all the money she had received. She had ₹560—three in a hundred-rupee denomination, five fifties, and one ten-rupee note. I told her to sit down. She sat down with a certain grace.

'Look Maya, you earn eighty rupees every day. So, for seven days, you add eighty rupees seven times—that should be your total earning for a week. Okay?'

She added the eighties up, one after another, seven times. Then she said that it added to the amount she held. 'That is wonderful, Maya. You are very smart indeed.'

She was pleased with my compliments and smiled. I said, 'Now you have one-hundred-rupee notes—three of them. That makes ₹300. Now you have five fifty-rupee notes—that adds up to ₹250, and here is one ten-rupee note. So, they all add to ₹560. It means you have got your wages for the week correctly. Okay?'

She was obviously satisfied with my patient explanation. I told her to recognize the different denominations. She quickly followed. Then I told her that she could buy a lot of things in the market with this money. For the first time, I said that I would tell someone to accompany her to the market. Then she could see for herself how to buy things from this money.

She was overwhelmed and wished to touch my feet, but I stopped her. 'Sir,' she began, 'you have really explained in a simple manner. I will explain it to the others from my village. Sir, I came to you because I was ashamed to ask the contractor. I thought he would laugh at me. What if he took advantage of my ignorance and cheated me? I had heard good things about you, so I ventured here. I am very grateful to you. I am very excited to know that I could buy anything from the market. I would like to try it out in today's Friday Market in Bagaha.'

She looked bright-eyed. I asked someone to go with her to the market to help her out with the process. I told her, 'Maya, I am very happy to help you. If you have any difficulty, you are always welcome whenever I am around. Giri Saheb can also help you. He is also very helpful.'

Her eyes were shining. She stood with grace to thank me with folded hands. There was something extraordinary about her, it was for sure, but I could not figure it out at that time.

She went away, a spring in her feet. She seemed very attractive and athletic. She turned towards her people from the village and told them that she had understood everything. Her delight was visible.

I turned and walked away in bewilderment. What was this age where some people did not have access to currency notes? They still had to depend upon a system of barter. I had no doubt that unscrupulous middlemen were exploiting the poor tribal people. Even after four decades of planning in India, its benefits had not touched the fortune of these village people. Now thanks to this project, for the first time in their lives, they had had the occasion to handle one hundred rupee notes and were obviously thrilled.

I watched as they headed towards the market to try the paper money, their first wages. My heart was content. As the head of the project, I had helped. Money now flowed into the hands of these tribal women, directly. I was pleased that I could successfully explain the differences between different denominations of the currency notes—like teaching a kid how to write the alphabet or the number.

It was particularly satisfying to see the look of joy in her eyes. I was also happy that I could gain her confidence in such a manner. I did not know why she chose to come to me. Did it mean that even an outsider had that kind of confidence in the chief of a project? If that were true, it augured well for the project and the many people associated with this project.

So much had changed for so many. Look at the Bajrang Dal. They had given up their former way of life to pursue a socially acceptable lifestyle. For the first time, these tribal people had come out of their village to earn a wage. They were introduced to a new monetary system.

Here was Barun De, the Chief Engineer, who had become a symbol of the aspirations of different people. Some people in the area looked up to the project, hoping that it would help them get rid of the problems caused by recurring floods. Some wanted to restore disrupted communications. For the project team, completing the work was important to tame the Great Gandak, which had defied solution for the past fifty years. So many people, so many missions. All these missions had brought different people and stakeholders together in a unique combination. This was nothing but the will of god.

We were to finish the work towards the end of the working season in May. Our main concern was protecting the slopes of the embankment. The pitching work and turfing of the slopes were progressing well. The pre-monsoon showers in May could cause heavy rains. We also wanted the drainage system to be in place so that its efficacy could be tested in the early showers. I used to visit the work site more frequently to this end, and would see more of Maya at work.

'It seems you guys have picked up the work nicely. Good work, Maya,' I said to her one day.

'Thank you, Sir,' she said. 'Actually, it took only a few days for us. You see, the turfing is just like sowing paddy saplings in the field. We are experts at this. We have to plant the paddy in a row and at a distance. So, we adapted it to the spacing required here to plant the turfing.

Likewise, slope pitching requires filling the stone pieces in a pattern over a layer of sand and pebbles. This we are also used to doing when we construct the stone walls of houses. So, there was no difficulty in picking up the work. We're grateful to the local supervisors here. We even sing while working as we do while sowing paddy. That has made the work enjoyable, Sir.'

'I'm glad. We were a little apprehensive about your inexperience. It is quite strenuous to work on the slopes of the embankments as well.'

'No, Sir, nothing of that sort. We are used to working in jungles and on the hills. This is our natural habitat. We do not find it particularly strenuous. And it pays well too. We discovered this when we went to the market. We got things we had never imagined before. Thanks to you, Sir. You have given us a new way of life. This satisfaction has given us great strength and encouragement. We want to do this work in the best possible manner.'

And so, the work continued. The more I saw her, the more my admiration for her grew. Her sincerity and its application were touching.

Once, Giri and I were inspecting the embankment at night. As we moved to the top of the bank, under the beam of the headlight of the jeep, we saw Maya standing with a gun in her hands. I stopped and got off the vehicle, leaving the headlights on. As we reached her, she recognized me and greeted me with a laugh. I was surprised. I asked her what she was doing here in the night with a gun in her hand.

'Sir, it had rained in the evening so I wanted to see the newly-planted turfing. So, Sir, I am also on an inspection.' Then she laughed.

'What are you doing with a gun? Where did you get it?'

'I had to walk through the jungle at night. So, I picked up the gun. However, I don't have to worry about my protection. Everyone is afraid of me. But I am a good shooter, Sir.'

She did not say where she got the gun from. I did not want to press further. I said anyway, 'There was no need for you to venture out like this during the night. See, it is our job and we are out for inspection.'

'Sir, it is also our responsibility. I had to. Had I known you were also here, I would not have come. But having come here, I also went to the Narayani temple. I was returning when I saw the headlight of the jeep. So, I stopped to see who it was.'

'No, it is very kind of you, Maya. I have not known a daily wage earner who takes her job so seriously. It is commendable. But you should go home now.'

When she spoke, she had a lump in her throat, 'Sir, surely we are daily wage earners today. But our tribe has a rich heritage. When we do something, we own it. I thought that since I am the leader of the community, I had to display that sense of ownership and responsibility as well. You have shown that trust in us, I must do everything possible to be worthy of it.'

I was completely floored. When she mentioned their rich heritage, I felt a tinge of recognition. I wanted to be patient and hear her more. I apologized and told her, 'Maya, you are truly great. May God bless you.'

She had said that she had a bicycle parked below and she would go back without any difficulty. She walked away with a regal grace. Her lantern swung in her hand, and the gun glinted from her shoulders.

I looked towards Giri who had not uttered a word so far. He also had a look of admiration on his face. We saw her reach the bottom of the embankment. She picked up her bicycle and rode away, disappearing into the jungle. We turned back to go back to our jeep. We thought how only recently, no mortal would have walked like this through the area. Here we were—riding a jeep alone, trying to inspect the work in the night, meeting a brave woman riding in her bicycle, disappearing into the dense forest without fear. Things had indeed changed. God had blessed us.

## IX
## Completion

The primary tasks involved in taming the Gandak River included the construction of the east guide bundh, eastern approach embankment, west guide bundh and western approach embankment along with their respective protective works. They were completed in the first working season—just as envisaged. Part of the bridge's foundation work was also completed. This had almost seemed impossible in the beginning of the working season. Many had expressed their reservations. But with blessings from Mother Narayani, this was successfully executed.

After the month of May, the rainy season started. Discharge from the river consequently increased. But all the structures behaved. Our main concern was ensuring protection of these slopes and earthen embankments. Maya's team and Bajrang Dal continuously helped monitor them and undertook emergency repairs wherever needed. These were routine problems and were expected.

At the end of monsoon, in the middle of October, the highest-ever flood discharge rushed in. We were satisfied by the bridge's tenacity. We even took a satellite picture that showed how the river, which was previously 8 km wide, had now almost straightened. It was flowing in a single stream down the bridge. After the floods, it filled us with delight to see a thick carpet of fertile silt lying all over the western and eastern parts of the river bed. More than 50 square kilometres of the river bed was reclaimed as fit for agriculture. And, both the banks were completely secured without requiring further protections.

The prophets of gloom had become silent not knowing which way to look. It was a moment of great satisfaction for us. A great sense of humility had descended upon us. We tried to remember how many seemingly unsurmountable mountains we had climbed on the way. All this could never have happened without the generous and divine help of Mother Narayani.

One day we were looking at the western bank. Many people had come to reclaim their lost land. Agricultural activity was in process. As we watched the happy scene, an old man appeared suddenly and asked me, 'Sir, are you the Chief Engineer?' I nodded.

Then, without any warning, he fell at my feet. I was greatly embarrassed; he was of my father's age. I lifted him by his shoulders.

He spoke thereafter.

'Sir, I was a young man of twenty-five years when Mother Narayani took away my land. It was the only source of sustenance for me. Many engineers had tried to build the bridge but I was told that it was not possible. I thought that I wouldn't be able to get my land. But Sir, you have made it possible. I came to give you my respects because for me, you are like God.'

I patted him and I said, 'We are very happy that Narayani has ultimately returned your land with such enriched soil. You see, Baba, others are also enjoying the moment.'

We embraced. It was an ultimate tribute! It was a great satisfaction for us. We would never be able to thank our Bajrang Dal gang, led by Suraj, and Maya's team enough. Without their invaluable contribution and support, it would have been impossible to complete the work. Nobody had imagined this in their wildest dreams. So, thank you, Mother Narayani, once again.

## X
## Mother Narayani

I believed that both Bajrang Dal and Maya's team were gifts from Mother Narayani. They had grown up in her lap.

Bajrang Dal was the face of the violent forces ruling the area, defying administrative control. They had raised real fears in the hearts of the people in the area as did the tigers. The forest, which provided cover to their operation, was also designated as an official tiger reserve. However, in the four years I spent there, I never came across a tiger. But unlike the tigers, the presence of the Bajrang Dal was writ large everywhere.

Maya's team from Tharu village was officially known as the tribals. They had very little interaction with the urban society and did not know much about economic development. They were brought by Bajrang Dal people. They fulfilled our need for labour. Mother Narayani had graciously presented us with an opportunity—the Tharu women joined the project as workers at a critical moment, ensuring they became its crucial stakeholders and earned a wage.

If not for the project over Gandak River, we would never have met either the Bajrang Dal or the villagers from Tharu. We would have had nothing to do with the Bajrang Dal because of their criminal activities; we would have kept them at a distance. Maya's villagers would have remained obscure, away from the light of civilization; we would have never found their worth. If not for Mother Narayani, I firmly believed, this kind of response would have never come. This was truly a win-win situation. And without telling their story, the story of Narayani would never be complete.

Maya, with her team, lent support in carrying out maintenance work at the embankment. The Bajrang Dal maintained the supply line of sand and aggregates for the bridge work. Once I was walking along the site when I heard Maya calling me. By now, I was familiar with her voice—very measured, never shrill. I saw her coming up the slope of the embankment. She was greeting me with her famous smile and a namaste. I asked her how she was. She said that she was watering the turf sods.

Then she said, 'Sir, she is my daughter.'

She introduced me to a small girl trying to hide herself behind her mother. She said, 'She wanted to meet you, so I brought her today.'

I smiled at her daughter and bent down to talk to her, 'Tell me your name, little girl.'

Maya said that she was not so little, 'She is five or six years old.' Then she told her daughter to tell me her name. But the girl was too shy and kept hiding behind her mother. I asked Maya, 'She is still little. What is her exact age?'

'Sir, I am not very sure. I confuse it all the time. In any

case, in our village and at her age, girls lend a hand to their mother in household work. So, we can't call her little, you know.'

'In our place, she would still be a small girl. If you are not sure, you should fix her age as five only. A girl can always be younger. So don't tell her she's five or six. From now, she is five years old. Okay?'

She laughed heartily, and the cheer pleased me. I asked for her daughter's name again.

'Payoli.'

'What a wonderful name, Payoli. You are wearing a beautiful frock too. So can we be friends?'

The daughter hid while Maya spoke up. 'Sir, we bought this frock for her from the Bagaha Market the other day. We also bought her this blue ribbon that she is wearing. We often talk about you at home. I tell her that Sir is nice and so she wanted to see you. She insisted on wearing this new frock and ribbon.'

I was very pleased. I told she looked wonderful in the new dress. She was pleased with my compliments but still did not say a word. Then I asked her, 'What else do you do? Do you go to school?'

The young girl looked bewildered and looked towards her mother for an answer. Maya said, 'Sir, no one goes to school in the village. We are all taught by word of mouth. I learnt from my mother. Payoli will also learn from me.'

I was astonished. 'Why not? Don't you know how much she will miss out in her life? Proper education can carve a beautiful life for her. Remember that, Maya.'

She looked towards Payoli with a look of hurt and guilt. I wondered if this was the first time, she had heard someone telling her about the virtues of education. She had remained uneducated because there had been no opportunities for her. But Payoli had that opportunity now. Perhaps, she was thinking about it and did not utter a word. I was not sure. I wondered if I had said too much. But it was the truth.

We left it there that day, but it culminated and grew into a mission.

In general, Maya was very sincere and attentive to the work assigned. I once asked her whether she was getting her wages alright. She smiled and said with a lot of satisfaction, 'Oh, yes Sir. I am now able to count quite well and I am sure no one can cheat me now. And Sir, do you know they are now paying me ₹100 and not ₹80 per day? They say that the rate has gone up.'

I was glad that the daily wages were being paid correctly, i.e. as per the recent wage hike. I was very happy to note the tone of satisfaction and contentment in her voice. That was important. Everyone working for the project should always feel happy and satisfied. That augured well for the organization.

The river too benefitted. I looked at it with sheer joy and contentment daily as it flowed under the bridge. It was a majestic sight for an engineer. I often found myself lost in my thoughts here.

What was it about a wild and unruly river that when tamed, it looked so elegant in its conduct? I thought about the film *My Fair Lady*.

I recalled the wild Eliza Doolittle selling flowers in a high-pitched voice. How she had been groomed by Higgins and the result was remarkable. After the training, she was a regal and royal lady.

It was the same with the river. Earlier, the river had flowed with gay abundance over a playing field of over 8 km, unbothered about the consequences of her unruly conduct. Today the river had abandoned its wayward style.

She behaved in a comely manner, bringing joy to all. I, of course, wanted to be humbler than Professor Higgins. I could not be like the master trainer, Prof Higgins. In the story, he had taken a bet to turn the ordinary Cockney girl Eliza into an extraordinary character. On the other hand, I had approached in the most humble manner. I wanted that humility all along in my life.

As I was absorbed in my thoughts, I heard Maya standing by my side. She had seen me absorbed.

She spoke very softly, 'Sir, is it very interesting? I see you still and absorbed in some deep thought.'

Coming back to my present state, I said, 'Yes, Maya, I was just seeing how the flow of the river had become so easy and majestic now. It appears that she has found meaning in graceful conduct. So far, she had flowed in gay abundance. Never bothered how her conduct affected others.'

Maya thought for a while and spoke to add to my thoughts.

'People who do not know the story of Narayani may not know how she had suffered. She was bound by a self-imposed vow to flow within the confines of the huge Himalayan mountain range. Only after she escaped that confinement, did she try to express her joys.'

'That is interesting, Maya. I never thought of it that way. I was thinking of what havoc her gay abandonment had caused others,' I said defensively.

'No, Sir, look at its spread, all the shaligram lying all along. As if Mother Narayani is sitting with all of them in her lap...'

Maya drifted off in deep thought, as if trying to recall something.

'I don't know what you are talking about, Maya,' I said.

'Sir, this is the story of Narayani. I will tell you. You will have an entirely different view of this river after you hear the story.'

'I do not know this story. I would like to hear it.'

Then, Maya began to tell me something that changed my life...

'There was once a girl named Gandaki, daughter of a prostitute. In those days, a child had to follow the same trade or profession they had been born into. Gandaki too became a prostitute.

She was a religious girl and an exalted soul. She performed her profession with religious fervour, considering each client as god. She treated him the whole night with utmost devotion. She entertained only one person per night. She followed this norm in order to maintain her single-minded devotion. People respected her for it and no one forced her to change her norm or practice.

'One day, a divine person came to her. As was her practice, she served him with her best. But the person did not even look at her. She said that she would like to have a husband like him. The person smiled and said that if she continued to do her service in such a devoted manner, then surely, she would have one. He said that whosoever came first to her place, she must serve him without any regard to his condition. All the clients would normally go away before dawn. He said that the one who would stay till the morning or the daybreak would be her worthy husband. The divine person left during the night.

'Gandaki continued to practice her profession with continued devotion. She would treat each visitor with utmost love and reverence. The first person to knock at her door would be admitted. Because of her lofty, exalted state, although she performed through her body, her soul remained pure.

'One night, there was a knock at her door. When she opened her door, she found a very sick person standing in front. He fell into her arms and she started to nurse him. Then, she found that he was suffering from leprosy. But she did not wince. She ignored his deplorable state. She bathed him, prayed for him, and placed his head on her lap. The fellow slowly found some comfort in her lap. He couldn't go anywhere. Now if he remained alive as the day broke, he would become her husband. Unflinching, her devotion did not waver at all. But as the day broke, the man died. Now, she was both—wedded to him and a widow. As per custom, she had to commit Sati and sit with his dead body on a funeral pyre. She told everyone that he was her spouse and must perform Sati.

'But as she sat on the pyre, there was a divine transformation. The dead man came alive as Lord Vishnu. The Lord said that she had passed the severest test and could now be his wife. But he said that he had been cursed to become a pebble. So, now, Gandaki had to become the river. All the pebbles in the form of Shaligram would lie on her lap. That river is known as Gandak, Narayani or Saligrami.'

Maya ended her story with a sigh. 'Sir, look at how Mother Narayani has respectfully carried all the pebbles in the form of Shaligram and helped Vishnu undergo the curse he had on his head. The pebbles are oval shaped—like an egg—they are very valuable and people keep them in their homes. She is not flowing in any gay abandonment. She was still following her duty with devotion. That is our belief.'

I had been spellbound by the myth. My respect for Mother Narayani grew.

'That is a wonderful story,' I told Maya. 'I think that we should build a temple on the guide bundh in the honour of Narayani, as a tribute for her cooperation. We will also request that she maintains her flow by the side of this temple of hers.'

She looked at me with her shining eyes. She told me that it would be the most befitting tribute.

'Maya, tell me, what religion do you follow?'

She answered quickly.

'We actually worship the Mother Earth. We were not taught any particular religion. We also observe some Hindu festivals but do not have any temple in our village. The only temple we go to is Mother Narayani's temple in the Valmikinagar Forest. You must have seen there is no temple as such. Only a thatched roof. No statue of Mother Narayani. Only the earth represents her. Some people wanted to build a proper temple here but Mother Narayani would have nothing of that. All attempts failed,' she said.

After I reflected on the story, I understood how firmly her beliefs were rooted to the earth. In its essence, every religion had to connect to the earth. It carried the entire civilization on its lap. In reality, the earth was basic to human existence. Marvelling at the story of Gandak, I thought that each civilization had grown next to a river. Every river, therefore, must have a story with its own significance.

As an engineer, I had looked at the river from its purely hydraulic properties—discharge, velocity, etc. But a river also sustained life, civilization itself. We have compartmentalized our knowledge into categories: engineering, social sciences, philosophy, religious beliefs, etc. So, when another aspect of knowledge is presented about the same thing, it dazzles. I was learning from the tribes, away from literacy, and from folklore.

I later told Giri the story, and he too mentioned that he had also heard about it before. Then, I said that I strongly wished to build a temple of Narayani on the top of the eastern guide bundh as a respect or tribute to the Narayani River. He readily agreed, as did everyone working there. I wanted Mother Narayani to make that her new home, and never have to shift again. All legendary river engineers were known to be very humble and would pay all the credit to the river's benevolence. Those of us, who had worked hard for this project, could not agree with it more!

## XI
## Felicitation

The construction of the temple began with haste. My tenure at this project was also coming to a close now that major work was almost over. My competent deputies would finish the rest. The project was completed within the scheduled time with considerable savings in terms of estimated cost. It was a great feat.

One evening, as I was staying in the guesthouse, I heard a woman's voice from the kitchen. I could hear a mild laughter. It sounded like Maya. I was surprised to see the cook and Maya emerging from the kitchen together. Maya stopped upon seeing me standing outside the verandah. Before I could ask what she was doing there in the evening, she asked me in Bangla, 'Barun Sir, how did you like the kesar payas?'

I was stumped. My mouth was open wide in complete surprise. She was standing gracefully with a mischievous smile on her face. Even the cook was looking at her with great surprise. Giri was not far behind and he too was surprised.

'Maya, tell me where did you learn this language? I have never heard you speaking Bangla earlier. I don't know about any Bengali family in or around Bagaha,' I asked in Bangla.

'Sir, I just wanted to surprise you. I learnt it from my mother. I am now teaching my daughter, Payoli, also. My mother had learnt it from her mother. She used to say that I should know a language other than the one spoken at home. She said that it was necessary to maintain secrecy, if needed. Sir, it runs in our family. I do not often use it. But knowing that you are a Bengali, I just wanted to try it. But Sir, I really wanted to know if you liked the kesar payas.'

The cook interjected, 'Sir, she came from home this evening with some milk from her village. She brought some pure milk from her home to cook the payas. She found out that you like the dessert and wanted to learn the recipe. She has been asking what you usually liked after a meal.'

More surprises. I told her that she should not have come during the night with milk. It is not safe for a woman to move alone during the night in the jungle. 'Thanks for the milk, Maya. The payas was excellent because of the pure milk you used to make it.'

'I'll call you Barun Sir instead of Chief Engineering Sir—it sounds much better. I'll address you this way unless you have some objection?'

I nodded.

She continued. 'Please do not worry about me moving in this forest alone in the night. I am a forest creature and all the forest creatures—animal or snakes—they know me. Suraj bhai is my brother as well. So why should I be afraid? I can see very well even in the night. The path is well known to me. This lamp is supposed to warn others that I am coming. Sir, I am very glad that this milk from our home has made such a difference in taste. Sir, I won't tell you why I was enquiring about your preferences. It is a surprise for you.'

I shrugged my shoulders. I went into my room and took out my three-cell torch and gave it to Maya.

'This is a gift from me. You can use this torch on the way back. It is better than your dim kerosene lamp. I do not buy your talk about everyone in the forest knowing you. It is always better to be careful during the night. Haven't you brought your gun along?' I asked smilingly. I explained how she could operate the torch.

She put her hand on her mouth in complete surprise. She said, 'Sir how could I bring my gun here in this place. That I had brought for inspection in the night. This torch is very good, Sir. I think Payoli will be excited to see it. I have seen a torch like this with my brothers—you know Suraj. They usually come to me in the village. I tie rakhis on their wrists and they love me as their sister. In our family, the rakhi has great significance and is respected very much.'

'Maya, you are springing surprise after surprise. It seems you have some wonderful and exciting story about you and your family. I am very keen to know it... the heritage and history ... which you have often talked about, but it remains shrouded in mystery. Unless you tell us all about it, we will not know. But not today, because it is quite late. You must return to your home as soon as possible,' I said.

'Oh Sir, that is a long tale of four generations. It is lying dormant inside me. Today, we are called tribal because of our obscure origin. I shall surely tell you, whenever the time is opportune. Thank you once again,' she said and then departed.

After she left, I turned towards Giri and told him, 'It seems like a big mystery. We must hear it next time I come. And what did she mean by saying that she won't tell me why she was enquiring about what I liked to eat?'

'She is a mysterious woman, but you must have noticed how confident she is. Otherwise, she wouldn't have talked to you in Bangla or addressed you as Barun Sir. I have heard something about Tharu people. It appears that they were from a princely state in Rajputana, which is in Rajasthan now. But I am not too sure. As to her inquiry about your food preferences, I can only say that I have heard these people talking about felicitating you. They might invite you to attend. But they have also not told me.'

I was alarmed. What did he mean by 'they', I asked. 'Who are these people inviting me?' I added.

'The Bajrang Dal team. They just revere you and it will be very difficult to say no to them. Maya must be a part of the felicitation team, if I am not very wrong. She has told us today that they are her rakhi brothers. So, it is natural that she has lent a hand in organizing the event.'

I looked blankly at Giri, not knowing what to say. In my heart, I abhorred someone felicitating me for a thing done in the course of my duty. But here the picture was somewhat different. But more than this, I was struck by what Giri told me about Maya belonging to some royal family. But I had to wait for the opportune time for Maya to tell her story.

I was supposed to be leaving for Gorakhpur the next day. I had some work to do before I left. I was told that Suraj, the leader of Bajrang Dal, wanted to meet me. I asked him to come in. Giri and Himangshu were present when they entered the room. Maya was also with them.

After greetings, Suraj told me with folded hands, 'Sir, we have come to ask for something, which we trust you will not refuse. Sir, we do not have words to express our complete reverence to you as an ambassador of God. He has descended especially for us to lead us out of the life of sin, which we were forced to live. Here, our sister, Maya, too feels that you have brought about a change in her life.

Sir, we have heard that you would be leaving this project soon. It is our deepest desire that you join us in our celebration to hail this extraordinary gift of god. Maya wishes that she would host this get-together in her village. The temple of Mother Narayani will also be completed in a fortnight's time. Please accept our humble invitation to come with Giri sir and Himangshu sir and grace the evening. After paying our respect to Mother Narayani at the new temple, we can go to the village.'

Those were the genuine words of love spoken by people who had never bent their heads before any mortal. Their feelings were loud and clear. It was not possible to refuse.

But I said, 'I am truly moved and overwhelmed. I cannot forget the kind of love your men and women have bestowed upon me. So, I am bound by your words and wishes. I must, however, submit that being a public servant, I cannot accept felicitations or any public honour. I shall come as a member of the team to celebrate an event. Felicitations should be reserved for political bosses who need them and also deserve it.'

They smiled and agreed, adding, 'Sir nobody can take away our feelings of respect or reverence for you. It is not dependent on your official position. We are addressing you as Barun Sir, a darling of our heart. No other person, much less some high political boss, could come between you and us. We have also seen this world. Nobody would have done what you and your team have done by going beyond the sphere of your official position.'

I looked towards my colleagues. They too smiled and said, 'Sir, better we say nothing and follow them.'

I felt embarrassed. That I did not doubt. Maya said softly, 'Sir, you will have a chance to have a look at our humble abode in the village also. You are already so much talked about in the village. All of us will be very happy to have you, along with respected Giri ji and Himangshu ji. We are actually looking forward to your visit. I am grateful to my brothers who have kindly and graciously asked me to host the occasion.'

I followed the advice of my deputies and decided to go. It was decided that Giri would finalize all other details. After the pooja at the new temple, we were to attend the evening programme in Maya's village. I was also keen to see her village. This programme would be an opportunity to do that.

I arrived as per the programme. At first, we formally prayed before Mother Narayani to accept the place as her permanent home. The solemn occasion was conducted with proper rituals, prayers followed by shlokas chanted by the priests.

Of course, it was with selfish interests that we had wished that Mother Narayani adopt the site as her permanent home. But it seemed to us that the Mother too had agreed to make this her home. She wanted to help all those whose lives depended upon her kindness. I would say this was a unique feeling. Because those who had suffered for so many decades from the vagaries of the river would only appreciate this blessing the most. I again thought of the poor old farmer who had retrieved his land. He had lost his land when he was a young man. He had given up all hope of ever retrieving it. His sense of delight and happiness could never be described.

## XII
### The Spectacle at the Village

We were looking forward to the evening programme with a strange feeling of curiosity. Firstly, we never had an occasion to see such a programme organized in a village that was inside a forest. Secondly, the programme was being hosted jointly by Bajrang Dal and the chief of a village who, Giri claimed, belonged to a princely state.

Evening set in and we were ready. Giri drove us there in our jeep. We were escorted by two members of the Bajrang Dal. At the entrance to the forest, we were greeted by a big contingent of the Bajrang Dal with an awesome display of firearms. The forest road was rather narrow. With the cavalcade in front of us, and even behind, progress was slow. There was a welcome portal made of banana trunks and leaves. Some flower petals and rice grains were thrown in to welcome us. At the venue, we were welcomed by the team led by Maya. They greeted us with mango leaves and sprinkled some water over us.

We were taken to a dais, where we were seated with Suraj, the chief of the Bajrang Dal team. He then explained that in that village the custom was to show respect by showering a small bunch of mango leaves over the guest. This was considered a pure and highly respected ritual.

It was an open ground lit by big kerosene gas lamps provided by the Bajrang Dal. We were later told that they did not allow any diesel generators in the jungle area, since it would disturb the ambience of the forest. The village was located at the end of forest. Thereafter, there were hills. But it was not considered wise to disturb the serenity of the forest. With the same considerations, no microphones had been placed either. There was, of course, no need for one as the gathering was not very large.

As we settled down, the first item on the programme was a welcome song and dance by Payoli. She was dressed in her new dress, garlanded with mango leaves and a headgear with a plume of peacock feathers. She looked adorable. When Maya had brought her to see me the other day, she was so shy that she hardly lifted her eyes. But today, she welcomed us with folded palms and some words. There was no sign of that shyness now. She put on a commendable performance.

After the welcome performance, Suraj, the Bajrang Dal chief, stood up to say a few words of welcome for me.

He said, 'It is a big day. Barun Sir, with his most competent lieutenants, are here with us today. We have seen many government officers and engineers in our life. But these officials have put service above the self. For forty or fifty years, engineers have tried to build the bridge over the river but they have not succeeded. But Barun Sir came to us and completed the work successfully in such a short time. We have seen him and his team working day and night.

'You have all seen the work. The team from this village helped as well. They left the village for the first time to work. You yourself have also seen the change in your fortunes.

Look at us—we were engaged in the business of abduction. That was how we earned a living. But we used to run like rats through the forest. We were continuously living under a feeling of fear and uncertainty. Barun Sir arrived and we were given a handsome offer to earn an honest rupee. We did not know the work, but he taught us what we could do.

Today, we go out in an open jeep to the bank at the Bagaha market, walking with a cheque in hand and pride in our chest. The fear and shame have gone from our life. We have learnt to live a life that had for years remained unknown to us.

Who is this Barun Sir? How did he come to us? What has he done for us?

'The answer is very simple. Barun Sir is an ambassador of god. He has been sent by god to redeem us from the curse that had been placed on our lives. He must have come from his heavenly abode to change our lives with a magic wand. He must have brought a paras—a stone that changes iron to gold. It is our great fortune that his feet have led him here. We and our children will remember this day all our lives. He will be our deity for all time to come.'

I was stunned and moved by the words. He had chosen every word of his speech and laced it with deep emotions. I understood that they had undergone changes in their lives. They were now honoured and accepted in civil society. Their fear and shame had left them. I did not know how to describe how I felt upon learning that there had been such a change in their psyche, having come out of utter darkness to the light.

Then Maya came forward to say a few words. 'Barun Sir, it seems, came to help all of us. He came for those who wanted a bridge to be constructed. For those who wanted their lost land. For those who were forced to live a life of disrepute and those who wanted their honour and pride back. He came for us to give us the means to live a life we had never known. He has come to show us freedom. Thank you, Sir.'

I was left speechless. I turned to the programme. After the short speeches, there was a tribal dance by Maya's group. It was meant to be in reverence of the earth. It was sung and performed when a marriage took place in the village. It was a lively dance. It appeared that the artists were very well versed in the performance.

Then it was time for me to speak. I wanted to choose my words carefully, trying to let all my emotions show.

I said, 'I am simply overwhelmed. When I came to do this work, I did not know this area. I had some experience with the work, yes ... but nothing else. My two deputies had joined me with a lot of enthusiasm. There were many challenges ahead of us. But all the credit must go to these two gentlemen who worked very hard, lived away from their families and risked their life to complete this work. I have guided them, but the real work has been done by these two silent gentlemen, and without you we could not have achieved anything.

It brings us great satisfaction that this project has brought change in your lives—the obscure villagers from Tharu and our respected Bajrang Dal men. It is true that people will talk about the completion of the work as a great achievement. But outside the work, I really am proud of the socio-economic benefits that have come about here. It has brought about a landmark change in all of your fortunes. It will of course also be cited as a great achievement for all time to come.

'I cannot appropriate all the credit to myself. Least of all, I cannot accept that I have been the cause of all this. I very humbly submit that the almighty god has chosen me to be the head of the organization. God has asked me to carry the mantle of glory, the kalash, on my head on his behalf. I accept all that you have said as glory to god.

I humbly pray and hope that this small change would soon grow, bigger and bigger. It should never be a flash in the pan. Your own will and belief will surely take you further to a higher position in the society. May god bless you all.

'Lastly, coming to Maya's village was our ardent wish. We have been very fortunate to witness a grand spectacle of your great cultural heritage. I salute all who have performed this evening with great gaiety and warmth. Thank you all.'

The space rung with applause. I bowed and then a feast was announced. We were served on neat banana leaves and cups made of forest leaves. The food was very simple and delicious and Maya had tried to replicate the cuisine I was used to. The best part was the kesar payas. We were touched to be served so warmly. The simplicity reflected the warmth and hospitality of our hosts.

As we were leaving, Maya came to me to say that she would like to come and meet me in the evening. I was to leave for Gorakhpur in the afternoon but I decided to stay back to listen to her.

We returned to our guesthouse. It was not very late. We had not spoken a word on our way back. Giri proposed that we have a cup of coffee before retiring for the day. The coffee before sleeping usually killed my sleep but after the eventful evening, I was not sleepy. So, I nodded and said, 'Why not?'

We quietly waited for the coffee to arrive.

As we sipped the coffee, Giri said in a low tone, 'Sir, what an evening! I still wonder how all this has come to pass. Everyone here knows how dreadful this area was after sunset. We are now invited to the dens of the same infamously dreadful guys. We are felicitated in the jungle in a village—a mysterious affair. Sir, I am overwhelmed. The only thing that seems to have made a difference is your entrance. It is a fact that cannot be denied. So, what the Bajrang Dal chief said in his speech is true.'

He spoke solemnly, and in a voice choking with emotion. I only looked at him in amazement. I did not know Giri was capable of such emotion.

The room was quiet. Then Himangshu spoke too. 'Sir, in the presence of everyone you praised us, you gave us all the credit. It reminded me of Lord Rama who after defeating Ravana gave all the credit to his army of monkey saying that he couldn't win the war without their help. It is your magnanimity. Everyone knows that but for you, this difficult work could not have been completed.'

I listened quietly, holding their emotions to my heart. Then, I said, 'It will be really wrong if I would have given you credit when you did not deserve it or if it was not true. It would have been worse if I had done this in public. It would have been a slur in my character. I didn't say anything of the sort. I was friendless when I had come here. I did not know you when you joined me as my lieutenants. But both of you shouldered the responsibility far beyond your known capacity. Is that not a fact that you faced all the ugly situations first and kept me as far away as possible? Giri handled the Bajrang Dal team by himself. You risked your life for the work. You had unshakeable faith in your leader. My words, my suggestions, became commands for you. You never talked about the difficulties and the dangers. I am being praised in public today. How can I walk away with all the accolades without acknowledging your contribution? Will it be honesty? I know your contribution is no less than mine.

'Then, I also look to god in amazement. Whatever has happened is unthinkable. Take the problem related to the dacoits as an example. We knew that we could not depend on the protection of the police. We were not saintly, not like Vinoba Bhave. We were not social reformers. To enable the dacoits to earn honest money was just an idea. It clicked, and we succeeded. What I mean to say is that everything is ordained. We were just agents in the hands of god. He chose us to dispense these benefits to them. There is change. Do not mistake it. It is real change. Nobody, otherwise, would felicitate you with such humility. I, therefore, said that this flame should keep growing. It shouldn't prove to be a flash in the pan.'

Our coffee had done us good. While getting up, I said that I was looking forward to meeting Maya tomorrow. 'Maybe she will tell us her story finally. I would go miles to hear it.'

Then, I held on to my two friends and associates and told them, 'Don't for a moment forget you are not ordinary. God knows and we also know that he does not make a mistake in this respect.'

We went back to our respective rooms for the night. I was sure that sleep would be elusive. I was also sure that my colleagues would also find it difficult to rest. One could possibly blame coffee for that but I knew the programme was simply intoxicating. It had opened the door for so many thoughts and emotions.

An engineer is wedded to facts, formulae and drawings; emotion had no place here. For an engineer, a straight line always had to look straight. Only a creative person could make a straight thing look curvy, only for them would a curve look straight. Today, all three engineers were fighting with their emotions. Of course, it was good that the work was completed and the engineers could justifiably take a break, leaving the field, to explore their emotions.

## XIII
## The Gift of the Magi

We were busy in the morning next day. We had meetings too. The evening came leisurely.

Maya came to meet us. I asked her to come in as she arrived at the door, asking her to sit with us, pointing to the sofa. She smiled and said that she would like to sit on the carpet.

She said, 'Sir, you occupy high positions. I am an ordinary person. You are very kind to offer me a seat equal to yours. That is your magnanimity. But I am pretty conscious of my position here. I thank all of you. But allow me to take a position to which I belong. So is our culture. In any case Sir, I am more comfortable and at ease on the carpet.'

We looked at her in admiration.

I said, 'Maya, we were really overwhelmed at the celebration yesterday evening. The programme was well organized. I was impressed to see the houses built so neatly in your village. The exterior of the walls are painted with some beautiful mythological paintings and I appreciate your style and customs.'

She smiled and said, 'I am very happy to know that you liked the programme. Payoli was so happy to receive your compliments. She rehearsed a lot for the show. Sir, in our village, such occasions come only during a marriage. It was for the first time that it was held without a marriage. So, you can understand how grand this occasion was for us. The celebration is normally held to welcome the bridegroom.'

I laughed and said, 'That is very interesting. In this case, you made an exception. Neither was there a bride nor a bridegroom.'

All of us laughed. Maya continued, 'The paintings on the walls depict the journey of Ram, Lakshman and Sita when they were banished into the forest. I don't know how this story has come to us because we do not worship them. In fact, you will not find any temple in our village. I cannot really explain this. I have never asked my mother about this either.'

'Oh, your mother told so many things about her background and history. And she of course taught you how to speak in Bangla. Did it not occur to you at that time why she was teaching you Bangla of all languages?' I asked.

'Sir, in our society a girl always holds a higher position. You may say that she is the heir or the head of the family, especially after her mother's death. So, my mother wanted me to have all the knowledge she had. Bangla was part of it.'

I asked her more.

She said that the language had been taught by her mother. She had told her that their grandmother was taught by her governess, who happened to be a lady from the royal family of Cooch Behar. The governess had told her that for a prince or princess, it was always very helpful to know a foreign language. In the princely state, nobody knew Bangla. And so, they settled for this language. Her mother told her that they had actually found this language very useful.

'That leads to your story, once again. We are yet to hear it from you. But tell me, are you teaching Bangla to your daughter, Payoli? Have you told her your story, the one you've heard from your mother?' I asked Maya.

'Yes, Sir, I have started teaching her Bangla. She has learnt a bit. But in the course of time, she should learn as much as I know. I have not told her our story. She should grow up a bit, only then I will tell her. This story may not mean much to others. But for us, it is our heritage. We must keep it intact as long as we live. My mother used to remind me of our past. She used to tell me that we had a royal lineage. It should be our pride. We must not forget it.

I think she was absolutely right. I, for one, have never forgotten it. I try to conduct myself with the same royal aplomb. Yes, true, we are very poor now. We have been designated as tribals. But our regal status cannot be taken away from us.'

On hearing this, I understood and appreciated the style and dignity with which she conducted herself. Her way of walking, her way of looking, talking—everything had an unmistakable style. It could not go unnoticed. Even now, while she was sitting on the floor, she possessed dignity and spoke in a measured tone. She looked at each of us with style, moving her gaze from one to the other in a considered manner. Her voice may have been charged with emotion, but she never seemed to be lamenting or seeking sympathy for her loss.

There was silence in the room. I had only talked in between. My other two colleagues had said nothing so far. I put myself in her shoes as the silence extended beyond us. There were no princely states now in the country. But the influence of the princely status had continued. Maya was acutely conscious of her lineage, and her ideals had percolated all the way down to four successive generations.

Maya stood up with grace. Looking at me she said, 'I have not told this story to anyone else. I realize that you have given us a new meaning to life. I am not very learned or knowledgeable. I can be called an illiterate since I have no formal education ... I suppose we felt that we needed to keep running. Now I know we should stop. We must face the present and live our life accordingly. That is why I must tell you the story. If I don't tell you now, it will never be told. And it is good that Giri ji and Himangshu ji are here to listen to it as well. They too have had a profound influence on us. You correctly spoke about them in the function last night. They have also played an equally important role in this project. I had come here with a different purpose this evening, Barun Sir. I must do that first before I tell you more.'

With that, she took out a small wooden box and walked towards me in a reverent manner. She opened the box and took out a beaded string chain with a pendant at the centre. She placed it in my hand.

'Barun Sir, this is a chain the Queen Mother had given to Sham Sher Singh. A man who was called to rescue her daughter, the princess. She had two such chains. She gave the other one to her daughter, the princess. She told them that this chain would protect them from all evils and dangers in their way.'

'Sir, you too are leaving us. You protected us while you were here. You have provided us with the means. You must keep this chain with you as a token. It is our gift to you. I shall give the other chain to Payoli when she grows up. She may also set out on a path of achieving something higher and different. She won't get anything from this closed society of ours. I am beginning to understand the virtue of education… Payoli deserves it.'

I stood up, holding the gift in my hands. It was a beautiful piece, likely to be priceless. A gift from the Magi, I thought. But I was overcome by sadness to say anything for a moment. When I gathered myself, I placed my hand on her head in order to bless her.

Then, I said, 'I don't know how to thank you, Maya. This gift is priceless. It is true that I embark upon a new path from here to seek a new fortune for me. I appreciate it.'

'This chain will remind me of all of you. I am happy that

you are considering Payoli's education. I would love to see her achieve greatness. She must receive some education, but I do not know how this can be done. I shall be very happy to help her.

'Maya, thank you. You will always remind me of the value of determination and a great fighting spirit. Otherwise, it is difficult to visualize how a simple tribal woman would emerge from the obscurity to be a true stakeholder of this project.'

Saying this, I sat down. Maya also resumed her seat on the carpet. She slowly started telling us the story in great detail.

Her tale took us to what happened to a princess from the small state of Jhaluk, located in the southern part of Thar Desert and contiguous to the Aravalli Hills. They were persecuted by the villainous Muslim chieftain Jia Khan who had set his eyes on the princess. She escaped with her manservant one night. The duo ran across lands and finally reached this faraway village across the Gandak River. This happened four generations ago.

Then, years later, the story was told to her daughter, who in turn, told her daughter.

After it ended, Maya stood up gracefully to leave. We stood up, meeting the eyes of the descendant of the royal family. We could broadly place the Jhaluk state to south of Thar Desert today. But there were many such small states earlier. It is difficult to identify the location of the state today in modern India. But nevertheless, Maya was present as a lawful heir. There was no doubt by her demeanour that she belonged to that princely state. We were in awe of the courage and grit of a princess—Sahiba, that was her name.

Maya left us to brood upon her story. That was the last time I saw Maya.

*Four*

# Sahiba

I was to be transferred to the offices in Delhi. I prepared for my return and was excited about being back. Nick too had planned a visit to Delhi after I settled down. It isn't difficult to settle down when you're single and I hoped to be done soon.

I did not want to stay at a hotel and had taken an apartment and thanks to the World Bank, everything was very well organized. I thought of Sahiba and how it had changed my life all of a sudden. Sahiba was still in Assam. She was expected to be back in Delhi by the first week of May.

I arrived in Delhi in April, and quickly found a good housekeeper and a cook, an elderly woman from Bengal. Sadhana was a quiet person, and she seemed to like me. Sadhana prepared the Bengali meals I liked, which reminded me of my childhood and my mother. Sadhana had made the apartment quite a comfortable place to live. We were happy with each other. She had her own style, it seemed. I found that quite acceptable. I never said anything if I did not like something she had cooked. She would know. She would also know what I liked.

My life in Delhi proceeded simply. I did not have many friends in Delhi. I was not a party-going creature, and would come home after work. I took a cup of tea in the evening and though I was not a connoisseur, I was picky when it came to the flavour and wanted my tea made in a particular way. Sadhana was quick to pick this up. I preferred a particular kind of tea that I received in Assam by some tea-loving friends—a mixture of Darjeeling tea and Assam tea. The Assam tea leaves provided a body to the brew while the Darjeeling tea provided the true spirit and character.

It was strange but I was sold. I had preserved this passion even now. People often say: 'This is the cup which cheers.' There is nothing truer than this, I am sure. The boiling water poured over the tea leaves throws out the aroma, which literally filled one's nostrils. That was the exquisiteness and spell of the tea. May god bless all who conjured up such a lovely and intoxicating drink. Sadhana in the beginning thought I was crazy. But she also realized soon that the aroma cast a spell on the one inhaling it.

As days progressed, I realized that Nick would be coming to Delhi from Washington. However, he was delayed. He told me that his wife, Edna, had some health issues and therefore he would not be able to come to Delhi for another fortnight. I didn't mind. I looked forward to Sahiba's return to Delhi by the end of the week. I wanted to spare some time to spend with her. I especially wanted to know how she had fared at the business school. She hadn't mentioned it, and I too had not asked. Somehow, I found myself expecting her to share everything.

'That is not a good idea, Barun,' I said to myself.

But the mind works in a strange manner. It could harbour expectations in the subconscious mind. I could not readily explain it to myself. I perhaps thought I was at the centre of everything that had happened with Maya and her daughter because of the Gandak Project. But it was also possible that I merely reminded her of her childhood in her obscure village.

I reminded her of where she belonged. She believed

in Barun now. She had not heard the tale of her great grandmother, whose name was also Sahiba. The only person, who could now tell this story was Barun. But I wondered if she wanted to hear the tale ... or had she forgotten?

I revisited the events of the Gandak Project after many years only to be able to tell her. But memory is a double-edged thing. It brings about some sweet or memorable events back to one's mind. It could also bring out things that one would like to forget.

Maya must have found it impossible to deal with the absence of Payoli. She would have missed her daughter. I recalled her steely resolve. Much like the Queen Mother in her story, she had handed over her daughter to the care of a servant. More significantly, I could not forget Maya's death. I remember how Maya had often said that others were afraid of her. She knew everybody, be it man, animal or snake. But she reportedly died of a snake bite!

We would never know how it had come to transpire.

## II
### Sahiba Arrives

Sahiba called. She said that she had arrived on a train in the morning and was dying to see me. Excited, I too told her that I would be free by around half past six in the evening. I could meet her then. I suggested that she come to my apartment for a quiet evening and some dinner. I could drop her home after.

'That sounds wonderful, Barun. Should I come after 7 p.m.? Once you are back from the office?' she asked.

'No need to wait. You can come whenever you want. I am sure Sadhana will look after you in my absence. I can send a car for you,' I said.

'Sadhana?'

'My housekeeper. She is a wonderful cook from Bengal. You can talk to her in Bangla. She will like that.'

'That would be nice. I know the place already; I can reach early and chat with Sadhana. I won't need a car.'

We agreed and Sahiba hung up. I realized I needed to tell Sadhana about Sahiba. I had not entertained anyone in my home so far. I thought that I needed to explain so she would not have any other ideas.

I called Sadhana. She was surprised because I had never called her from the office before.

'All fine, Sadhana?' I asked.

'Babu, I hope everything is okay? Tell me, what is it?' She wanted to know.

'I will have a visitor this evening. She is the daughter of my colleague, Maya. Her name is Sahiba. She speaks Bangla too. Please look after her. I have given her your number, so she might call you before coming. I shall come around my usual time.'

Curiosity has no end. I did not believe that she would be satisfied with whatever I had told her about Sahiba. Sadhana said nothing else, except that I should not worry. But I knew from her tone that she was concerned. But Sadhana had been a wonderful host. I was pretty sure that Sahiba would be quite comfortable in my absence.

After work, I reached home quickly. When I rang the bell, it was Sahiba who opened the door. I had already expected it, anticipating her excitement. She held me by my shoulders in welcome and said, 'Barun, it has been ages! It's so nice to see you again.' I lightly embraced her and led her to the sofa. Sadhana was standing behind us, grinning from ear to ear. She took my office bag from my hand as I sat down opposite Sahiba.

I told her that I wanted to look at her properly? since it had been so long. She blushed.

'Sahiba,' I said, 'it is good of you to come down to meet me here. I hope Sadhana took care of you.'

'Oh! Didimoni and I have found many good things to talk about. She is so sweet and affectionate. I was perfectly at home.'

'I am glad. Give me five minutes, Sahiba. I shall just freshen up and join you,' I said, rising.

I headed out to take off my jacket and tie and washed up. I returned in haste, joining her with a smile.

'I feel like you seem a bit shaken—not as bubbly as the last time. I hope everything is fine?' I spoke.

'Barun, please,' she said, 'do not be that keen an observer. Is it a habit of all engineers? I may be a bit tired after the long train journey. After I arrived here, I had gone to my office. Reports had to be filed. All routine work. But I am relaxed now after talking so much with Didimoni'

Sadhana brought in the tea. I looked at the special brew. I wondered if Sahiba would like it. 'This is a special blend of Darjeeling and Assam tea. Many people don't like it. I don't know if you will like it. I can ask Sadhana to prepare a different cup for you.'

She looked at me strangely. She began with some sarcasm. 'Barun, I do not have to remind you that I have spent some long years in Darjeeling. I pretty well know how aromatic Darjeeling tea is. Or, do you still consider me a girl from the forest?' She mocked me with her mischievous smile.

'My apologies, Madam. I did not mean it that way,' I said smiling.

She started laughing, which she always did whenever something like this happened—as if she had scored a point. Then, from her bag, she took out a small packet of Darjeeling tea from Happy Valley Tea Garden, an exquisite quality of Darjeeling tea. And then one more, a packet of Assam tea.

She gave it to me, 'With my compliments, Sir.'

I looked at them with great pleasure and stood up and bowed down to her. I wanted to express my gratitude for such a beautiful and thoughtful gift. She acknowledged it with a tilt of her head and said, 'Barun, let us have the tea lest it will get cold.'

'You should have taken a flight back to Delhi instead of taking a long train journey. That would have been less tiring.'

'Barun, you remember that I used to ride on the pillion of a bicycle? When I first got on a train, I had Sister Jane who put my head on her lap and comforted me. With great difficulty, I am now used to trains. I cannot board a plane unless somebody is with me on whose lap I could put my head for comfort,' she laughed as she said this.

'But a more important reason for taking the train was to stop at New Jalpaiguri and go to St. Joseph's Convent in Darjeeling. I had to tell Sister Jane and Mother Grace so much. I had two proud possessions to show them too. One was my Management Diploma,' she said, without taking a breath.

'And what was the second thing?'

She held my head in both her hands and seemed lost in thought. Then shyly, she said, 'I got you, Barun.'

She continued. 'You have been the reason for me to leave my village and venture out to the church.'

Then she dropped her hands, leaving me to gather my own thoughts at such a heartfelt statement. Finally, I congratulated her. 'Congratulations on the unique achievement, Sahiba. I too am so proud of you. I am sure Mother Grace and Sister Jane were happy about your twin success. You are blessed, my dear,' I said, caressing her shoulders.

Then, I called for Sadhana saying, 'Sahiba has passed her

Management exam and we should offer her some sweets. I don't know what you are going to cook for her for dinner.'

Sadhana arrived with a smile. 'Sahiba Bibi has got this kesar payas. I was going to get some sweets but she told me this would be best. As for dinner, Sahiba Bibi has already told me what to cook.'

'For heavens' sake, Sadhana, where did you learn to call her Sahiba Bibi?'

Then I turned back to Sahiba. 'I am amazed ... kesar payas?'

I turned to Sadhana again. 'This is Sahiba's handiwork.'

It suddenly occurred to me that Sham Sher Singh used to call princess Sahiba Bibi too. It was strange how Sadhana had chosen to address her the same way.

'It is fine, Barun,' Sahiba said. 'I call her Didimoni. We talked a lot. I found that she did not know you were so fond of kesar payas but she knew how to prepare it. I helped her prepare it this time, just as I learnt from Maya. Maya too knew about what you liked to eat. I told Didimoni. She was surprised. She told me that you have never told her what you liked.'

I laughed at their scheming.

'I never told Maya what I liked either, but she prowled into our kitchen to find out from our cook. I do not care too much about what I eat as long it is edible. But you are hooked on the payas, Sahiba.'

She laughed. I added, 'But the name is more intriguing to me. Don't you know that Sham Sher Singh used to call your great grandmother Sahiba Bibi?'

'Really? It fits me so well,' she merrily said.

All this time Sadhana had been standing at the kitchen door and looking at us in great amazement.

She hastily said, 'I am sorry if I have addressed her in an

offensive manner. In our side of Bengal, a respectable lady is called "Bibi" and a respectable man is a "Babu". Since we spoke in Bangla, it was natural. It was so nice to hear her talk, Babu. She talked all about you, Babu. And, she has made all the difference to our usual evenings and has brought me this mekhela chadar from Assam...' She trailed off.

Both of us told her that it was alright and there was no offence involved in whatever way. 'Sadhana, it is very famous and a prized piece from Assam. They give to a lady as a mark of their respect. To gentlemen, they offer a handwoven towel,' I told her.

'Oh! Thank you, Bibi. Thank you so much. I really love it,' Sadhana said. 'What time will you have dinner?'

'Our usual time. She has to go back after dinner. I have told Bahadur to be ready.'

Sahiba then got up from her seat. She took out two things from her bag. One was the handwoven towel, which she respectfully wrapped and placed on my shoulders. Then there was a beautiful hand-crafted Assam silk tie, which she also gave me.

It had a note. It read, 'with love from Sahiba'.

I was overwhelmed. I said, 'Thank you so much, Sahiba. It appears you have seen a lot of Assam. It reminds me of the days I spent in Assam. Now, I would like to know how your visit went. Will you tell us?'

### III
### Sahiba visits Assam

Sahiba smiled and said, 'I am so glad I went to Assam. You know, Barun, at first I was not very keen to go to Assam to cover the exhibition on Assamese silk and other handicrafts. It was supposed to be a three-day programme.

I have a friend—Rupa from my management programme—who is from Assam. She told me that Bihu was the most celebrated event in Assam and was called Rangoli Bihu. It is a festival of dancing and feasting. Then she said that she could take me to the Kaziranga National Park, which is home to the one-horned rhino. The lure of the forest and wildlife really hooked me. She even said that her aunt was a forest officer living inside the forest reserve. She said that we could visit and spend some time in the forest.

I was sold. Jungle life has always attracted me—it is in my genes. So, the decision was made. I told my office that I would go.'

'I travelled by train to Guwahati. Rupa met me there and we had a lovely time together. Bihu festival expressed the true spirit of the Assamese. They are so simple and warm. They trust you easily and embrace you as their own. They danced in gay abandon.'

'Yes, I know,' I said, 'Their music is so exhilarating that your feet start tapping in response.'

'You know, Barun, there is so much love that it touches every heart. Since Bihu marks the harvest, a feeling of contentment is in the air. The folk dances seem to express this contentment. I didn't know the language but it resembles Bangla and was easy to pick up. I could not, however, understand why they are a little hostile towards the culture or people of Bengal.'

I said, 'As far as I know, Britishers ruled Assam with the help of desi babus from Bengal. These Babus thought they were superior by virtue of their education. They would also boast of a particular cultural heritage and did not treat the Assamese with any kindness. Hence, there is an inherent hostility against them.'

Sahiba shrugged and continued. 'Well, it was noticeable.

It was not on the surface all the time. It was an oddity but also forgettable. They showed a genuine interest in me, and were very helpful. The exhibition went well. We had tried to give this programme a global or international theme and wanted to provide a window to their art and handicrafts. From that point of view, it got some encouraging coverage. The village craftsman and weavers of the Assam silk sari were presented at the exhibition.'

'The three-day programme was quite hectic in many ways. After that, Rupa and I left for Kaziranga by road. The view of the villages on the way was thrilling and the weather was quite pleasant.

On the way, we passed the city of Nawgaon, and then, a small village known as Nelly. Rupa told me that this place had a dubious history during the time of the Assam agitations. Minority communities resided in the village. One night, the agitators consisting of local people encircled the village. The entire village was burnt down. There were very few survivors. Apparently, it got quite the media limelight then. But the Assamese seemed so peace-loving ... it is unthinkable how, in a fit of frenzy, they attacked so many innocents.

Rupa mentioned that the agitation was going on at that time to deport the migrated minority community from Bangladesh. Rupa also said that her aunt had something to tell her—a sequel to this incident—and that part was quite interesting.

'What was it?' I asked.

'I'll tell you,' said Sahiba and continued. 'We reached the park in the afternoon, beside the mighty Brahmaputra. We received a warm welcome from Rupa's aunt. Next morning, we were taken on an elephant to look at the famous one-horned rhino. They looked so innocent and harmless. We were told that they did not like to be disturbed and resent it;

then they get violent. I thought that was perfectly okay. Why should we disturb someone's privacy? Anyway, we saw other animals and a lot of birds. Did you know that sometimes, when the river is flooding, water enters the park? The animals have to leave the park then.

'In the evening, we sat down for a typical Assamese dinner. After the dinner, I asked her aunt to tell me the story about the agitation. Her aunt became very grave.

She said, "I was a small girl, about ten-years-old then, when my father was posted in Tezpur, where the railways were building a bridge over the Brahmaputra. My father was an officer then. Our colony was located near the bridge site; the adjoining village consisted of many people from the minority community. The Nelly incident … a fortnight had passed since it happened. Media congregated and fuelled the flames … The media described some of the gory details of the incident. This had fuelled a sense of revenge in the minds of the minority people.

We had no inkling that we could also be targeted for the reprisal. We were around a hundred, most of us Assamese, who lived in the colony. We used to live peacefully and the women from the adjoining village worked in our homes."

"I don't know how to describe it. One night, around 2 or 2.30 a.m. we woke up because of a lot of noise, hearing shouting all round. In the distant, we found people had formed a ring around our colony. They held torches and were beating drums and shouting chants. We realized that our colony was encircled and there would be an attack. We did not know how to defend ourselves.

We all assembled in front of the project-in-charge's house—a young man. We cried and pleaded for our lives to be saved. But he told us that there was no response from the police. Then, he swiftly moved amongst us, reassuring that nothing would happen to us as long as he was alive. He called the local headman. The headman was a contractor. He was given some job as contractor in the project. He told the headman sternly that this attack had to stop if he wanted the project to continue."

The headman had found the project work very profitable. He did not want the project to be over. I was small then. I was so afraid that I was crying. Uncle placed his hand on my head and told me that nothing would happen, but we were not very hopeful. We doubted how much control these two men would have over the crowd.

Outside, the men were baying for our blood. But after some time, we could see that the people were turning back. The shouting had ceased. In fifteen minutes, all was clear. Then we also heard police sirens. But the project head had nerves of steel. He went person to person trying to comfort them. The person was Barun De—a remarkable man.'

I jumped on hearing your name. 'I beg your pardon ... What name did you say?'

'Barun De, chief of project from the Railways.'

Sahiba looked into my eyes and said, 'Barun, I couldn't believe my ears when I heard your name spoken with such reverence. You were carrying out miracles elsewhere as well. Rupa's aunt was overwhelmed when she called out your name.

I told her that I had just met you in Delhi. I told her that I and many others in my village were beneficiaries of Barun. I told her what you did at Gandak. You should have seen her. She was beaming as she listened to your tales. I was dying to tell you this, Barun.'

I thought about it for a while, trying to recall the time.

'She must be the daughter of Gohain, our Personnel Officer. I am glad she is a forest officer now. I forget her name, though ... actually, now that you mention it, Sahiba, I too can recollect that horrible night. I don't know how these things go around in cycles. After the riots on the Muslim minorities, we should have known that there would be some reaction. I blame the media. They spread the hatred and violence. I remember waking up to the noise and saw all the Assamese assembled and crying ... behind them ... an advancing ring of people shouting and beating drums.

'I called Noor Ahmed, the local leader of our small village. I had told him that he needed to act immediately. We had been living peacefully for so long. This must be stopped. I had earlier called on him for some minor work. He had done well for himself through it, and had given others employment. At that time, I did not think he would be able to quell the mob. But in my heart of heart, I hoped... Others told me that he could not be trusted. But there was no way out. Our phones were not working and no help from police was forthcoming. We were without any arms. And in any case, we could not defend ourselves against an invasion. I prayed and told myself that nothing would happen.

'Sahiba, those fifteen minutes were the worst. I did not remember what I was doing then. I was told that I was running from one family to the other trying to comfort them. I remember how relieved I felt when I saw the crowd turning back. Soon, the drumming ceased and the flaming torches moved away. In twenty minutes, everything was clear. Then we heard the sirens. But quiet had already descended in the colony and around us.

'You know what I believe, Sahiba. The people of the area should always be made stakeholders. Noor Ahmed was one. I had told him that this project could be a golden hen, which could continue laying golden eggs as long as it was served and nurtured.

But because of any capricious and greedy action, if the

hen was killed, there won't be any more golden eggs. It had struck him and he must have used all his strength to convince the crowd that these people must not be harmed. I don't know what happened between him and the vengeful crowd, but there was absolutely no damage to the colony.

Sahiba, I had no other power except that of prayer. But if people do not choose to acknowledge god's help, and instead try to put an ordinary person like me on a pedestal, it is not fair.'

Sahiba interjected and said, 'Barun, your faith and belief has been extraordinary. Many of your actions, you consider ordinary. But those little things have actually brought a sea change in the fortunes of those people who had no hope.

I know what happened with me and others in Gandak. For ordinary people, god is not visible. But godly acts can be seen and realized. They see them as extraordinary events. They consider people like you to have wielded extraordinary powers. It is good that you are not considering yourself god and assuming a role that has been assigned to you by god. You symbolize the presence of god.'

I did not want to prolong the discussion. I said nothing, asking Sahiba to continue her narration. I marvelled at the philosophy she had expressed.

Sahiba continued, 'Rupa's aunt is Reema. I told her that Barun had done something like this in Gandak. I was an example of it. I told them that you were coming back to Delhi shortly and I would tell you about this.

I returned to Guwahati with so much love and pride for you, Barun. I had to return to Delhi quickly. But I had to visit St. Joseph's Convent in Darjeeling.

'From New Jalpaiguri, I took a bus and reached the convent before noon. The school bell had rung and all the children and staff were heading for lunch. They were overjoyed to see me, and even more so when they heard that I had successfully completed the management programme. Sister Jane told me that they were very proud of me.

'In the evening, I went to meet Mother Grace. She rose from her chair to embrace me. She put her arms around me and made me sit down beside her. She looked at me with such love and affection that tears rolled down my eyes. Mother leaned forward to wipe my tears and said, "Sahiba, I am so glad that you came here after obtaining this degree. You did not forget your home. I am so proud of you, my child. Now tell me, what you are going to do?"

'I told Mother that there was no question of ever forgetting the convent. It was where I received my early education and shelter. I had come here with nothing. But they had embraced me and made me into a worthy woman. Then I told her the truth.

"Apart from this degree, Mother, I have also received something I must share. I don't know if Maya had ever told how she had decided upon my education. Mother, the person who brought it about is Barun De, the chief engineer of a project in our village. He had made the villagers stakeholders of the project, and our community gained the most from it. He told my mother that she must provide me with proper education. That idea propelled my mother to stealthily send me away. He had gone away and we had not heard of him for a good twenty years.

"Mother, you recall that you suggested that I earn this education myself. With references from the church, I got the job of an event manager, which helped me complete my studies.

A couple of months ago, I was covering a seminar in Delhi with the company. Among the experts, I surprisingly found Dr Barun De! He was attending this seminar. I was excited but I was not sure he would recognize me. But a mention of Maya's name was enough. He had not forgotten anything. He was still Barun. Then he told me so many things I had no idea about, and even promised to tell me the story of our royal family, which Maya couldn't tell me.

Mother, he is a prized possession for me. If he had not advocated for me so strongly, I would still be a girl from the jungle, likely married off to the son of the blacksmith. Mother, I am going back to Delhi. He is also in Delhi now. He is an amazing person and I look towards him with awe—it's an emotion I have not felt so far.'

Mother had listened to me intently. Then she asked, "You have not told me what you are going to do now."

"This company has offered me the position of a Business Executive. The salary is quite good. But we have to discuss things. Barun had also told me that he would help me find a good position. Mother, I think I owe this company something. It might be a good idea to serve them for some time."

She agreed and said, "That is a wonderful idea. I am very happy to learn about Barun from you. It looks like a lot of things are bound to happen now when both of you are together. It looks as if you have to climb some more mountains. One cannot explain your meeting simply, it is no ordinary coincidence, my child.

So, in the days to come, you will be confronted with making some choices in life. If it comes, as I perceive it should, don't blink. Look at its face and decide. We can see that you are an extraordinary person, Sahiba, and god has chosen you to give some extraordinary messages. May god bless you.

But I would love to see both you and Barun here. Let's see what god thinks about it.'

I looked at Mother in wonder. She had spoken so slowly

and with such a strange faraway look in her eyes, I was left to wonder about what she meant. Finally, she wished me farewell with love. "May god bless you, my child."

Barun, her voice is still ringing in my ears. It was full of depths I cannot comprehend.'

I had listened to her story all this while as my feelings coursed through. It moved me. I said, 'Those are stunning words, Sahiba. But one thing is certain. You do still have to climb a number of mountains. But that should not worry you. I think you have decided upon accepting the offer of your company. Mother also seems to have blessed your choice. That's fine. But at the moment, dinner is ready and we can eat.'

'Are you tired?' I added. 'You can then go back to your apartment and rest. You look pretty tired, Sahiba.'

'You are right, Barun. Let me go to the kitchen and help Didimoni lay the dinner.'

'I forgot to ask about your mate, Shruti. How is she?'

'Oh, Shruti? She is not here. She has gone to Bhopal. It appears her parents have fixed her marriage. She should be getting married shortly,' she said with a laugh.

'She is a good girl. It is good to follow the suggestion of your parents in this respect. Shouldn't her marriage ring a bell for you, Sahiba?' I said rising and moving towards the dining table.

'If it is ringing, I do not have time to hear it, Barun. But Shruti is fine and I am very happy for her,' she said in mirth.

We sat down at the table in gaiety. I was amazed to see the fare produced by Sadhana.

'God bless you, Sadhana,' I said. 'You have outdone yourself.'

'Most of it is Bibi's idea and handiwork, Babu. She was busy with me in the kitchen before you came back from the office,' she replied.

Sahiba came and sat down opposite me. I wanted to start eating, but she raised her hand and said, 'Let us say grace first, Barun.' Then she bowed her head and said the prayer. I followed her. I was used to it. Edna too often insisted on it whenever I went to Nick's place for dinner.

I greatly enjoyed the food, but when I looked up I found that Sahiba was hardly eating a thing.

'Why aren't you eating?' I asked.

'I'm tired, Barun. But it is all quite delicious. Thank you.'

I understood. I quickly ended my dinner and I took her to the car. Bahadur dropped her off to her apartment in Vasant Kunj. A good night sleep would do her good, I thought.

## IV
## Sahiba is Sick

Busy in my office, I rang Sahiba up in the afternoon. Her voice sounded sleepy and low. I asked her whether she was at the office. She said that she was in her apartment and not well. I was alarmed.

I told her that I would meet her straight away.

I reached her apartment within fifteen minutes. I went up to her door and knocked. She opened the door and tried to smile feebly. I looked at her pale face and touched her forehead.

'Sahiba, you have high temperature. Have you checked?' I asked. Saying nothing, she fell into my arms, shaking. I carried her inside and helped her onto the bed.

She said that she was not well during the night and had thrown up. Then she felt feverish. She had taken a tablet of Crocin but it did not help.

'You are too sick. I am taking you to the hospital to

have a quick check-up and for some proper treatment. You cannot be alone here'.

She feebly protested but when she saw I was firm, she relented. She picked up a few things and held my hand and followed me out.

I soon left with her to the hospital, entering through the emergency gate. She was quickly attended. The doctor took her blood for some tests. After half an hour, the initial results were available. We were at a loss.

The doctor said that she had typhoid!

I was surprised but kept my cool.

'It would be better to admit her to the hospital. Most of the drugs have to be given intravenously,' he said.

I nodded.

Sahiba now began to protest again.

'I ... won't be able to stay in a hospital.'

I comforted her.

'Look Sahiba, it is essential for you to be in the hospital for two to three days. This type of medical attention won't be available otherwise. Come on, I will come and stay in the hospital with you, if you like.'

At once, she smiled and nodded.

She was admitted into a good private room. She was settled down and the nurses administered some medicine, which seemed to have soothed her immediately.

'Is it fine if I go home and bring some things for my stay? It won't take much time,' I said to her.

She just smiled.

I was out and back within an hour.

The medication had started working. The fever had come down.

When I entered the room, Sahiba turned towards me to ask what I would eat. The doctors had advised certain restrictions in the diet for her.

I told her not to worry because normal food was also available for me. Then, I sat down near Sahiba. I placed my hand on her head to comfort and assure her. She immediately began to speak, 'Barun, thank you so much. I am so scared of hospitals. I could not stay here without you. Shruti is likely to come back by Monday. I can go back to my apartment then.'

'Don't worry about it. You will be fine soon. Tomorrow is the weekend. So, it isn't an issue at all. You come first at the moment. That is for sure,' I told her, my resolve growing firm as I spoke.

She held my hand in hers. 'Barun, you are so nice. I don't know what would have happened to me without you. I wonder where I contracted this disease?'

'This is a waterborne infection. You have been travelling...'

She interrupted me. 'I think it is a good thing. Otherwise, could you imagine me holding your hand like this? It feels as if I have found what I was searching for,' she said with a sparkle in her eyes.

I was struck dumb for a moment. Then I laughed it off.

'You are absolutely crazy, Sahiba. You don't have to fall sick for this.' For god's sake, think good. Don't unnecessarily vex your mind on this,' I said.

'Okay, I will remember that Barun,' she said, her eyes glinting with characteristic mischief.

Sahiba began to improve quite fast. I could see the colour returning on her face by Monday. The doctor said that she could go home if she liked; he too was happy with her rapid recovery. Addressing me, he said, 'She can take oral medicines now. Should be fine in ten days.' Then, turning to her, he said, 'Be careful with your diet. Take the medicines regularly. Don't exert unnecessarily. If you are not careful, there can be a relapse. Okay?'

She nodded obediently.

Sahiba had called Shruti. But she turned to me with worry. Shruti was stuck with work and could not return before the next Monday.

I said, 'Shruti or no Shruti, you are not going to your apartment in this state. The doctor has warned that good care has to be taken. Sahiba, you are coming to my place. With Sadhana around, you will recover fast. Both of you can gossip to pass the time. That will be best.'

She clapped her hands and said, 'Really Barun, can I? That would be wonderful.'

'Of course, you can. Let me call Sadhana. I wish we had a piano at home. Then I would have listened to your music'

'Now don't show me the moon, Barun. This time you are becoming crazy.'

## V
## Sahiba Recuperates

Sahiba was wheeled out on a wheelchair to my car. She resented using the wheel chair, but I had insisted. As soon as we were in the car, she said, 'I looked so sick on the wheelchair. Everyone was looking at me.'

'Good for you, Sahiba. Remember what the doctor said. People were looking at you because you are beautiful.'

She blushed. I told her to cheer up. She gave me a hard look and then smiled.

On reaching home, Sadhana greeted us. And Sahiba hugged her, 'Didimoni, I am back to bother you.'

'Come to your room, Bibi. I have looked after my brother who had typhoid. You have to be very careful. Please lie down, I shall bring some coconut water. It is very good for typhoid. It will soothe your stomach.' Sadhana escorted her to her bedroom, reciting instructions all the way. Then she brought her some coconut water, which Sahiba seemed to like.

Later, I spoke to Sadhana, 'It is good that you have experience handling a typhoid patient. I am sorry for the inconvenience but you will have to take good care of her.'

'It is very good that you brought her here, Babu. She won't be able to manage alone in her apartment. I know what kind of food suits typhoid patients. There is no workload, Babu. Doing anything for Bibi is enjoyable,' Sadhana said warmly.

Then Sadhana noted down all the schedules of the medicines Sahiba had to be given. Sadhana proved to be very strict with Sahiba. She would not allow her to undertake any kind of unnecessary exertion. As a result, Sahiba kept making good improvement throughout the day. She took complete charge of Sahiba and offered to stay during the night also. But I insisted that she go home. I could manage myself. Sahiba was in much better shape now.

For the first two–three days, I spent the night in her room, sleeping on the couch. I often sat down by her side on the bed and slowly caressed her head, which Sahiba was very pleased with. One night, I dozed off next to her. After quite some time, I felt Sahiba's soft hands on my head and woke up.

She kept stroking the hair on my head. I remembered my mother used to do this in my childhood. The soft touch of her hand made me close my eyes once again, almost drifting off. When I looked up, I was surprised.

Sahiba was crying.

'What is the matter?' I asked.

Sahiba said nothing. My mother too used to cry while caressing my head. I looked up again and said, 'Sahiba, try to sleep. Crying is not good for you.'

'These are tears of love and joy, Barun. You must be

tired, but you are awake so that I sleep better. I have never felt a loving touch before. I feel as if I have grown wings now, Barun,' she said, crying.

'Where does my little fairy want to fly to?' I asked, trying to cheer her.

'I will not tell you now. But Barun, you must sleep. You have work tomorrow.'

I smiled and said, 'When you caressed my head, I felt my mother's touch. I've seen her cry in the same manner. She never told me why. She too would smile lovingly when I asked her about it. Sahiba, you have kindled that old love. I had forgotten about it completely. When I saw you crying, I didn't know what was happening to me. Were my mother's tears also tears of love and joy?'

She held my head in both her hands and looked lovingly into my eyes and nodded.

'The tears of joy were always spontaneous. They were a mark of love in its purest form,' Sahiba said.

The doctors had said that she would need care for three weeks at the least. With the help of Sadhana, Sahiba made rapid progress. She started sitting in the living room by herself and would talk to Sadhana, who also seemed to enjoy the gossip. Sadhana would make some simple Bengali dishes without spice and some khichdi. I also partook of the dishes sometimes and quite enjoyed it. Sahiba insisted that I eat what I normally liked, and usually, I would tease her. 'You are becoming possessive of your Didimoni. You don't like to share what she prepares for you.'

'Don't try to be mean Barun. It is out of your character,' she would retort.

Finally, one day she mentioned that Shruti would be back and she could go back to her apartment. I was aghast. I did not want her to leave. I immediately countered. 'That is out of question, Sahiba. You also know it. Moreover, Sadhana would be heartbroken if she comes to know about it. But I have an idea. Why don't you invite Shruti to come and stay with us? Both of you have a lot of things to talk about. You can continue to enjoy the hospitality of Sadhana as well.'

'That would be kind of you, Barun. Shruti is a fine person. She is very affectionate. We have grown very fond of each other over the years. But this would add workload and crowd your house. We should ask Didimoni first,' she said gaily.

'You can ask your Didimoni, of course. But be prepared for a reprimand.' I joked.

'No, no. We cannot take Didimoni for granted in these matters,' she said. She called for Didimoni and apologetically said, 'Didimoni, my friend and roommate, Shruti, is coming from Bhopal. Barun suggests that we invite her to stay here with us. If you agree, of course.'

Sadhana gave her a hard look and then disappeared into the kitchen. She appeared after a while and said, 'Bibi, good that you and Babu are asking me if I can serve your friend. I have only two hands, you can see. It will be really too much for me. Have some mercy, Bibi,' she said with mock sarcasm and went back into the kitchen.

I looked towards Sahiba with a look on my face. I had told her so.

Sahiba looked at me sheepishly, then got up and followed her to the kitchen.

'Didimoni, I am sorry. Actually, Barun had warned me that you would be angry but I thought I should ask you. Please forgive me.' Sadhana laughed, then hugged her. She said if she called her Didimoni, she would never ask again. Sahiba took her hands and made her sit down, wiping tears from her eyes. Sahiba was so overwhelmed.

With that little dramatic scene, it was settled that

Shruti would come straightaway from the station. Shruti's arrival raised the spirits of the house. Sahiba looked at the engagement ring shining on her finger and held her in deep embrace. 'Congratulations, Shruti. You never told me that you were held up because you were getting engaged. Anyway, what a beautiful ring on your lovely finger. Look, Barun. She is a gem.'

I came forward to congratulate her. 'You are really glowing. May god bless both of you, my dear.'

Sahiba even introduced her to Sadhana, 'She is Shruti, Didimoni. Look, she has come here after her engagement. My sweet Didimoni, my dear, you can't believe how she cared and nursed after me. You will love to eat what she cooks. Didimoni, shall I take her to my room?'

Sadhana said, 'So lovely Mishima. What a lovely ring. Our blessings.'

Shruti asked her, 'What is Mishima, Didimoni?'

'We call our little sister as Mishima.' Pointing towards Sahiba, she said 'She is Bibi—the elder one.'

Saying this, Sadhana took her to her room.

I got ready quickly and left early as the two friends talked to each other. I was glad about Shruti's visit because I was going to be busy for the next three or four days. Nick was coming from Washington. We were supposed to be travelling to Bombay for a meeting. After some quick breakfast, I left for the office. I had told Sadhana that I might be going away to Bombay either today or maybe next day early morning, usually preferring to go a day earlier to avoid the early morning flight.

Shruti and Sahiba came out together after I left. Shruti had helped Sahiba get ready. On learning that I had gone, Sahiba was very disappointed.

Sadhana comforted her. She told her that Babu was in a hurry. His big boss was coming from America. He might have to go to Bombay today. She said that the driver was here and if Shruti wanted to go somewhere the car was ready.

At the office, Nick was very warm. I asked after Edna.

'She is much better now,' he said. 'She told me that she could manage by herself. I was told Sahiba was sick and that she is now with you,' Nick said.

'She had been travelling in Assam and caught typhoid somewhere. She's been living with me since her roommate was not here. Her friend has returned now. I can go to Bombay for the meeting. When do you plan to go? This evening?'

'A good Samaritan all the way, Barun. I am glad you could help Sahiba. I only met her briefly in Delhi last time, but I am glad that she is recovering. I know you like to travel in the evening. If we finish our engagements here by 3 p.m., we can take the 7 p.m. flight to Bombay?'

I agreed.

We were able to finish our schedule as planned. We left the office by 3.30 p.m. I thought I could spend about forty-five minutes saying goodbye to Sahiba before leaving for the airport. Nick left too, saying that he would come to the airport after checking out from his hotel.

Sahiba welcomed me warmly at home. She was wearing a pretty kaftan-like dress.

She said, 'Barun, I am sorry, I missed you at breakfast. I wanted to know everything about Shruti, how did the engagement take place and all that. Shruti's parents knew Manish's parents rather well. It is a wonderful way of getting married. Manish seems to be very nice. He is a software engineer in Delhi.'

'That is great! I'm glad they all approve,' I said.

'Yes. I am dying to see Manish.'

'Where is Shruti by the way?' I asked.

'We had left for the hospital in a hurry and I did not

have my things. Shruti had gone to our apartment to get them and also to get the room cleaned. Here she is,' she said as Shruti walked back in.

Shruti had brought her things and some bags from the market.

As we were talking, Shruti also joined us. I thanked her for helping Sahiba.

Then I told them both, 'Sahiba, I am leaving for Bombay. Nick has come from America. We have a meeting there. I shall be back in Delhi the day after tomorrow. Both of you enjoy yourselves in my absence. Sahiba, you must take care. I am sure Sadhana will also take care of you.'

I packed up and as I was ready to leave, Sadhana brought out my evening tea, saying, 'Bibi reminded me to give you the tea you like. Bibi can also join you for tea.'

I thanked her.

It was true. I would normally not get it if I was away from home.

Then, I told Sahiba, 'Look I am putting on the tie you brought for me from Assam. It looks so nice.' She got up from the sofa and adjusted the knot a bit. 'Barun, you look smashing. I am sure you are going to kill someone.'

'You are hitting under the belt, baby. I won't kill you for sure.'

'Don't talk of me, Sir. I am already dead. You can't hurt Shruti. She has Manish to care for now,' she teased relentlessly.

'Shruti, I am sorry. You have to take care of your friend. I find that her sickness has made her lose her balance. She won't spare anybody. I am the most vulnerable at the present. So, I must escape,' I said, getting ready to leave.

Then I bid goodbye to Sadhana, smiling at the two friends, and was out of the door.

I was quite in time. Nick was waiting for me. We boarded

the flight together. Nick seemed tired after the overnight flight from Washington. He dozed off as soon as we were airborne. I kept thinking about Sahiba. I had started to care for her while she was sick. I always thought that she was still an innocent child. It was cruel that she had nobody from her childhood who could give her emotional support when she needed it.

She had found me, even though my interactions with her were minimal. But she thought that I was central to her destiny. I too felt that destiny had again brought us together. She needed help and I had an obligation to support her. If her mother was alive, she would have got it from her mother.

Nick had jokingly said that I had acted like a good Samaritan. But I believed that I had wanted to provide emotional support. She had said that nobody had caressed her head before, even if she was really sick. Was it an act of deliberate show of care or concern? No, it was spontaneous. I felt that I caressed her aching head lovingly. In the process, I had fallen asleep. She had caressed my head too. This meant that we both had crossed some line. My words of caution to Shruti were real. Sahiba had lost that fine balance and I truly was vulnerable.

The two days I spent in Bombay were hectic. We returned to Delhi for lunch the next day. Nick was going back to Washington that very night. I told him that he could spend some time with us in the evening and have dinner before leaving for the airport. He agreed and I informed Sadhana. 'That sounds wonderful, Barun. I have not seen your new apartment also. I would love to meet Sahiba,' Nick told me. I told Sadhana that Nick would be coming in the evening—so, she could do whatever was manageable before Nick arrived.

I came back in the evening by 6.30 p.m. to see the house done up already; flowers had been placed around the house.

Both Sahiba and Shruti were dressed.

Sahiba hugged me. 'You look beautiful,' I said.

She held my hand and brought me in. Then, as I was still looking at her admiringly, she said, 'Shruti helped me dress up. It is good that Nick is coming. What time does he come?'

'He'll be coming around 8.30 p.m. for dinner; he'll leave in an hour. He is specially coming to see you, Sahiba. He was quite concerned when he heard about your sickness. He said that he would be glad to meet Shruti too. Oh, I hope Sadhana has made something special for dinner. Nick is not very particular, but he loves Indian food.'

Sadhana popped out from the kitchen wearing a good sari. She smiled and said, 'Bibi told me to put it on as Nick Saheb is coming. She and Mishima have also made some suggestions about what to prepare. I think it should be good enough.'

'You look great Sadhana. I like it. Don't worry too much about food ... so long it is not very spicy. Let me also get ready. After dinner is ready, you can go. We can manage. Nick is a homely guy,' I told Sadhana appreciatively.

'No, Babu. Don't worry about that.'

Nick arrived in time and went straight to greet Sahiba, 'How are you, my dear? You're looking much better. It is good that you are with Barun. He is a very indulgent and caring man. We call him a good Samaritan.'

Then he looked at Shruti, 'Nice to meet you again, Barun tells me you have been recently engaged. How wonderful. Congratulations!'

Sahiba asked him about Edna's health.

'She's much better now.'

Then Sahiba said, 'Barun has been wonderful. He devises means to help. I was very young when we first met at the Gandak Project. Had it not been for him, I would have still been in the forest village.'

'And been married to the son of the blacksmith to live a contented life,' I teased her.

'Nick, can you see how mean he can be? I don't know about contentment but I would have been married, Mr Barun. That is for sure,' Sahiba retorted.

'And not still be an unmarried dame. That is also sure,' I continued teasing her.

'Barun, now stop it. Sahiba, I can see a lot of things clearly now,' Nick intervened.

'Such as?' Sahiba asked.

'The blush and colour on your face. It is a beautiful sign,' Nick said.

Everyone was enjoying the light-hearted banter. Sadhana came out of the kitchen and announced that dinner was ready. Sahiba got up to go to the kitchen for help, but Sadhana forbade it.

Then, she looked towards me and said, 'Babu, look how Sahiba enjoys the light air. I suggest that you take her out of Delhi for some time. It will do her really good.'

'That is a wonderful idea,' Nick said. 'Change of air would do a world of good. Barun, why not take her to Austria for about ten days? The weather would be wonderful now. I can help you organize it if you wish.'

'That's a good idea, Nick, but it is sudden. It has to be discussed. Sahiba has to decide for herself,' I said.

We ate heartily and Nick left soon after the dinner. Sadhana had stayed back and helped put away the dishes. I thanked her for the excellent dinner and all other arrangements, and all of us went off to rest.

The next day was a weekend. We were all free. Come next morning, and we were just enjoying our morning tea. Sahiba told me that Manish had already come. Shruti would be going today to spend some time with him. She said that she could also go back to the apartment with Shruti now. It was fine with Shruti.

'Oh my, Sahiba. Do you mean to say you are going to join Manish and Shruti? Let them enjoy their time together. It is better that you stay put here. Sadhana has also said that you should have some good change of air. It will help you recoup faster,' I said.

Before she could reply, Sadhana went ahead and said, 'Babu, I know how weakening this disease is. Bibi does not realize this. I am sure an outing of a week or ten days will do her so good. Look how pale your skin looks, Bibi. Good air will restore the colour, Bibi.'

'I don't know ... where can I go?' Sahiba whined.

'Yes, that is what should we think about,' I cajoled. 'In summer it is not worth the effort going to Goa. The hills involve a lot of climbing, which you should not do. That brings us to what Nick suggested. Austria is a beautiful country. You have forests and lakes there and the air is wonderfully cool and pleasant. Should we have an excursion of about fifteen days in Austria?' I asked.

'You mean, you and I go? What about your office, Barun?' she asked in surprise.

'My dear, we are also entitled to some holidays from the bank. It is paid for. You heard Nick talking about it. That is not a problem.'

'But...'

'Can you go alone? Can you fly alone?'

'That is out of the question. And you know that, Barun. But it must be pretty expensive. I don't want you to spend so much money on me,' she said with apparent indignation.

I took her face in my hands and looked her in the eyes.

'And why should I not spend my time and money on you?'

Sadhana was listening to both of us. She added, 'Bibi it will be good for both of you. Babu is also tired. I have never seen him taking a leave. So, on this pretext, he will also benefit. And I too will go and see my aunt in Bengal.'

Sahiba got up and hugged Sadhana, 'That is perfect. You are wonderful, Didimoni. It is for Barun's sake that I'm agreeing to go. If he enjoys himself, even for a moment, my life will be fulfilled. I have seen him working like this for years, Didimoni. He deserves the biggest break. And we will all be so happy if you take a vacation too. You have been working so hard to look after me, Didimoni.'

'So, we will all have a break,' I said. 'That is the best solution—a win-win. I thank you for the suggestion, Sadhana. I will make all arrangements for your travel to Calcutta. If you want to fly, I shall organize that,' I said.

'No, no. I won't fly. My younger brother will go with me. We will go by train. I shall go only after you have gone and I will be back by the time you are back,' Sadhana said.

Now that all of us have agreed, I started working on the programme. Shruti had gone back to her apartment. Her fiancé was in Delhi with her. It was a good idea to leave them alone. Nick had told someone in Vienna to make local arrangements; Sahiba had a valid passport too. Nick knew someone in the Austrian Embassy and Sahiba got a visa for the EU. I had a UN passport and I didn't need a visa. The travel agent made all the other arrangements. The programme included three days in Switzerland as well before returning to Delhi.

I told Sadhana that we would leave on Friday. She could also go to Calcutta that evening.

She said that her brother would be off from Saturday, and so she would leave the next day. She said that she would return after ten days. We were set to return after about thirteen days. That suited everyone.

I told Sahiba that she would have to shop; she needed some clothes for the tour. Immediately, Sahiba wanted to go to the bank.

'Why bother?' I asked. 'If you insist, you can give me a cheque. I will give you the cash. I shall also get you a forex card, which will take care of your local use there.'

But she insisted. I told her that we could go to the bank before we left, and she was relieved.

All the arrangements were made in time. Sahiba seemed giddy with excitement. But now that she was well, I wanted to tell her about Maya. It was time. One evening, I told her that I would tell her the story Maya had told me.

'Yes, Barun, I remember. I fell sick and was not in a state to listen. I wanted to be alert when you recounted the story,' she said, agreeing to listen as she sat down next to me in the living room.

'Actually, Maya had told us the story long ago. I had almost forgotten it. You told me your version when we last met and I had shown you the chain Maya had given me. Only after all that did I remember it clearly...'

'Thanks for everything, Barun. I think we may sit down for the session today after dinner. Don't you agree?'

I agreed.

*Five*

# Sahiba, the Princess

She had said that the story was traditionally told to daughters by their royal mothers. Maya told us the story in Bagaha. She had come to give me a chain as a gift; then she had told us a story, breaking family tradition. Had she already made up her mind to send Payoli away? Did she hope that we would get a chance to tell Payoli? I don't know. It was merely a story for us. We never knew we would meet Payoli ever again.

When I met her after twenty years, Sahiba was not aware of her royal status; she did not know why her name was changed from Payoli to Sahiba. She did not know the significance of the engraved necklace. She did not know why there was only one chain instead of two. Had we not met, she would have never known.

So, when I sat down that Friday evening to tell Sahiba the story, I trusted my memory. I did not want to miss any essential part of the tale because I was fond of Sahiba. I felt as if Maya had entrusted this responsibility upon me. So, with serious intent, I started the tale.

## II
### The State of Jhuluk

Thar desert was once a large and monstrous arid region, inhospitable as it spread over the western part of India.

Today it extends beyond Pakistan and has a good presence in Rajasthan as well as parts of Gujarat.

The desert is known for its numerous sand dunes, and cross-country winds make the region quite devastating. People still travel on desert mules and camels. In early AD 1500 or so, the site was significant. It provided the only trade route, popularly known as the Silk Route (earlier silk was the most famous export item), to outside India via Jaisalmer. Traders from all parts took this route for their trade. But this route was also rampaged by camel-riding pirates.

Jaisalmer's rulers provided some security to the traders from the attacks and in return, the traders paid some specified sum or fee. In the southwest, the desert housed many other princely states: Barmer, Marwar, Udaipur, etc. The other princely states located in the trade path also provided protection against these pirates. The fee charged by the princely states for the protection was also one of the sources of their revenue. And so, the interests of these pirates were in conflict with the princely states. In order to retain their respective supremacy in the area, wars often broke out between them.

The people in this area were very hard, weather and war beaten. There are many stories of personal valour described in the history of the region. They say that in the princely states, people were fierce and brave. They even say that the bandits were cruel, deceitful and unscrupulous.

Within these areas stood the small princely state of Jhuluk, perched between two hills. In its heyday, the kingdom was known to have great power, exerting a strong influence over the area. The kingdom was reputed for patronizing cultures and arts, even as they trained their people in warfare.

As Rajputs, they took pride in their historical and cultural heritage. In the course of time, their influence declined. It was said in history that after an apparent decline, a stronger heir would emerge. He, by dint of his sole personal show of power, would bring back the past glory of the state; the state would never show any sign of its depleted strength. That was the hallmark of the Rajputana, as Rajasthan was then called. A very high premium was placed on personal and family honour, and people would sacrifice their lives for such purpose.

King Raunaq Singh of Jhuluk had died some years ago in a battle. Since then, Queen Chandni Bai had ruled the state. Her daughter, the princess, was named to ultimately succeed her mother. The name of the princess was Sahiba.

## III
## Grooming Princess Sahiba

The Queen Mother was a good warrior. Even though Sahiba was young, she was trained to take over from her mother in all aspects. She was an expert horse rider and good at sword fighting and spear fighting. She was rigorously trained in warfare by the experts. Sahiba was beautiful as well. People talked of her beauty and her expertise as a fierce warrior.

Her governess, Pratibha, belonged to a princely family in Cooch Behar in Bengal. Sahiba's father, King Raunaq Singh, had specially brought her to groom Sahiba in stately manners and music. He felt that when Sahiba took control of the kingdom, she should be adept at more than fighting. He used to dote on her daughter as she had shown a lot of promise even at her young age.

She soon grew to be a fearless and expert fighter. The princely states of the area were known to have faced many invasions or assault from outside and all of royal blood had to learn to fight. Sahiba was thus trained to be a good and expert warrior.

But as she grew up, she had turned out to be a beautiful

princess. She caught the attention of many rulers from many neighbouring states. Sahiba was to be the ruling princess and had no time for these frivolities. She, therefore, devoted most of her time to honing her skills as a good fighter.

Sahiba had a manservant by the name of Sham Sher Singh. He was a tall and well-built man, with enormous strength and skill. He served the princess as her bodyguard and trainer in arms and warfare. He was very subservient to the princess and would hardly look into her eyes. Sham Sher Singh was aware that one day the princess would take the reins of Jhaluk. She was the king or queen-in-waiting.

Sham Sher Singh had been specially selected by the Queen Mother. He was sworn to loyalty towards Sahiba, his finger dipped in his blood to show his devotion. In Rajputana, this was custom and meant that he could be trusted to take responsibility of the safety of the princess. Sahiba considered herself quite strong and competent and would have strongly resented someone being in charge of her safety. So, Sham Sher Singh never mentioned his role to the princess. Instead, he would tell her that he was to help her practice higher skills in sword or spear fighting. She was quite comfortable with that.

In the course of training, he often took her to a nearby forest to practice throwing the spear at a running deer. Sham Sher Singh also asked her to practice hitting the tree with a spot marked on it. Sham Sher Singh was an ace shooter. He would never miss a target. He had explained everything to her—how to grip the spear, what the position of her feet should be and how her body should bend. As a coach, he was never allowed to touch her.

The princess was a good learner. She would imitate the action by observing her trainer and then shoot, learning to hold her own. Once while chasing a deer from her horse, she did not notice a low-hanging branch. She was hit by the branch and fell down. She had hurt her shoulder a little. Sham Sher Singh was following her on his horse. Having seen the princess fall, he got off his horse. He wanted to touch her shoulder and help her up. The princess suddenly grew furious and shouted, 'Sham Sher Singh, come back to your senses. How dare you touch me? Keep a distance or you will regret it.'

The fury in her reprimand was enough for Sham Sher Singh to fall back. He apologized profusely for his indiscretion. The princess said, 'Remember this your entire life. I am a warrior. I know how to recover from a fall. I am also a princess. No man can dare to touch me.'

Sham Sher Singh was taken aback by her furious demeanour. He had never seen this side of her. He of course knew that he was not supposed to touch her in course of the training. He came closer to take a good look at the injury suffered by the princess after her fall.

But the warning now set the tone. It was good enough for him for two reasons: one, he now knew where to draw the line in his conduct and two, he now had to appreciate her courage and grit while dealing with a setback. She was emphatic that she could stand up on her own. During her fighting lessons, she wielded the sword as if Sham Sher Singh was her equal. Sham Sher Singh was an ace swordsman. His riding skills on the horse or a camel was well known. Sahiba was also gradually acquiring that level of expertise. But his superior skills never awed the princess. She was fiercely conscious that she was a princess destined for the throne.

The Queen Mother and Sahiba were both aware that a ruler had to be strong and also excel in many other ways. Sahiba was determined to demonstrate her steely courage, strong grit and fearful fighting skill.

Alongside, she also took her lessons with her governess with equal keenness. Sahiba was not a great lover of music but she wanted to learn the nuances of music to develop an appreciation for the court. She learnt from Pratibha who was well versed in courtly manners and conduct. Pratibha also wanted the princess to learn a foreign language. She had explained that it would enable them talk in a language the public could not understand. Sahiba decided to learn Bangla because nobody spoke the language in the state.

She learnt to converse with her governess and her mother in Bangla. The governess also helped her learn how to dress, take care of her face and keep her body healthy. Sahiba was made conscious of her beauty and she learnt to preserve and enhance it. So, even though she was learning to fight with the likes of Sham Sher Singh with weapons used by strong men, she learnt to look after her skin also. She also learnt dance because she felt it would make her body and limbs supple. This would enhance her power to be a good warrior. It had improved her gaze as well.

In a nutshell, Sahiba was on the path to achieve great things. She was being taught well, quickly acquiring the confidence and power that would make her a worthy ruler. Everyone was pleased with her progress.

Even after her father died, Sahiba continued to grow. The Queen Mother took steps to make sure that Sahiba was cared for and taught to be a powerful ruler, known for her valour and her beauty. For a mother, her daughter's beauty and personality are a matter of pride. For a father, the valour in his offspring is endearing. The Queen Mother was a combination of both after the king had died. So, she was naturally very happy how Sahiba was progressing. Sahiba also saw in her mother the picture of her father, who was the king. That is why, when her mother told something firmly or sternly, she would not question or argue. She would accept it without demur.

## IV
## Ominous Clouds Gather in Jhaluk

Everything appeared to be going on well in the state of Jhaluk. Or so it seemed. One perceptible difference appeared in the revenue collection of the state—it was declining. In course of time, an alternative sea route had been developed for the purpose of trade. The new route went around the earlier hostile trade route through the Thar Desert.

Apart from the hostility of the terrain, the business was also being taxed at multiple points. The danger from the camel-borne pirates had not ceased. In the past, this collection was well regulated. Over the years, some of the states had also become more demanding. Therefore, when alternative sea routes became available, traders preferred it and as a result the volume of trade through the desert route had declined.

This decline in the revenue from the trade route and taxes had affected everyone in the area, including the princely states and pirates. The pirates lost their only source of income. The states lost a major part of their income. The pirates were more desperate now and they wanted to ensure that the trade business thrived. Everyone had realized that the protection fee had to be reasonable. They were, thus, keen that the hen laying golden eggs was preserved and not killed.

The states consulted amongst themselves to reduce tariffs at major trade routes to entice traders. The pirates also wanted to be a part of such consultations. In order to assert their authority, they started attacking the local people in the villages of some states.

One such pirate was Jia Khan, a daredevil leading a gang of desperadoes. Jia Khan was smart and cunning, with the farsightedness to secure his influence in the region. He intended to form an alliance with some of the princely states. He advocated that such an alliance would enable the states to collect all the revenue from the trade business at a single window. Traders would not have to pay at each juncture. This collection could be then shared between the states and himself. It was clear that he sought legitimacy for himself and his group. He wanted to be treated as a partner in the business, not an adversary.

However, he strong-armed the smaller states for this purpose. On paper, the scheme looked attractive. But there was no guarantee in terms of distribution. Smaller princely states were threatened. These states were reluctant to join hands and challenge the threat posed by Jia Khan. It was a tragedy. The Indian history is replete with incidents like this. That is how Mughals overwhelmed state after state in India despite having a small army. The combined might of the local forces would have easily defeated the invading army. Had it been so, the Indian history would have been written differently.

In this manner, apprehensions grew in Jhaluk. The wily Jia Khan eyed this state with particular interest. He knew the history of princely states. He knew how they would refuse to help a neighbouring queen in times of distress. He was sure that no one would come to help Jhaluk if he twisted their arms. In willful act of provocation, he raided and looted some villages in the bordering areas. Then, in the name of carrying out negotiations, he obtained a degree of legitimacy and sought a meeting with the queen.

## V
### Indecent Proposal

Jia Khan could not have dared to do what he had just done earlier. He had submitted the same old proposals and shamelessly feigned ignorance regarding the attack on border villages. His misdemeanour or mischiefs were becoming frequent. The clouds of trouble seemed to be gathering over the state of Jhuluk.

Jia Khan was cunning. He had heard about the beauty of the princess. His greed therefore had crossed all limits of decency. So, he sought an audience with the Queen Mother in a respectful manner. The queen had agreed to meet him to listen to what he had to say.

He saluted her with great respect. He placed an expensive gift at her feet as a token of his regard for the state. Then, he took a seat. The queen faced him, partly hidden by the veil.

Jia Khan began by praising the valour of the late king. He congratulated her for ruling the state in a befitting manner. Then he said, 'Rani Ma, I must tell you that your neighbours have some evil designs against you. They think that a state ruled by a woman can always be won over. They also say that there is no male successor to the kingdom. They are very petty. It would be wise to be careful and vigilant against them.'

The queen replied, 'There is nothing new in what you say. That is their typical trait for generations. We are not particularly worried about them. Now, Jia Khan, tell me the actual purpose for this meeting with me.'

'Rani Ma, I am sorry. Don't misunderstand. I have a powerful outfit with me and my only interest is to see the welfare of this state. I have earlier said that we can form a powerful alliance in the area. I know that people in the borders are feeling disenchanted with your rule. You should not take their loyalty for granted. These are not good signs, you know. There are many challenges around you. It is time to reassess your own strength.'

The queen was angry but she somehow controlled it and said, 'I know what is happening here. I also know who is fomenting the trouble. But I am yet to hear what you have got to say.'

Jia Khan smiled, 'I must thank you for your patience. Of course, we are not here to talk about niceties alone. I have a wonderful proposal. The might of your state and that of my humble self can be united to form a formidable alliance. It will turn the fortune of the state. We will jointly be able to regain the past glory of Jhaluk.'

The queen was seething in rage but said nothing.

Encouraged by her silence, Jia Khan continued, 'Rani Ma, I have thought over a great deal. To make this union strong, like that of a rock, I propose to seek the hand of your dear daughter, the princess, Sahiba, in marriage. The union of the two powerful forces will rule over the region. Although I could have sent this proposal through my emissary … I wanted to be the one to present it to you, Rani Ma.'

She had had enough. The queen got up in a trembling rage and said, 'How dare you suggest or even think of such an unholy thing? It is preposterous. Leave this palace at once.'

Jia Khan was unfazed and said very soothingly, 'Rani Ma, don't be angry, please. But just remember that the Rajput King Bharmal of Amber had offered the hand of his daughter Jodha Bai to the Emperor Akbar to buy peace and maintain the sovereignty of his state. You are placed in a similar situation.'

The queen hissed, 'He was an Emperor and you are but a bandit! What sort of a similar situation?'

With hurt in his voice, he said, 'I am a bandit? I have to remind you that today I also rule. The grandfather of Akbar was also an armed bandit who invaded this country. If you trace the history of all the princes in this region, they were all bandits once upon a time.

Rani Ma, do not stand on this false sense of honour. Honour lies in one's strength and power, in the power of his sword. I have that power now. The powerful man does not have any religion or propriety. Whatever he does, it becomes proper. His strength is the religion. That is why King Bharmal did not consider religion as a condition to marry his daughter to a Mughal king. Sahiba Begum can practice her own religion even after the marriage.'

'Get out,' the queen said simply.

Jia Khan looked at her arrogantly. Finally, he said, 'Yes, I am going. I had come with your welfare in mind. But I shall strongly advise you to reassess your power. Please check and recheck the loyalty of each of your men. The power has a great sway over the loyalty of persons. After all, loyalty is earned by power alone.

Secondly, also remember your recent power has not been tested. Anything can happen in this condition. Your daughter may even be abducted. God forbid it. But I am cautioning you before you finally spurn my offer. I shall patiently wait for a month. I know such matters cannot be decided in a huff. So khuda hafiz, Rani Ma.'

Jia Khan left in style, leaving the court in panic.

Jia Khan had been right. Two things which he had uttered were of great significance. One was to reassess the power the state of Jhaluk could wield now. It was a fact that Jhaluk had not been tested in a warfare in recent times. The last war the king had won was ten years ago. Many old soldiers were either no more or were too rusty. Their weapons were old and rusty too.

The loyalty of her people was also in question. Loyalty could not be absolute or it could not be taken for granted. It was true that power generated loyalty. Loyalty of a few can be on emotional account. But would that tilt the balance in the case of a war?

Why had Jia Khan made this remark? The queen

pondered. He had also talked about villagers along the border feeling disenchanted. Why were they disenchanted? They were attacked by Jia Khan's men. The state administration of Jhaluk did not even visit them. There was no retaliation. It could lead to disenchantment. The state had the responsibility to protect the lives of its subjects and their property. She had let them down in this respect.

The Queen Mother learnt where her weaknesses lay now. She had to think beyond the individual valour of her daughter and the fighting Sham Sher Singh. She had to reassess her firepower. Yes, it was an indecent proposal, but it sounded the signals of danger.

## VI
### Reassessment

The Queen Mother told Sahiba what had happened. Sahiba was enraged and told her mother that she was strong enough to fight him alone.

'It is most preposterous, mother. I wonder how the fellow got away alive after insulting us. I know how to protect my honour. We have many strong and brave men who can give him a befitting reply.'

The queen shushed her. 'Never be angry while dealing with such matters. This is what your father used to say. Anger shuts the door of reason and intelligence. I was also angry. But I wanted to restrain myself. One who comes with such indecent proposal is either a lunatic or knows his strength. Jia Khan is not a lunatic. Do I have people who can overpower him? We have not fought any wars for the last ten years now. Our weapons are rusty. We have not recruited any soldiers into our armies. You alone have been training every day with Sham Sher Singh to remain fit. But that is not true for the army. Do we know who are still loyal? If you enter into a war without knowing your own battle strength, it may turn out to be an avoidable defeat.'

'Does that mean, we are giving up even before the war?' Sahiba asked in dismay.

'No, I have not said that. Jia Khan has pointed out our weakness. How did he have such a read on our weakness? We did not retaliate when our villages in the border were attacked. Our reaction should have been exemplary. We did not do so. That was either due to lethargy, indifference or inherent weakness in our defence system. All of them are dangerous to the well-being of a state,' the Queen Mother said.

Sahiba was still angry. She could appreciate her mother's cold logic but she wanted some quick action. She thought her mother was dithering.

The Queen Mother continued, 'We must reassess our preparedness for war. That is the immediate task. Strengthen our army. We have to procure some new weapon. We should visit the villages which were attacked. Assure our people. The most important concern is to check and recheck our people's loyalty.'

'You mean to check the loyalty of people like Sham Sher Singh?'

The Queen Mother nodded. Then said, 'Loyalty is earned through a display of power. That is what Jia Khan said as well. Fear makes people loyal. We have not displayed our firepower for a long time. It is necessary to reestablish a fear of state power again. It is time we weigh all the options before us.'

'Then marrying off to a bandit is also an option in your mind, mother?'

'Don't be stupid. You can clearly see that his design is to get hold of the entire state without bloodshed. After such a marriage, he would coolly throw us off or kill us. No, there is no question of accepting such an indecent proposal. But we have to look for an option beyond this. And we must do it the right away. Remember that we cannot count upon the valour or loyalty of Sham Sher Singh alone. We want many like him to be with us,' the Queen Mother said.

The next day, the Queen Mother asked Sham Sher Singh to come with her to visit the villages that had been attacked. They met the affected people. The villagers were happy to see the queen. They did not have many valuable things and had only lost some cows and food grains. She immediately announced that their losses would be compensated by the state. She said that it was clear that the intention of the invaders was to just harass them. By doing so, they were perhaps sending a message to the state that they could attack them at will and without any fear. The queen promised quick action before she left.

While returning from the village, she told Sham Sher Singh, 'Some difficult times are ahead Sham Sher Singh. Jia Khan is threatening us. You have pledged your loyalty in blood to us, and particularly to Sahiba. I suspect that Jia Khan has secretly tried to poison the trust of our people. I respect and honour your personal loyalty. But perhaps the time has come for everyone to renew or reaffirm their loyalty to Jhaluk.'

She then became silent and looked towards Sham Sher Singh.

He understood the meaning of her stance at once. He drew his sword and was in the process of striking his thigh to draw blood. The Queen Mother stopped him. She smiled at him, 'That will do. You must preserve each drop of your blood, Sham Sher. Jhaluk may have greater demands on our blood. Remember, for the last ten years, we haven't shed any blood. But listen, we are talking as we ride. I have a premonition. The palace may not be a very safe place to talk about the secrets of the state.'

Sham Sher Singh was still holding the sword in his hand. He slowly put it back in its sheath and said, 'Rani Ma, I have also heard that Jia Khan has increased his strength many times. This fellow is strong and cunning. But he has certainly made a grave mistake if he thinks Jhaluk is an easy catch. He has not tested the strength of our army. We have not lost any battles so far.

Rani Ma, you have seen that they did not find a sizeable loot after attacking the villagers. Those villagers did not have any thing valuable. It meant that their purpose was only to provoke us. He also wants to check our strength. From that point of view, your personal visit should serve as a warning.'

'One has to be careful all the time. However, a small incident comes to mind. After your mention of trust, it might have some larger significance. I was standing at a distance as Jia Khan came out after meeting you. He probably did not see me. After riding a small distance, he stopped and looked towards a big tree. He appeared to be saying something to the tree. He then nodded and rode away. After a while, I saw a palace guard emerging from behind the tree. He soon disappeared. I couldn't see his face. Actually, it did not occur to me that he was saying something to the bandit. The important question is this: how does Jia Khan have access to a palace guard and for what reason?'

The queen heard him, masking her alarm under a calm guise. She said, 'This fellow wants to know whatever is happening here. Likewise, he must have infiltrated other places too. Inside information is going to be his added strength. It is easy to lure people. Sham Sher Singh, I want you to be very careful. I want you to explore all options very carefully. I am particularly concerned about the safety of the princess.'

'Nobody can dare to come near Bibi, Rani Ma, as long as I am alive. She is herself very brave and can account for many on her own,' Sham Sher Singh thundered.

'Yes, I am sure that you can face any threat in front of you. But a person like Jia Khan has no scruples, you know. So, you must prepare a course of escape for the princess, should such an eventuality arise. Remember that Jia Khan must have also visualized that in a war, she might escape. So as soon as hostility begins, he would mount guards on all the escape routes. So, timing and preparation for it is most important.'

'You leave it to me. I know a secret route and nobody can get wind of it. Be assured, Rani Ma. I shall work on this secretly with the help of my trusted men. Don't worry. We will face this threat. Victory to Jhaluk, Rani Ma!'

They rode back to the palace in silence thereafter. On meeting Sahiba, she instructed her to speak only in Bangla if she had to say anything of importance. As the ruler, she had the safety of the state in mind. But as a mother, she was also concerned about the safety and honour of her daughter.

The Queen Mother called a meeting of her army commanders. They were told that some provocative actions were being taken by Jia Khan who had also met her. From his talk, it was evident that he had set an evil eye on the state of Jhaluk. She never mentioned that he had proposed to marry her daughter. She then told them about her visit to the villages, which were attacked recently. She had said that Jia Khan had not taken any responsibility for the attack. She said that it was quite evidently the handiwork of his men.

'The looting of the village was a pretext. It was actually meant to send a signal to the state. They want to say that they could do anything with impunity. It is a challenge to our sovereignty. It is true that we have not fought any war for the last ten years. But it does not mean that we are weak. The only difference is that all the wars in the history of the state were fought between two states. Never against a bandit. We have to be ready for a war. There's no time to lose.'

All the commanders voiced their support and readiness. They assured the queen that they were ready to give a befitting reply to the evil design of the enemy.

But the enemy had all the information. His spies had infiltrated deep into the system. He struck once again as if to mock at the strength and preparedness of the state.

In broad daylight, four armed men arrived in a village and before anyone could realize, they picked up a girl returning with a pitcher of water and abducted her. It clearly demonstrated that they could enter without any warning. They could completely surprise their adversaries. This was an unethical act. But for Jia Khan, whatever a strongman did would become right.

Cries rang through the state. Two days later, the girl's mutilated body was again dropped in the village during the night. The invaders had come and gone unchallenged again.

## VII
## The Great Escape

As a matter of precaution, the Queen Mother stopped Sahiba from going to the forest for training. She was sure that Jia Khan must have eyes on the princess and knew all about her regular routine. He had also told the queen that an abduction was possible; he had demonstrated it by abducting a village girl in broad daylight.

The evidence was perhaps enough for the queen to see the writing on the wall. She had two options. Wage a war against him on his known hideout. It was an unknown territory. Or, face the danger of a surprise and unwarned attack. She was not sure if she could protect the princess against such an attack. She was also apprehensive of Jia Khan's espionage network.

She thought of engineering an escape for the princess. Sahiba could go into hiding for some time. She could return after the war against Jia Khan was won. The queen had not told anyone about the indecent proposal of Jia Khan. But Jia Khan must have told others about this. The queen made up her mind—the princess would have to escape immediately. What would she say to her people and commanders? The princess was the weak link in defence which Jia Khan could exploit. It was also necessary to protect the heir to this state. Sahiba would return as soon as the war was won. That seemed like a plausible explanation to her.

Then, she visited the village where the tragedy had occurred. After offering her condolences, she assured the families that action would be taken soon. There was terror marked all over the village. She was now determined to strike back. But before that, a vital step had to be taken in the larger interest of the state of Jhaluk.

While returning, she looked towards Sham Sher Singh, who was riding along with her. She asked, 'Ready?'

Sham Sher Singh looked towards her and nodded.

'Tonight,' she ordered and then she rode away to the palace.

Once inside the palace, she called Sahiba into her chamber and held her hands. She said in Bangla, 'You are leaving tonight, Sahiba. Sham Sher Singh will escort you out to a safe place for some time. War with Jia Khan is imminent. The war will start as soon as you are in a safe place.'

Sahiba was taken aback and protested, 'How do you want me to leave the state when a war is imminent? I am a good fighter. Sham Sher Singh is good too. We can make a lot of difference in the war. It is shameful to run away like this.'

The queen said, 'You know it is not going to be a fair war. Jia Khan has set his eyes on you. He will stoop to any level to catch you. We are not sure whom we can trust in the palace. We also know that there is no support from any of the neighbouring states. You are the heir to this state. It is my responsibility to protect you under all circumstances.

We are sure that with the blessings of Shiv Baba, we will ultimately win. You can then return. There should be no argument, Sahiba. Do what I tell you. Sham Sher Singh will come around midnight. You should be ready. You will ride on your favourite horse, Pawan. You will be in disguise. Hopefully, it will be a short get away. Keep enough money with you. Nobody should have any inkling about what you are doing. Sham Sher Singh has made all the arrangements. Trust his advice. May Shiv Baba protect you and bless you, my child.'

Sahiba emerged from her mother's chambers with a very heavy heart. She had never imagined that she would have to leave like this. She had believed that she would be able to fight, shoulder to shoulder with the others, in case of a war. But she knew that it was a different kind of a war. She was heir to the state and her safety was paramount.

With a firm resolve, she went to her chambers. She told her chambermaid that she wanted to retire for the night. She was soon ready with her sword and the spear strapped to her back. At the appointed time, there was a knock at her door. She opened to find Sham Sher Singh and her mother standing at the door. Her mother had a small bag. She took out the engraved necklace with the insignia of the state embossed on it.

She said, 'Sahiba this is the necklace, which gives you the authority to rule as the heir of state.' Then she took out two chains from a small box. She put one chain on the neck of Sahiba. The other chain she gave to Sham Sher

Singh. She solemnly said, 'This is for your protection. Now Sham Sher Singh, I am handing over the heir of Jhaluk for protection and safe-keeping. May Shiv Baba help you carry out this sacred task.'

Sham Sher Singh knelt down and with his hand on the sword said, 'Rani Ma, please do not worry anymore. I shall protect Bibi with the last drop of blood in my body. So, help me Shiv Baba.'

The Queen Mother told them that she had given all the guards some opium in their nightcaps. They would not get up. You can leave by the rear gate of the palace. She then hugged her daughter. Both of them had tears as they disengaged.

With a bow, Sahiba left with Sham Sher Singh. This was the last time she saw her mother.

They rode away on their respective horses with Sham Sher Singh leading the way. There were no words exchanged.

Sahiba was an ace horse rider. Her horse, Pawan, was known for his speed. Sham Sher Singh was riding on Bahadur. Both the horses were very fast. It was a moonless night but Sham Sher Singh knew the route. They went towards the east and then, to the northeast and soon crossed their borders. They skirted the forest on their right and proceeded at a good speed. After a while, they were on an open terrain. Sham Sher Singh stopped beneath a tree. They had had been riding for nearly two hours by now. There was a well at a distance. Sham Sher Singh had located a water tank.

'Let the horses drink and rest a bit. The next part of the journey was going to be difficult,' he said.

Sahiba also got down. Sham Sher Singh took both the horses to the water tank where they had their fill. About half an hour later, they were again riding away. After about half an hour, Sham Sher Singh got down and said, 'Bibi we must walk on foot for about three kos as the horse's hoofs may attract some people. We'll guide the horses so that they make no noise.'

She nodded and they walked like this in silence for an hour. He signalled for Sahiba to ride as soon as it was safe to do so. After half an hour, they saw a couple of figures. As they came closer, they found that they were two men on the horse.

One of them spoke up in a rough voice.

'Who are you? Where are you coming from? Nobody crosses this area during the night. This is the area of Jia Khan. Don't you know that?'

Sham Sher Singh immediately took out his spear and hit one of them with absolute precision. Seeing Sham Sher Singh, Sahiba also drew her spear and hit the other one with equal precision. The spear had hit their hearts; their strike was so swift that they had no time to draw their swords or to make any noise. Sham Sher Singh retrieved the spears and put both the corpses on the horses. 'Good hit, Sahiba Bibi. They made no noise. The horses will carry the corpses to their camp. They won't be able to locate the exact spot of the fight. It is important that we leave no trace,' Sham Sher Singh said as they rode away in a northernly direction.

After some time, Sham Sher Singh spoke very slowly. 'Bibi, this is not a good sign. It appears these two men were sent to prevent the escape of the princess. That means that the attack on Jhaluk can take place any time now. I just wonder. These two guys did not expect us to shoot with a spear in the dark. They never got a chance.'

Sahiba looked at Sham Sher Singh as they galloped, but said nothing.

Sham Sher Singh was keeping an eye on all sides. His horse was galloping at a fast pace. Sahiba's horse was also keeping up. He said, 'Bibi, by early morning we should be away from the zone of danger. We would now go eastwards, north of Gwalior. We will stop outside some village for the day. We will have a wash and can eat.'

By early morning, they were near a village. They stopped near a well again. They had travelled for close to six hours by now. The horses needed rest. Both of them also needed rest. After freshening up, they rested under the tree. It had a big pedestal for people to sit on. Soon, some villagers came to draw water from the well. But nobody paid any particular notice to the two of them as it was common for many wayfarers to rest there.

One woman from the village came to them to ask if they needed something. The woman said that if they were going far, it was better to pack some roti for the journey. It was a good idea. The woman went to the village and brought some roti and also some butter milk for them to drink. She refused to take any money from them.

It was late in the afternoon. The sun was going to set. They started again. After riding for an hour or so they turned towards the northeast. Sham Sher Singh said that they should be close to Agra and would cross the Yamuna soon. He said that they would be perfectly safe thereafter.

By early morning, they were near the bank of Yamuna. They crossed the river with their horses. The boatmen were used to such traffic. Tradesmen were used to travelling in such a manner. They again took shelter under a big banyan tree.

Sham Sher Singh said, 'Bibi I shall go to the village to find a place to stay here. I shall also get a few things to eat. Be careful while I am away. I shall go on foot. Going there on a horse will attract people. I want to avoid that.'

Sahiba still said nothing. She took out a golden coin from her bag and offered it to him. He refused saying, 'Bibi, Rani Ma has also given me some money. I don't need it. Bibi this is the usual route taken by traders. I found it from them. We may stay here for about ten days. We shall try to find what is happening in Jhaluk. I am worried about them. This is going to be a crucial time. So be careful while I am away.'

Sahiba looked at him and just nodded.

As Sham Sher Singh walked away, Sahiba grew more alert. Two horses were tied down nearby. After a couple of hours or so, Sham Sher Singh returned. He was carrying some food and looked pleased with himself. He said that he had found a small cottage where they could stay. A local villager had helped him. He was getting it cleaned. Some essentials had also been arranged. They could occupy it in the evening.

Sahiba again looked at him and said nothing.

Sham Sher Singh had already noticed that Sahiba had not said a word since they had left Jhaluk. She would mostly nod and say a monosyllable or so in response. He guessed that Sahiba was brooding and thinking of her home and her mother. By nature, she was a very brave woman so she was not afraid of anything. She was just not given to talking much.

She had maintained her royal status in dealing with Sham Sher Singh—a royal servant. Did she want to assert it? But now, for all practical purposes, she was dependent on him. Queen Mother had also told her to follow Sham Sher Singh. He thought to himself that he simply had a responsibility of escorting her to a place of safety, her superior position did not change. Sham Sher Singh was fully conscious of his own position.

They went over to the cottage in the evening. It was made quite liveable. There was a small courtyard also. A bed had been pushed to a corner. Sahiba looked at the bed curiously. There was a small place to cook. The village women told her that she could cook some food in her home and bring it for them.

A village woman came forward and said, 'Bhai ji told us that you belong to some royal family. It is our good fortune that you have come here to stay. Bhai ji said that you will be here for some time only. So, there is no need for you to cook.'

Sahiba was pleased and thanked her for their help. She gratefully accepted their offer and smiled.

Sham Sher Singh left to look after the horses. He procured fodder and water from the village for them. When dinner was served, the women first served it to the princess. After she had eaten, Sham Sher Singh took the food away to eat in the verandah.

After his dinner, he told Sahiba, 'Bibi you can sleep in the bed and close this room. I will sleep outside. I shall also keep an eye. This place appears to be safe. We will decide what course to adopt after a week.'

Sahiba again looked at him and turned her gaze away. Then she nodded in appreciation. She was quite tired. She fell asleep as soon as she lay on the bed.

The travesty of fortune; how they had changed. The princess slept without a royal bed. She ate cold rotis with some curd. All the luxuries of her past were gone in one night to be replaced by hardship.

Nobody would have ever imagined fortune twisting in such a manner. Was it the price she had to pay for being a princess and for being beautiful? However, for Sham Sher Singh, all this did not matter. He was still serving the princess. Even now, he bore the responsibility for her safety. It was greater now. He had the queen's mandate to bring back the princess safely to Jhaluk again. Thus, he could not sleep. He had to be careful and alert.

He stayed awake, only closing his eyes now and then. The horses were sure to raise an alarm in case of dangers. He trusted them.

## Sahiba, the Princess

After the two nights of ride, Sahiba slept on the cot peacefully. Even if she dreamt, she did not remember it. She woke as the day broke. She dressed and came out of the hut. The rays of the morning sun were falling on her face. She looked towards Sham Sher Singh who was tending to the horses. He saw the princess from a distance. Her face was glowing in the morning sun. He looked towards her and smiled. He welcomed her and said, 'It looks like the princess has slept well. You look fresh, Bibi. You can walk around. The morning air is very good here. I shall then bring some butter milk for you and something to eat.'

Sahiba smiled for the first time since they had left the palace. She nodded and still said nothing. Then she gracefully went for a morning stroll. The Yamuna was not very far and the breeze from that direction was pleasant.

This soon became her morning schedule. Back in Jhaluk, she would wake every morning to practice wielding the sword. But there was no practice now. She wanted to tell Sham Sher Singh to resume their practices, but he was quite busy in the morning, tending to the horses. She still thought that practicing was important and needed time. She could not do without it.

Sham Sher Singh would take both the horses to the river to give them a wash; the horses also liked it. He kept watch over the banyan tree to see if any wayfarers had come from the direction of Jhaluk. He wondered whether Jia Khan had sent any men.

On the fifth day while he was out for his daily morning chores, he saw someone waiting under the tree. He contemplated whether he should inquire after the man. The guy looked at him and called out to him with joy.

Sham Sher Singh recognized him! He was one of the tradesmen who would often come to Jhaluk to pay protection money. He knew Sham Sher Singh.

He hailed him and said, 'I am just returning from Jhaluk. I had gone there to pay the fees. But everything has changed. I was told that Jia Khan has taken over the palace in one swift move. It was given up almost without a fight. Most of the commanders have been captured and are in jail. A few have run away. I looked for you but did not find you. People said that you have also run away.'

Sham Sher Singh was taken aback but he asked him, 'How is the Queen Mother?'

The man narrated his tale.

'I reached in the morning. There was a deathly silence everywhere. I met someone peeping from the window of his house. He beckoned me to come inside. He asked me why I had come. Jia Khan had invaded two days ago. They entered the palace without any resistance; the palace guards let them in. The commanders of the army were quickly overpowered by the enemy. Two or three of them ran away. The queen had been arrested and they were looking for the princess, but she was not to be found.

'The man told me that the queen had refused to tell them anything about the princess. Jia Khan was outraged and perhaps killed the queen in his rage. I'm sorry, Sham Sher Singh. But I learnt that he has told his men to find the princess.

'Jia Khan has now declared himself as the king. He has asked that nobody should come out of their house. He asked me to leave immediately and get out. Nobody knew where you had gone. With great luck, I was able to escape. Now I see that you are holding two horses, Sham Sher Singh. That means that you have escaped from the palace with the princess, likely before the palace was invaded. But be careful. Jia Khan is frantically searching for the princess.'

Sham Sher Singh was stunned. He realized that their escape had been miraculous. And he realized that the trader had found him.

He bade him farewell and returned to the princess with a grave face. She looked at his face and spoke for the first time, 'Sham Sher Singh, you seem to be the bearer of bad news. Tell me what has happened.'

Sham Sher Singh said nothing and went to tie the horses. He brought the food for the princess. He said, 'Bibi, please eat first. We may have to leave as soon as possible.'

'Sham Sher Singh, I thought you knew that I am not an ordinary weakling. I can bear it. Eating has nothing to do with that. Have you ever seen me crying or wailing? Go ahead.'

Usually, he was very courageous, but this news had struck a nerve. He was born in Jhaluk and had a lot of pride in the state, the king, the queen and now, the princess. He was in awe of them and they too had looked after him well. The cruel hand of fate had wiped everything out in one stroke. He was likely to be the only surviving soldier of the state. Did he not have to stand to defend Jhaluk? He had carried out the orders of the Queen Mother. The heir had to be protected at all costs. If not for this, both he and the princess would have fought hard against any enemy.

He spoke with anguish. 'Bibi, there is no question of quivering. We are Rajputs. It is in our blood to fight. We have heard many kings who have had to withdraw and have returned with renewed energy and power to wrestle their kingdoms back. To be a good fighter is our religion.' Then he told Sahiba what he had heard from the trader.

The princess stood still in horror.

Sham Sher Singh continued, 'Bibi, we must leave this place. According to the trader, Jia Khan is frantically searching for you. He must have found out that I am also missing. He is likely to be searching for both of us. The trader has also seen me with two horses. He has correctly guessed that the princess is with me. If Jia Khan's men meet him, he will surely tell them about us. We will go further north of Bareilly and see what happens. Whatever is to happen, must happen in a week's time.'

Saying this, he started preparing the horses for the ride. He quickly informed the village woman that they would leave.

The princess stood still in a pensive mood.

When Sham Sher Singh came to her after making all the preparations, she suddenly sprang into action and was ready. She said in a low voice, 'This is not the time to grieve the fall of Jhaluk. This is also not the time to mourn the death of the Queen Mother and the many others who have lost their lives. Queen Mother had great foresight. If we had lost even a few hours, we would have been caught unawares just as the others were. Her main concern was to keep the heir of Jhaluk safe. She has succeeded in this campaign. I agree with you that we should move away from this place.'

Sham Sher Singh nodded.

She continued. 'All the carefully drawn out plans of my mother should not be lost because of our negligence or complacency. But I can tell you this. No one will capture me alive.'

She drew out a small knife from her blouse and showed it to Sham Sher Singh. She would end her life and take away the life of her assailant if it ever came to that.

She patted her horse Pawan. The horse seemed to nod in agreement. They swiftly rode on, following Sham Sher Singh, who was amazed by the courage and grit of the princess. She did not shed a single tear. She was a worthy daughter and heir of the state of Jhaluk, he thought.

She may have been the daughter of King Raunaq Singh

and Chandni Bai, but this relationship was secondary. At the moment, she thought only of Jhaluk. That is why she would not allow anyone to sully her honour. She was prepared to kill herself and would also take the life of anyone who dared to touch her. This did not surprise Sham Sher Singh much. The women of Rajputana were known to sit on a burning pyre after their husbands died.

They rode at a good pace and reached halfway to Barielly by the evening where they found a shelter to spend the night. The well nearby provided water for them as well as the horses. They ate what they had brought from the village. The princess slept on the floor after spreading a sheet. Sham Sher Singh sat down on a haystack. He remained alert during the night.

They got up early. After freshening up, they rode forward. They skirted Bareilly and settled down in a small village near it. Again, a village woman provided them with some shelter and food. They stayed there for three days. They kept following this routine.

One day in the afternoon, Sham Sher Singh headed out to Bareilly to buy a few things. The shopkeeper began to question him. 'You don't seem to belong to this place. Where have you come from?'

Sham Sher Singh was guarded in his reply. He did not name Jhaluk. He responded with the name of a place nearby.

The shopkeeper said, 'What a coincidence! About two hours ago, four men riding on the horses had come. They said that they were from Jhaluk. Two days ago, a trader had come this way and said that he had narrowly escaped from Jhaluk where a new king had taken over. These men were looking for two persons on horses. I told them that I had not seen anyone passing by this town. I don't know what the matter was but I did not like the faces of those guys. They have gone towards the Sarai.'

Sham Sher Singh just shrugged his shoulders in response and was gone.

It was very clear that these men were sent by Jia Khan. It was certain that some people would learn of the two strangers living in the village nearby. It was no longer safe to remain in that area. They must forge ahead. Thinking about all this, he returned to Sahiba. He again told her everything that he had heard in the town. He said that those four men were still resting in Sarai. They would certainly continue to make further inquiries about the princess.

The princess said, 'It appears that Jia Khan is desperate. I think we should go so far that he cannot reach us. Why don't we go to a jungle far away? It is no use running like fugitives. Think of it. Ask someone, if you don't know.'

Sham Sher Singh said, 'That makes sense Bibi. But we cannot ask anyone here. We can go ahead to the Terai region of the Himalayas in the north. So, we can go north and move eastward. Then we'll decide.'

Sahiba nodded. They again left their temporary hideout. They reached a peaceful village in the evening where they spent the night. They rode again in the morning turning eastward. After sometime, they stopped again near a well under a tree. While they were resting, two wayfarers also arrived from the direction towards which Sham Sher Singh was heading. He asked them, 'We are new in this area. Where are you coming from and what do you do?'

They said, 'We are traders from Gorakhpur market. We are now going to Punjab's side. Actually, we are from the other side of Gandak. We bring cotton fabric from Gorakhpur area there. On the other side of the river, there is a deep forest.'

Sham Sher Singh was interested. He inquired about all the details. They appeared to be simple fellows and were heading away; they would have little chance of encountering

Jia Khan's men.

The forest seemed to be a three-day ride.

He discussed with Sahiba. The decision was made. They would go beyond the Gandak River and find a place to stay in the forest. They were used to the life in the forest. She thought that they could perhaps resume their training once again in the forest. Most importantly, they thought Jia Khan's armed forces could never reach that far. They couldn't find them in the jungles.

## VIII
## Sahiba in the Jungles

Now knowing the direction and the destination, they rode away with ease and quiet. Only stopping to pick up some food or to rest for the night, they moved forward towards their destination. For the first time, they felt no lurking danger.

They began to enjoy the scenery and villages. The area they were headed towards was much greener. Sahiba had seen nothing like this in Rajputana. She saw a number of streams and a lot of cultivation in the area. The people she met were warm and hospitable. This part of the flight from Jhaluk was the most enjoyable for them. At that time, there was no thought about what they would do after they reached.

They kept their minds from drifting towards thoughts of Jhaluk, and Sahiba was relaxed. Sham Sher Singh too felt better on seeing her glow.

Towards the end of their journey, Sahiba started to hum a popular folk song. Sham Sher Singh smiled on hearing it. The song was about the harvest, about a woman coming home after the harvest with the bundle on her head.

It was an expression of contentment and joy. Sham Sher Singh looked on with amazement at how Sahiba seemed to be coming alive; it was as if she had been set free after a long period in a prison. He could understand the reason for it. There was suddenly no fear. They had crossed the boundary where fear had tried to strangle the free spirits of a person... But there must be more to it. Sham Sher Singh could not fathom a reason for it and he did not have the courage to ask her.

The tune she was humming had a chorus. He could have joined her. But he had learnt to keep his distance. He just enjoyed the sweet music which reminded him of Jhaluk.

This time they did not need to avoid Gorakhpur. They passed through it. There was distinct change in the culture of this area. Most of the women were wearing saris and not lehengas. Sahiba also realized this change and stopped to buy two saris. After another half-day of riding, they were on the banks of the Gandak River. There was a boat, which they could use to cross with their horses. They had planned to head to a small village on the outskirts of the jungle named Madanpur, belonging to a tribal community.

Upon reaching, the people of the village came out to welcome them. They were provided with a small room to stay. The villagers said that if Sahiba and Sham Sher Singh wanted, they would make a hut for them.

They wanted to tie the horses in the open. But the villagers said that the place was frequented by a tiger and the horses would not be safe. No one slept outside here. They helped Sham Sher Singh take the horses to a site where they secured their cows during the night. The horses were also tired and did not seem to protest. Sham Sher Singh was amused. He thought that he would have to tackle the menace of the tiger soon. He had to build a separate enclosure for the horses if they were to live there; they would resent the company of cows. Then, for the both of them, he found another place to sleep at night. He asked Sahiba to secure the door from inside. For the first time, both of them slept peacefully and deeply. That was their first night in the jungle of Madanpur.

Next morning, he woke up to the singing of many birds. There was a sweet fragrance in the air. He found Sahiba was already up and walking around. She was trying to spot the birds with a particular note. The villagers were already up, gathered about the well in the village.

They were told that there was also a stream flowing close by. The women of the village would go there to wash themselves and their clothes. Sahiba also joined them and enjoyed a bath in running water. It was refreshing.

Then, Sahiba wanted to change into the sari, but she did not know how to wear it. The tribal women helped her put on the sari. They saw her beautiful athletic body and believed she must be royalty. The women did her hair also and put some flowers in it. The result was captivating—a village belle in a sari and flowers. It was an exciting and freeing time for Sahiba. She was feeling very excited. The wash in the running water was a unique experience for her. There was no such stream in Jhaluk. A princess could not, in any case, be allowed to bathe in the open. It was exhilarating.

Sham Sher Singh saw that she seemed to enjoy the simple disposition of the village. He too liked them. She was now much like the others. It was a good sign, Sham Sher Singh thought. It had been a month since they had left the palace. The innate charm in the princess had free reign here. The tribal women too seemed to be attached to Sahiba.

Sahiba had a natural grace in whatever she did or the way she walked. After all, she had been groomed to take over the reign of Jhaluk state. A month ago, nobody had imagined that she would have to escape from the state which their ancestors had ruled for generations.

Destiny and fate have a queer way of bringing events in one's life. Sages have said that when that moment came, one has to take them without qualms. Sahiba was just showing that trait in the most normal way. Sham Sher Singh thought that the trait was that of winners. The losers always whined and complained.

Sham Sher Singh wanted a hut made. He asked the villagers for their help. They said that they would bring materials like some bamboo from the forest. They, however, said that a tiger was causing a problem in the area. They had lost their cattle. Sham Sher Singh said that he would get rid of it as soon as he could. They didn't think it would be possible; Sham Sher Singh had a strong build but they felt that tiger would not be an easy prey.

Two days later, the tiger appeared in the late afternoon to attack cows. The villagers made a lot of noise to drive the tiger away. It infuriated the tiger. Sham Sher Singh rushed towards it with his spear. The tiger wanted to silence them by growling at the shouting men. Sham Sher Singh challenged the tiger. The tiger was angered and jumped at Sham Sher Singh. He aimed his spear and threw it hard. It hit the tiger's neck as it leapt forward. The spear had pierced the tiger's throat and the mighty creature fell with a big roar.

Everyone started applauding and soon the drums were brought out for celebration. He was hailed as a hero. They narrated the story over and over, embarrassing him with their praise. Sham Sher Singh told them that Bibi could have also hit the tiger with the same precision. They were amazed and would not believe it until one day, a deer started running away at the sight of them. Sahiba came forward and hit the deer with her spear in an effortless manner. Thereafter, both of them were respected for their valour.

The hut was soon built at some distance from the village.

They wanted some space and privacy. Then a stable for the horses. And thus, life in Mandapur continued.

Bagaha was a small village market not very far away. Villagers went there to buy a few things like salt. They did not have any money. They used what they produced in their fields to exchange what they needed. They also got some clothes from the market. They got a needle and thread for the princess from the market. This was the most valuable purchase for the princess.

They took to cultivation and started growing paddy and other cereals. The field was very fertile. Sahiba did not know anything about cultivation, the normal practice in the village. She also did not know how to cook. Sham Sher Singh did know how to cook. He also knew how to sow paddy. The princess started to learn even as Sham Sher Singh insisted that he would take care of all these things. As she settled in, Sahiba firmly opposed him. She helped in the kitchen as well as in the field just as the other women in the village.

## IX
## Sahiba is Sick

It seemed to Sahiba that after the long flight, she had finally reached her destination. They had now settled down in their hut in the jungle. They had not told the villagers where they had come from or why. They had also not told them how they were related. They had told them that they belonged to a royal family and had come to stay here. The people in the village were not inquisitive. They had begun to see them as a normal couple.

Sahiba, for some strange reason, had forgotten that she was a princess. She was reconciled to her present state. She did not see any immediate prospect of her return to Jhaluk.

She also did not see any way to retrieve her lost kingdom. Queen Mother was dead. Their army had given up without any fight. Thus, Jia Khan was firmly in the saddle and could not be easily dislodged. She knew that brooding over the lost kingdom would only make her more miserable. Nevertheless, she had still maintained that old distinction between herself and Sham Sher Singh. She appreciated his services as that of a servant of the palace but nothing more. For Sam Sher Singh, there was no change in his position. He could never dream of any other role for himself.

Life rolled on for some time in this manner until fate brought another twist in her life.

Malaria was a common disease in the area. Villagers had a few methods to rid themselves of mosquitoes; they would burn some leaves in a pot inside their hut and the smoke would drive away the mosquitoes. Sahiba did not like the smell of the smoke and avoided using it in her room. Sham Sher Singh did not mind the smell because he worried about the dreadful disease. He could not afford to be sick. The princess, used to more subtle fragrances, found the smell utterly distasteful.

One afternoon, Sahiba felt unwell. In the evening, a fever came on. She did not have an appetite and fell asleep for some time. But she soon woke up with terrible shivers. Sham Sher Singh went near her to find her tossing in the bed; her body was shaking with convulsion.

He was bid not to touch her. But it had become unavoidable. He touched her forehead. It was burning up. He brought his blanket and covered her, but it did not help much. He immediately brought some water. He put a cloth soaked in water on her forehead, which seemed to cause some relief.

Then he lifted her into his arms and poured some more water on her head. As the fever cooled, Sahiba let her head rest on his chest as he poured the water. After some time, the fever seemed to abate. He wiped her body dry and wrapped her in some dry clothes. Her trembling had ceased and she slept. He did not know how to handle a patient with malaria. In the night, the fever again shot up. But it was not as high. He repeated the same methods every time the fever returned.

In the morning, Sahiba got up with a lot of difficulty. Sham Sher Singh left her in the room. Sahiba then came out and sat down outside. She was very weak. She did not look at Sham Sher Singh.

He called for the villagers to check Sahiba. The women came and touched her forehead. Sahiba still had fever.

The woman said, 'A decoction prepared by boiling some leaves in water is the only medicine which has worked against this deadly disease before. This decoction has to be taken as many times as she can. It is quite bitter so she can take it with some jaggery.'

Sham Sher Singh heard patiently.

'It is likely that she will have repeated attacks. But she should be alright soon. This decoction is really effective'.

She said bathing her in water when the fever was high would certainly help. She brought some green leaves and then made a decoction so that Sham Sher Singh could do it. The decoction was really bitter the first time Sahiba took it. But she was made of steely resolve. She mustered the necessary willpower to take it without making too much of a fuss.

For the next three days, the attacks returned with equal severity. Every time the high fever caused trembling, convulsions and delirium in Sahiba. She had a strong nerve but the fever made her miserable. Sham Sher Singh continued to serve her. And when she was well, she continued to take the herbal decoction. After the fourth day, the intensity of the attack started to decrease. After a week, it was manageable.

She had no attacks after fifteen days. The medicine seemed to be working. But she had become very weak. She had lost all her appetite. She had to be raised from the bed and taken outside for her daily needs. She was completely dependent on Sham Sher Singh who even had to feed her.

But Sham Sher Singh never left her for a moment. He watched as her body became paler with the passing of days.

Sahiba only looked at him as if pleading to take her out of her wretched condition.

In the morning, Sham Sher Singh dressed her up as well as he could. He would then take her out of the room. He would provide a cushion for her to rest her back against the wall. He thought that the fresh air, coupled with the sweet fragrance of the forest, would do her good. The village women brought her some fresh honey from the forest and also brought some fruits and berries. Then they sat and looked after her, which gave Sham Sher Singh time to look after the field. The horses also needed attention. They seemed to be adversely affected by their idleness. Ace horses needed hard exercise every day to keep their systems fit; Sham Sher Singh did not get time to provide it. He was completely devoted to Sahiba's well-being.

The village women sat and helped Sahiba comb and tie her hair. They praised her husband and his care, and said that she was lucky to have such a wonderful man. She had never told them that Sham Sher Singh was not her husband. Hence, when they spoke of Sham Sher Singh like this Sahiba would shut her eyes or would look away, saying nothing. But now, she even avoided looking at him.

Sham Sher Singh too felt a pang of guilt. He was distracted in her presence. When they spoke, they used only monosyllables, as if both were pricked by guilt. But touching and tending Sahiba's bare body had become necessary, her life depended on it. But once the feeling of urgency left both of them, moral righteousness had raised its head to stare at both of them.

All these feelings apart, Sahiba continued to make very good progress. The villagers told her that there was no need for her to continue the medicine. With the bitterness gone, she got back her appetite quickly. She started taking a few steps out of the hut by herself. In a month's time, she felt that she had now completely recovered. She began to smile again.

## X
## A New Page

As more time passed, the colour returned to Sahiba's face, leaving a distinct glow. The village women came to help her. One day, she wanted to wear the sari again. The women dressed her up and put a string of flowers on her hair. She looked rather pretty as she sat outside her hut, waiting for Sham Sher Singh to return.

Sham Sher Singh had taken both the horses to the river. He washed and bathed both the horses to their pleasure. Walking them to the river had provided some good exercise to both the horses and Sham Sher Singh.

The cool river water seemed pleasing and Sham Sher Singh couldn't help relishing it as he washed himself. As he passed through the forest, he found a bloom of lilies. He also found some berries. He knew that Sahiba liked them both. He plucked a few ripe ones and carried them home in a big donga made of the leaves, along with a big bunch of the flowers. He rode on the horses, gently trotting. As he arrived, he saw Sahiba sitting there, beautifully decked in a sari. She looked innocently and eagerly at him.

Sham Sher Singh was surprised. He had not seen her

so beautiful since her illness. Why was she waiting for him? He climbed down the horses and she got up. She had not patted her horse for a long time. She came up to Pawan and stroked his head. The horse was very happy and nodded in recognition of her loving touch.

She then turned towards Sham Sher Singh and smiled, 'It appears Pawan is feeling down. As I stroked him, he cheered up.'

'Princess, Pawan has been missing you. He would keep looking towards the door to see if you came out.'

She again patted him and said, 'Don't worry, Pawan. I am fine now. Sham Sher Singh has looked after me so much. We will ride again. Be good.'

The horse neighed in pleasure.

Sham Sher Singh then said, 'Princess, I have brought these lilies for you. I found them in the forest. I have also brought these berries since you like them so much.'

'Oh! Sham Sher Singh, thank you. The lilies are so beautiful and I love these ripe berries. Come inside. Let me put these flowers somewhere to capture the sweetness,' Sahiba said in giddy excitement.

Sham Sher Singh went to tie the horses and followed her into the hut. He saw her walking with her usual grace. He watched as she placed the flowers by the window, standing by with the berries in her hands. As Sham Sher Singh entered, she went forward and offered him the berry to taste.

'Princess I have brought them for you. Please taste them. Tell me how they taste.'

She took one berry in her fingers and put it in his mouth. He was taken aback. Then she said, 'Not today, Sham Sher Singh. You must have it first.'

Then she held his face for a while and he waited. She held both of his hands and took him towards her bed. She sat down still holding his hands. Her gaze was fixed on him with overwhelming intent. He was totally confused and tried to withdraw. Then she said, 'Sham Sher Singh, please take all of me. I now belong to you.'

Sham Sher Singh was completely confused. He tried to say something ... but no words came to him. Sahiba continued, her voice shy and full of emotion, 'You remember, Sham Sher, I had rebuked you once when you had touched me. But now I have been touched and tended. You had held me in your strong hands. You had held me in your arms so that I would not be blown away. You bathed me with water to quench the fever. I would not have survived without you.

'Sham Sher, you know that I was born with conviction that nobody had a right to touch my body or hold me except the person whom I loved. The one whom I would marry. To him, I would submit. And nobody else dared to touch me.'

'I was very sick. I only had you to depend upon. I was so sick, helpless and senseless. I remember how your strong hands felt all over my body. They never quivered when you touched me. It was a touch without any passion. It was the touch of a person who only wanted to heal me.'

Sham Sher Singh felt lost in her words. He did not know whether she had a change of heart. Did she mean something by it? He did not know. He tried to pull away but Sahiba held on to him and would not let him go.

He said, 'Princess, I am overwhelmed. I never for a moment thought of you as anything but a princess. I have pledged myself to serve you. The service above self, Bibi. I felt as if you were sinking. Someone would snatch you away from me. And so, I mustered all my courage and told myself that I would not let it happen. I have to hold you, come what may. So, I did what I could as a servant. Nothing more.'

He cried. 'I am grateful to God who saved me from any

indiscretion. I know how it has ruined so many sages also. 'Bibi, forgive me. It was unavoidable. I can swear that you are as pure as one could imagine.'

Sahiba had tears in her eyes as she continued to hold Sham Sher Singh. She would not let him go.

'I know Sham Sher. I felt it myself. But it is also true that I have been touched. My body has been bare. I am remorseful and if I do not correct this, it will now continue to needle at me.

Sham Sher, now there is only one way. That is the direction that the providence has taken today. You have to be my husband now. It is impossible for me to find any other person worthier than you to be my husband. I submit to you. Our fate is intertwined with each other. It has to be like this. Women already sing praises of you as a husband. They do not know that you aren't my husband. It is a mere ritual now. Accept me, please, Sham Sher.'

Sham Sher Singh was in shock. He did not know what to do in a situation like this. He took his hands away.

In a voice full of desperation, he said, 'Bibi, it is impossible. You are the princess and I am your servant. In the palace, a servant like me has to pledge one's life to the service of the princess. I have even renewed my pledge before the queen. To do what you say would be going against the solemn pledge, princess.'

He knelt down before her and said with tears in his eyes, 'Forgive me, princess. I cannot do it. Please try to understand how I am bound by the solemn pledge I have undertaken.'

Sahiba held his face in her hands and spoke with a smile, 'Which princess are are you talking about? Where is that state of which I am supposed to be a princess? Where is the Queen Mother? You had given that pledge to me. I am asking you to revoke that pledge. After the fall of Jhaluk, there is no princess. Can you think or entertain the thought that you and I would be able to wrest control of the state once again? It is meaningless. I am reconciled to the present position. All I have is the necklace my mother had given me and two horses. We're on a new path, Sham Sher. We have to write a new history now. Do you refuse to belong to this new history with me?'

Sham Sher Singh struggled to respond as she continued. He stared at her.

'Think about me, Sham Sher. Whatever the circumstances were, Sham Sher, I now have been touched. Whether it has been with pure intentions or not, it is a fact. I have been touched by you. I have thought over it a great deal, Sham Sher. My conscience is now ridden with guilt. It is much worse than the breaking of your pledge. That pledge is defunct. Our union is ordained now, Sham Sher. If you accept me, we are both absolved—you of your pledge and I of my guilt. God points in that direction. We have to follow. There is no other choice.'

Sahiba said this and pulled his head towards her. She pressed him against her bosom in ultimate acceptance. Sham Sher was weeping and so was Sahiba. It was only proof that a man proposes and god disposes. Sham Sher Singh embraced her tightly, unable to say a word. Then he slowly lifted his head and looked into the eyes of Sahiba.

'Bibi, I accept as you wish. But please don't deprive me of my service to you. Tell me what else I can do.'

Sahiba pulled his head towards her and kissed his forehead. 'Thank you, Sham Sher. Everybody here believes that we are married. So, there can be no pretense of a ritual marriage. Here, our only witness is the mother Earth. We can take a vow, we can touch the earth together as we become husband and wife. I think I will go to the temple of Mother

Narayani to seek her blessings.'

They slowly rose, holding each other they went to the courtyard where Sahiba had planted a Tulsi plant. They sat down and touched the earth.

'Oh, mother. Accept us and give us all the happiness, which your daughter and son deserve.'

With that Sahiba put her arms round the neck of Sham Sher Singh.

She then smiled and said, 'You can now carry me inside the room.'

Sham Sher Singh smiled as he lifted her in his powerful arms and carried her.

Once inside the room. Sahiba said, 'I have gifted myself to you, Sham Sher. What are you going to give me at this occasion?'

'My loyalty, Bibi,' he said.

It was a marriage without a ceremony, but it was full of the ritual purity. Sahiba said that she was content and very happy. Sham Sher Singh went out and brought both the horses. Sahiba came out and kissed both the horses as if saying thank you very much. As she had mentioned earlier, the two horses—Pawan and Bahadur were witnesses from the erstwhile state of Jhaluk.

They rode in abundant joy. They went to the temple. They sat down together to seek her blessings. Both of them walked down together for some time, their horses following. They stood beside the Narayani River also to seek her blessings. Then Sahiba turned towards him and fell into his powerful embrace.

That was beginning of a new life. This marriage had sealed her fate as far as the state of Jhaluk was concerned. She was sure that she could never go back to that state. It was god's way of beginning a new life for both of them.

*Six*

# Recuperation Abroad

Maya's story ended there. The two of them continued to live in the forest, soon growing comfortable with the mores of married life. They adopted the traditions of the forest and the community and raised a family. Maya's mother was the first daughter, and Maya the grandchild of Sahiba, the princess.

The village saw the new couple as protectors and heroes and as time passed, Sham Sher Singh's service to his wife had become the norm.

Sahiba listened to the tale in rapt attention.

I watched her; sure, she was trying to revisit the things from her childhood. But Maya was gone, and there was no one who could answer her queries.

After this, we shared a cup of coffee and left to sleep. It was pretty late already. Sahiba said little as the story ended.

As I was leaving the room, she said, 'Thank you, Barun. I am really grateful to you for remembering this story and telling it to me. I think my mother wanted you to tell me. But what am I to do? By marrying Sham Sher Singh, my great grandmother burnt the bridge that could have taken her to Jhaluk someday. Jhaluk is simply a necklace with the insignia now.'

I listened as she shrugged it off. 'Beyond that, you are now part of my life, Barun. That's all I know. Good night.'

I agreed with a smile. At this stage, we were helplessly drawn towards each other.

In my room, I tossed and turned in my sleep. But I was not worried. We had a holiday to plan.

I got up early since I was not given to sleeping late. I always thought that the morning hours are the best to liven my day. Sahiba too was up quite early; knowing that I was an early bird, she wanted to join me for morning tea.

As she freshened up and sat at the table, I smiled and greeted her. 'Good morning, princess.'

She laughed in embarrassment. 'Oh my god, Barun. As my great grandmother said—what princess, which state? They are all gone. I was Payoli but my mother chose to rechristen me as Sahiba. Although I can appreciate why she did it now, yet all that is history now,' Sahiba said.

'What is your last name, Sahiba?'

'Deb.'

'Your mother chose your name as Sahiba Deb. Why Deb? Isn't that a Bengali surname?' I asked.

'It is simple Barun. Deb is simply after you. Barun De—De, Barun. Elementary, my dear Watson,' she answered with trademark mischief.

'You are such a tease. Take care lest you should trip, my dear.'

'I will. Shall we enjoy the tea now? Thank you, Didimoni,' she said. She was still smiling as she poured the tea for me.

I do not like to talk too much while taking morning tea. I don't want to lose the taste or aroma of the tea while talking to others. Sahiba knew and respected that idiosyncrasy of mine. After tea, I told Sahiba that we needed to buy a few things.

'I don't have any idea about what to buy.'

'Some woollens at the least. Anything extra you can get

in Austria. Their shops are trendier.' Then I asked, 'Do you want to continue wearing a sari there? You will receive a lot of attention.'

'What do you mean? A sari is so elegant. Don't you like it? I am very comfortable in it,' she said in all seriousness.

'I am sorry. You look marvellous in sari. But people there are more accustomed to denims or skirts. It's only a suggestion, take it or leave it.'

'I now understand your mischief, Barun. I don't wear pants usually. I don't know how I will look in a skirt. Don't try to dress me up like a European lady. You can try this idea on someone else.'

'No offence meant. You have an opportunity to look all modern. Otherwise, who will object to you dressing like the wife of the blacksmith's son,' I teased.

'That will do. Don't forget that I am a princess. I will see what your wife will wear,' she said in an angry huff.

'You will be disappointed, princess. But anyway, let us go and get what you like.'

## II
## The Trip Begins

Usual repartee apart, we were making all necessary preparations to leave on Friday night. Sahiba was doing much better, but I wanted her to avoid unnecessary exercise.

She was keen on meeting Shruti before she left. I told her that she could invite the engaged couple for dinner, if they were free. Shruti was also keen to see both of us. Her fiancé could find time on Tuesday. They came over. It was so nice to see both of them together. Shruti was apparently very happy. Manish was a little shy in the beginning, but Sahiba was soon able to win him over. I liked both of them.

I was sure that they would make a fine couple once they were married in November. After dinner, they went back and made us promise that we would call them when we returned from abroad.

After they had gone, Sahiba complimented Shruti's choices. She said, 'Barun, it is not a bad idea to depend on the choice of one's parents in the matter of matrimony. Manish is nice and they seem made for each other.'

'Surely, they make a fine two-some Sahiba. God bless them. It is good to depend on the parents, I suppose. Present result seems to prove that—'

Sahiba cut me short, 'Now don't say anything further. I know you will again start talking about the poor blacksmith's son.'

I laughed. 'May god certainly bless the son of the blacksmith. But in this case, your mother did not consent. So, praise be to her, Sahiba. If that had happened, you would not be here with me today, planning to fly away on a European tour. In many ways, the blacksmith's proposition became a turning point in your life. That spurred your mother to smuggle you out to Darjeeling.'

'You are a wise man, Barun. I had really not thought that way. Yes, that is so true. May god bless the blacksmith's son too,' she said with a smile.

'Yes, there should be some celebrations, Sahiba. My teasing has opened your eyes to this. You must thank me.'

Sahiba sighed exasperatedly. 'Barun, I have to thank you for everything. If I start thanking you now, one life won't be enough for it. I really don't know how to do that. Let's just say that every breath of my life is meant for you.'

'Come on, Sahiba. Save a little breath for the trip also. I want you to enjoy it.'

We both laughed and wished each other good night,

making plans for the market. As I left to my room, I saw that Sahiba was still deep in thought. I did not want to bother her. It was amazing really. The proposal to marry Payoli to the son of the village blacksmith had become the turning point. It changed the life of not only Sahiba but also that of her mother. Sahiba was now ready to launch herself on a different path or trajectory in the future. I stood between two of them, it appeared. Did I have any choice? I didn't know.

We met in the morning and headed to the mall. Sahiba seemed to be quite excited about the forthcoming tour. While picking up a few woollens from the mall, she also picked up a long skirt—likely just to please me. I said nothing but she smiled while showing it to me.

We were flying in business class. According to our itinerary, we were to go to Vienna first. The flight had a change at Zurich. I had chosen to fly with Swiss Air because they were known to be good.

We were soon through with all the formalities—immigration, security check, etc.—and were placed in their business lounge before departure. I thought Sahiba was feeling a bit nervous for her maiden air journey. I just patted her, trying to comfort her to relax. She would not talk either. As the boarding was announced, she looked very uncomfortable. I held her hand and she dutifully followed me, almost leaning against me.

On the flight, we were given very good seats. Sahiba refused the window seat and sat down very stiffly. The attendants brought us a welcome drink. I teasingly suggested in her ears, 'Take some wine. It will soothe your nerves, Sahiba.'

She hissed, 'Don't joke with me. I am not able to breathe. It is so awful.'

'I suggested some wine for it. Of course, I don't need it.'

'If I have any wine, I shall start dancing. Don't induce me to dance on an airplane.'

'All the guys and cabin crew members are probably thinking that this lady is madly in love with me because you won't let me go. Let the plane take off, you will be fine.'

'I don't care what others think of me. At the moment hold me tight, Barun.'

'I would actually love to see you dance. Anyway, fasten your seatbelt now. You will at least not fall. You can rest your head on my shoulders. You are welcome.'

I told the airhostess that Sahiba would have something after we were airborne as she was a bit tense. The hostess laughed and gave Sahiba a few cushions to rest her head. But Sahiba found my shoulders to be more comfortable.

The aircraft started to roll out very smoothly. As we were airborne, Sahiba started to relax. Soon the seatbelt sign went off. I advised Sahiba to keep the belt fastened for safety for a while. In ten minutes, Sahiba felt much better.

'Thank you, Barun.' She sighed in relief. 'I am alright now. I feel like we are floating. I am now a little thirsty and maybe, I can eat a bit?'

'I am going to have some orange juice. Do you care for some wine? I can eat some dessert with you. But let me see what they can offer you.'

'Why are you so hell bent on wine? I can dance for you without the wine. I can also have orange juice.'

We then ordered some ice-cream, Swiss chocolates and a cheese sandwich. Once she had eaten, I told her to sleep it off. She then comfortably placed her head on my shoulders on the recline and slept. Her soft breath sounded like music to my ears. I was just wondering how the hands of fate worked. This village girl, not even used to wearing a footware was now flying in a business class in an international flight. She was most comfortable—I could tell from her breathing. I did not know if she used any perfume. In the convent, they were not allowed to use any make-up. So, using any perfume was also out of question. But there was something intoxicating about it. Breathing it in, I too slept, my head on hers.

We were due to land in Zurich at around 6 a.m. Then we were to take a connecting flight to Vienna in an hour and a half. Indian time was 9.30 a.m., and the crew served us some Indian breakfast. After a cup of tea, we were ready. Sahiba was also cheerful now. From the window, she gaped at the Alps in glee as I marvelled at the Swiss countryside.

We landed in time at Zurich. The transfer was pretty fast and well organized. We were soon on the other aircraft which was headed to Vienna. This flight was rather short. We landed in Vienna, our destination. It was pleasantly cool as we came out of the terminal. Nick had organized everything from here. A car from his friend's office had come to pick us up. It took us to central Vienna where we had booked a hotel.

The room was lovely—we had a suite with a marvellous ante-room.

'So, Sahiba, our vacation starts now. Get ready. We can have some breakfast at the hotel.'

'I am full,' she said as she walked around the room. 'But we can go there to have some fruits and coffee.'

### III
### Sahiba in Vienna

While having our coffee at the hotel, I told her that we would stay in Vienna for three days.

'We will take it leisurely. There are a few places to see. There is some travel information you can look at. Do you like anything in particular?'

'You are my friend, philosopher and guide, Barun. Wherever you decide to go, I shall follow.'

'In a foreign country, I could be dangerous. Seeing you alone in such a beautiful country could be dangerous. Don't follow me blindly,' I joked.

'You are also welcome to be a dangerous guide, my dear. Is it why you are so insistent that I take some wine? My great grandmother carried a small knife with her. I don't keep anything like that.'

After coffee, we left the hotel and took a cab. We first went to the SchonBrunn palace. It was a magnificent piece of Baroque architecture with 1,400 rooms! Walking around the palace would have been very interesting, but I did not want Sahiba to strain herself. She was wearing a beautiful sari and she had caught a lot of attention. Other tourists asked her if she was from India and she smiled at them intermittently.

After the palace, we sat down at a place to enjoy the scene.

Sahiba said, 'Look, people are so carefree. The sky is so blue. It is almost sparkling under the sun.'

'It is a beautiful country. When we go towards the hills, you will find its brilliance even more captivating. Enjoy it, Sahiba. Everything belongs to you, right now.'

She stared at me like a child who had got everything she had longed for. I felt a strong sense of contentment on seeing her smile that way. After sometime, we went to a cafe. I ordered some tea, fries, and some bread with honey. The sight of fries excited Sahiba.

'Oh! I love them, Barun. My only worry is my waistline,' she said.

'It is my staple diet when I am out in unfamiliar surroundings. And don't worry about your waistline. You have been sick for long, so your waistline should not be a matter of any concern. Secondly, the sari you wear can easily camouflage it. Enjoy it. You will like this tea also. The bread is also good.'

'Ah, god bless the sari, after all! But don't worry. I am going to put on a long skirt the next time we are out of the hotel.'

We returned to the hotel as I thought Sahiba should rest a while. She just lay on the bed for a few moments and quickly fell asleep. I also lay down on the sofa. She got up after a while. She came to me and sat down beside me quietly.

I got up and said, 'Did you sleep well, Sahiba? We will have some tea.'

She just nodded and said nothing. We had brought some tea bags, sugar and milk powder to the table. There was a kettle in the room. I made some tea and we started sipping it quietly.

'Barun, I was wondering. Do you have to sleep like this on the sofa while we are on this trip?'

'What a question! No words about the tea, princess?'

'Princess, my foot! You are avoiding my question, Barun.'

'Calm down. You are a Christian girl. There has to be some propriety, no? We could have taken two rooms. But you won't stay in a hotel room alone. We have to compromise,' I quietly said.

'I have been raised in a convent. I don't know anything more than that about Christianity. I trust you, Barun. What can I do? I am scared of being alone in a hotel room. That is why I feel so guilty.'

'Don't be distressed. Let's not discuss it any further. We can go out to have some Indian dinner—put on the skirt if you like. We can see how the city looks during the night.'

'You are a master of persuasion. Of course, you know the art of dodging a question. I am feeling fresh after the nap. So, I am game. And I am going to oblige you, Barun,' she said standing up. She washed the coffee mugs and put them back on the table.

Soon, she was all dressed, looking gorgeous in her long skirt. I had seen her for the first time in something so chic. She asked me how she looked.

'Sahiba? You are not putting on perfume? I am sorry if it is too personal a question.'

She quickly came close to me, 'Do I smell foul? I am so sorry. I don't have any perfume. I don't have a make-up kit either.'

'I am so sorry. You look perfect without any make-up. And you smell very sweet indeed. I felt it on your breath while you were sleeping with your head on my shoulders.'

She blushed and I continued. 'Everyone uses some kind of perfume here. Men use some kind of deodorant. I don't use any. You can have some. There are some fine specimens of them in the market.'

'Thank you for clarifying. You had taken my breath away for a moment. I'll see. Tomorrow, if you please.'

Outside, the city looked incredible at night. I told the cab to take us on a scenic route to the Maharaja Indian restaurant. The driver was pleased and became a good guide for us. He showed us the glittering golden Vienna Mozart concert hall. I told Sahiba that Mozart had spent a lot of his days in Vienna, the capital city of Austria, which was the great centre of art in Europe. The driver also told us to visit Stadpark during the day.

Sahiba stared at everything as we passed.

We were warmly welcomed at the Indian restaurant. They had a lot to offer, but I requested them that we would go for some Indian cuisine provided he put less spice. We had dessert too. After a truly enjoyable dinner, we walked for a while on the wide footpath.

'We can take a cab, if you are tired,' I said.

As we walked hand in hand, Sahiba said, 'Barun, it feels like Darjeeling. It is very quiet.'

I smiled and we held each other for some time. Then, we took a cab to the hotel. We reached our room ready to crash.

Sahiba put up a wall between us with some pillows on the bed. She then led me to the bed and said, 'Now, sleep like a good boy.'

'Well, I will try my best. Good night.'

I slept soundly next to her.

The next morning after the complimentary breakfast at the hotel, we went to the Hofburg palace. It is the centre of the Habsburg dynasty and is presently the official residence of the President of Austria. We also passed the majestic St. Stephen's Cathedral on the way. Then, we went to the well-manicured park of Stadpark in Vienna. The statue of Franz Peter Shubert, the famous Austrian composer of the late classical and early Romantic eras, looked magnificent.

After some light lunch, we returned to the hotel for some rest. We saw some of the Museum Quartier as we did not have much time. It was interesting to note that it was a cultural hub in the world of Baroque and modern art. We learnt that Baroque art was of ornate architectural style of the seventeenth and eighteenth century. That way, Austria boasted to be the hub of cultural and heritage art in Europe.

Then to Mozart Café, which was a famous meeting place of intellectuals like Mozart, Beethoven, etc. The coffee there had a rather different taste. It had an amazing ambience. We appreciated the decor as we raised our head and looked at the walls, the ceilings and the photos in frames.

We again took a short walk around the place and finally found ourselves at a store. I told Sahiba that she could get some clothes here. I also noticed a fine collection of famous perfumes. She picked up a gown and a skirt. Then, she stood before the array, and whispered in my ears, 'I have no idea about these, Barun.'

I picked up a Christian Dior-Poison perfume for her.

'It is a present from me,' I told her. She took a sniff and looked enchanted.

'You are poisoning me, Barun.'

I only laughed. Leaving the place, I said, 'Care for another Indian joint, Sahiba?'

'Why not?'

I was steadfast when it came to Indian food. Given a choice, I always went for it.

After the dinner, I said, 'Barun is happy, young lady. Praise be to thee. Now we can go back to the hotel. We are now going to bid goodbye to Vienna, Sahiba. We take a train tomorrow morning to Salzburg.'

'Oh, good. I would love to be on a European train. How long will it take?'

'About two and a half hours. It is 240 kilometres away but the train is pretty fast. I am sure you will enjoy the ride, Sahiba.'

She seemed excited as we returned to the hotel. Sahiba was looking very happy and she seemed to be enjoying. I sat down in the ante-room while she changed. I told her that our train was at 9 a.m.; we had to leave the hotel by 8.15 a.m. and be ready early.

She came and sat before me. She took my hands in hers and said, 'Barun, it is so nice. Thank you. I am just wondering how a simple village girl by the name of Payoli has been transformed. It is all because of you.'

'It is just the beginning my dear. I think you must thank the Vidhata for it, if you have some reservations when it comes to thanking the blacksmith's son.'

'You are incorrigible Barun. Don't tease me anymore.

I have the good fortune of having the good company of Dr Barun De now. May god bless the son of the blacksmith.'

'But the blacksmith's son was set on marrying you. That point you have missed, Sahiba.'

'I have not missed anything. Be careful now, Barun.'

I frowned and said nothing and just went away to change. Then I returned and lay down without saying anything. She came near me and said, 'Very angry. You won't wish me good night?'

'Good night,' I said.

## IV
## The Sound of Music

After three wonderful days in Vienna, we were now on the train to Salzburg. It was a pleasure to look out of the window. But I had not spoken much since the last night. Sahiba sensed that I was upset and must have felt that her words had angered me.

But if I were to be honest, I was upset with myself. For the first time, I realized that there was no real need for me to be travelling with her. I would never have imagined travelling with a single lady and staying in her room. I had tried to do my best to look after her when she was sick and needed attention, but I felt there was no need for me to expose myself like this. Had both Sadhana and Nick set me up by suggesting this outing? It was supposed to be beneficial for her. But it was bound to raise certain serious issues of propriety. Why did I fail to realize it? It was totally avoidable. That is why I was angry with myself.

I tried to come to terms with it as the train sped through the countryside. I only saw a little village girl before me. Following my advice, her mother had sent away her only daughter to a faraway place in Darjeeling. Although this girl lived and grew in that Christian environment, she was not really a devout Christian at heart. In fact, she had not known any religion in her family. She had lost her mother and never returned to her village. She was now completing her MBA, after which she would be happily working again. But again, due to the twist of fate, she had met me. My advice had led her to this position. Then when she had fallen sick, I had reached out and helped her. She was advised to travel, but was scared to stay alone in a hotel room. She had chosen to stay with a person many years senior to her, a man she had treated like a god.

Could or should I have left Payoli alone? Didn't I have any responsibility towards her? I did not have to accept such a responsibility. I did not have to answer to anyone if I did accept such responsibility either. I had reached a certain stage in my life or in society where nobody could be bothered what I did. There was nothing wrong in helping her. Most importantly, Sahiba was an adult and had no qualms about me. That was for sure. Otherwise, she would have refused to come on a trip like this. She was sure to feel protected by someone she saw as her mentor. By being angry, I was perhaps doing her some injustice. With these considerations, I started to recover from my abysmal depths of self-inflicted remorse.

I had not looked towards her so far. Then, I looked towards her and put my arms around her shoulders. She turned towards me, and I saw the innocent face of the little village girl, of Payoli. She looked at me with tears in her eyes. I slowly smiled at her. She put her head on my shoulders and closed her eyes.

'Don't you want to see the lovely woods through which the train is passing?' I said.

She did not open her eyes and said very softly, 'I am seeing you through my inner eyes, Barun. You are so beautiful.'

I suddenly realized that here, Sahiba or Payoli, they were both depending on me. I could not leave her alone. I held her till we reached Salzburg. I woke her from her sleep.

'Here comes the city of *The Sound of Music*, Sahiba. There is music everywhere here. Mozart was also born here. Feel every tree and hill singing some song.'

She woke with a yawn and we got off the train. We took a cab to the hotel by the side of Salzarch River, which divided the city in two. The river had its own history. It was used to carry salt in barges to Germany. Salzarch joins the Inn River downstream, which flows into Germany. Sal in German meant salt and 'ache' meant river. It is also popularly known as Salzburg River.

The hotel room was good, but it was not as large as the one in Vienna. I had brought along a copy of the film *The Sound of Music*. I asked her whether she had seen the movie.

'Yes, I remember having seen it long back. But I don't remember it much, I must say.'

'We are going to Mira Bell palace in the evening after dinner. We will watch the concert—musical performance by some Austrian singers. Tomorrow we join *The Sound of Music* trip. It is going to be very interesting. If you want, we can watch this movie and you might enjoy the tour better.'

'Why not? We can see this movie in our room after some lunch. Barun, it will be great fun seeing a film together. I already napped on the train so I am game.'

Then she sang. 'I still remember its famous number 'Do-Re-Mi'.

'There are so many other beautiful things in this movie, Sahiba. But you still have time. I suggest some rest because we will be late in the evening after the concert. The trip starts early so we must leave after breakfast.'

'Okay, Boss. I follow your orders.'

Then we ate some lunch and turned in for some rest. I slept well since I had been disturbed at night. When I woke, I found that Sahiba had gotten the laptop ready for the film.

She said, 'I tried the TV, but it seems like it has some issues. So, we will see it on our laptop. I am getting some tea, then we give ourselves up to *The Sound of Music*.'

She brought the tea in no time.

'You are divine, my dear. Now I am ready for the show.'

It was a film I loved and I could watch it over and over. I liked that Sahiba too seemed to enjoy the film. After the credits rolled, I told Sahiba to get ready.

'The evening looks very pleasant. We can have a walk around and I can treat you with more Indian dinner. After the dinner we will go to the concert'.

She quickly got ready and joined me in the ante-room, glowing and spreading the fragrance of a flower.

I smiled. 'Oh my god! Sahiba your poisonous perfume is killing me. And your sari is simply gorgeous. You are going to set Salzburg aflame.'

She smiled mischievously and said, 'You have poisoned me already. So, if I let it spread a bit, I am not to blame. If the flame touches you, tell me. Don't complain.'

She seemed to be ruthless when it came to these jokes. I disappeared to change. I returned after a while and we went out together. The evening was very crisp and cool. We walked along Altstadt, the birthplace of the famous composer Mozart. Sahiba held my arm as we walked down. She was drawing a lot of attention because of her beautiful sari. We sat down in the Central Plaza for a while. The evening was really beautiful. We walked down and reached the Indian restaurant. The food was delicious. Sahiba too seemed to prefer the food we ate.

We took a cab to reach the marble hall of Mira Bell palace for the concert. It took some time for us to be soaked into the sounds of the performance. I had never attended something like this before, but Sahiba was used to it at church. I found myself captivated. After the music ended and we left the hall, we stood on the bridge for a long time, lost in thought. But as we came out, I was feeling so good. Sahiba was also feeling elated.

Then, we returned to the hotel to sleep. We woke early and as planned, reached the point from where the bus trip was to commence. It was right opposite the Mira Bell palace. We found a good seat and the tour guide was a wonderful fellow. He reminded us of many scenes from the movie. We were shown all the locations where the film was shot. We had a look at the abbey and the gazebo where the famous song 'You are sixteen, going on seventeen' was taken. We looked at the lake and the iconic castle where the Von Trapp family lived.

In the movie, the scene of Maria's wedding was beautifully shot. We looked at the Parish church of Mondesi, where the wedding scene was shot. Walking the aisle in the church brought back the beautiful scene when Maria walks for the wedding. In the tour, the background music of many of the famous songs from the film was being played. All the tourists were really enjoying. Sahiba was humming many of those songs. The entire tour lifted our spirits up in a musical crescendo. We were back to the Mira Bell palace where the last part of the song 'Do-Re-Mi' was shot featuring Maria. We moved around the palace garden after the trip was concluded.

The guide had told us that in the last scene of the movie, when the Von Trop family escaped to Switzerland, it was shown that the family was climbing the hill and crossing over to

Switzerland. He explained that hill was actually the border with Germany. In actual case, the family had escaped by taking a train to Italy from where they had gone over to Switzerland. He also said that strangely, Austrians did not by and large like the movie. He said that Germans had just crossed into Austria. Locals had actually welcomed Hitler's army. He also said that in the movie, Captain Von Trop was shown as searching some point to tear the Nazi's flag put by the authorities in his villa. He explained that the fabric of the flag was strong and could not be torn. To facilitate tearing, a cut was made where the Captain Von could tear the flag. The hero was fumbling to locate the cut. It was so interesting.

We then returned to the hotel for some rest. We went out in the evening for a walk again and the cool breeze from the Alps was invigorating. This time, we walked and had some pizza for dinner. It was light and good.

Back at the hotel, Sahiba was still humming the song 'You are sixteen, going on seventeen'

I said that this was a very romantic song. 'You are neither sixteen, nor seventeen, so don't you worry,' I teased her.

'No, Barun,' she said. 'Don't you realize that this song is not about the number. It is about a person who is stepping out into the world of men and she needs someone to look after her?'

She continued to sing in a jovial mood.

I looked at her. I did not know what she was up to. Then she continued, 'Barun, when you are with me, I don't really worry about anything. I too am entering a new world. Look at me with my background. I have no experience at all. But I have to face it. So having you around is so assuring. No?'

'You are too lost in thought, Sahiba. It is bed time. No?'

On the last day of the stay at Salzburg, we took a trip to the Bavarian Mountain and saw its breathtaking views and took in the air. We also learnt that the salt was mined from some salt pits here, which we did not enter.

Our last evening dinner was again spent at an Indian restaurant, followed by a walk in the evening. Sahiba was feeling much better, and had enough energy to walk. I was glad she was recovering so quickly.

## V
## In Innsbruck

It was our last night in Salzburg.

Sahiba was still impressed by the movie. She spoke about it excitedly, 'Barun, you know, the film reminds me so much of my own convent in Darjeeling. I can recount the days I spent there. Reverend Mother treated Maria the same way that Mother Grace treated me. You remember the scene where a new postulant is welcomed by the Reverend Mother? It reminds me of Darjeeling. The most exciting part was the wedding when she walked down the aisle.'

Sahiba was entirely engrossed, as if in a dream. I could imagine her excitement. She was a village girl presented before Mother Grace as a postulant. She lived the lives of the nuns. When her time came to fly, Mother set her free and did not bind her down to the life of a nun. In the movie, Mother had told Maria that the abbey was not a place to shut people. She had encouraged Maria to climb every mountain till she reached her dreams.

I held her arms and said, 'Sahiba, I understand how you feel. Mother Grace did not sing the lines, but the song by the Reverend Mother is so apt for you.'

I sang it for her.

*'Climb every mountain, ford every stream;*
*Follow every rainbow, till you find your dream...'*

'Don't you realize, Sahiba, the most important thing that happened to you, was your being set free to fly. You were asked to face the world. I think you should feel very proud of yourself and of how far you've flown.'

Sahiba twirled in glee, with tears in her eyes. 'Yes, Barun. You are right. I am so glad that you brought me here. I would never have realized these things... Had it not been for *The Sound of Music* tour, I would not have realized that mountains have to be climbed, streams have to be forded and rainbows have to be followed.'

'Have you found your dream, Sahiba?' I asked, looking into her face.

She smiled and said very softly, 'I think I have. I know I have. But I have to follow the rainbow still. Barun, I shall tell you when I get to it.'

'Congratulations, Sahiba. Now it's time for bed. Our train to Innsbruck is at ten o' clock,' I said and led her to her bed.

The next morning, we were in time. We boarded a good express train and were comfortably seated. The train rolled away from the station and ran through picturesque scenes. Sahiba looked out of the window to see the beautiful view.

I said, 'We will be in Innsbruck for two days only—'

Sahiba stopped me. 'I don't need to know where I am going and how long it will take to reach. I am with you, Barun. Wherever you take me.'

'I have told you before that I can be a dangerous driver. Be careful. Never give control of yourself to others. That can lead to danger.' I told with a smile.

'It is too late to consider your advice, now,' she winked.

I let out a deep sigh and said nothing. The train was moving at a good speed. It was scheduled to reach in less than two hours. Sahiba was engrossed in deep thought and was not very communicative. I did not want to disturb her.

We reached Innsbruck in time and noticed how beautiful the station was. We were soon at the hotel. After a short lunch, we went out for the cable car trip.

The height of the cable cars provided a wonderful view of the Austrian mountains. We travelled up to Surgrube, which gave us a bird's eye view of the steep-gliding slopes beyond us. We breathed in the clean mountain air.

Later in the evening, we took a stroll around the main city and looked at the glittering Swarovski World of crystals.

We returned to the hotel after a light dinner. Sahiba offered me a cup of coffee. One could not say no to her.

'Don't want to sleep?' I asked her.

'I want to watch the movie again, Barun. After the tour, I felt like I had missed a few things. For instance, I did not notice the original Maria at the party—on whose life the film is based on. I also want to relive the scene connected to the abbey. It reminds me so much of my days in Darjeeling. If you want to sleep, you are welcome to.'

'Immediate sleep is unlikely now that I've had some coffee. I want to see you watching the movie. Go ahead,' I said.

I sat down and relaxed, watching her take in each scene. I drifted off to sleep on the sofa. I woke up and found Sahiba had put her hand on my head. She said, 'It is so lovely to see you sleeping like this. I was just wondering how one could sleep like this. I am sorry for waking you, Barun. Now go to bed.'

I let her lead me to the bed and we both slept soundly. The next day, we went to old Innsbruck to see the Hofburg Castle of the Emperor. We also saw the old cathedral. Then we walked about the countryside, taking in the views of the mountains. On the outskirts, we located a small Indian restaurant run by a couple. We sat down there and ordered a few things. The food was simple and homely.

We returned to the hotel in the evening. It was our last day in Austria. We had spent eight days in this country, I realized. Sahiba said that she would not like to go anywhere that night so I got some sandwiches from the hotel's restaurant.

After dinner, I found that Sahiba was still absorbed in thoughts of the film. I stared out of the window and hummed a tune from the movie:

> *"How do you solve a problem like Maria.*
> *How do you catch a cloud and pin down;*
> *How do you hold moonbeam in your hand?"*

Sahiba said, 'I was wondering why Maria was a problem. I have thought it over. Barun, can you tell me your views on this?'

'Okay. In the song, the Reverend Mother says that they wanted to say many things to her. Maria should have listened and understood them. But she obviously did not. That was a problem.'

'Barun, but the basic reason was that Maria did not conform to the ways and the discipline of the church. She had pledged to be a nun. But she was wayward. She would sing and dress up unlike the nuns. Why did not she conform? She was still committed to her pledge, but she could not stop herself from going to the hills to see the clouds and birds.'

I nodded.

'She longed to listen to her heart, which was still that of a child. A child does not relish regulations or restrictions. It wants to be free. The Reverend Mother realized this when she said that Maria was still a child. The Mother also told Maria when she ran away from the Von Trapp family that the church was not meant to lock a person within its walls.

'So, the Mother told her to go and find whether the person who could love and set her free, actually loved her. Barun, the key issue of the problem was that she was locked and bound to the church. That problem had to be solved by looking for a solution beyond the confines of a church. That was the liberty.

'Barun, I too have realized that in my case Mother Grace thought that it would not be correct to insist that I be a nun or I be confined to the nunnery. I was sent by my mother to receive education in the convent to be able to lead a better life. By remaining a nun, that objective would have been lost. So, she set me free to receive professional education, giving me a small amount of money. She advised me to earn my way.

So, setting a person free was the solution and being confined inside the walls of the church was the actual problem. Am I not right, Barun?'

'Absolutely, you are right. Liberty is always a solution. Both Reverend Mother and Mother Grace have been very sagacious in this respect. But I am afraid your liberty is still incomplete, Sahiba.'

She got up and held my hands and said in a low voice, 'I know Barun. I still have to climb a few more mountains. But thank you so much.'

I smiled and told her we would be leaving for Zurich next day. We would bid adieu to Austria.

## VI
### Over to Switzerland – Zurich

We took a 1.30 p.m. train from Innsbruck for Zurich. The beautiful express train covered a distance of 215 km in three and a half hours. We were enchanted by the view, especially after we crossed the Swiss border at Liechtenstein. We were in Zurich by 5.00 p.m.

We were going to be in the city only for a day. So, we were in a rush. After checking into the hotel, we left to explore a bit of the old city. The city is divided by the deep-blue Limmat River. Walking along the river, breathing in the atmosphere, was a worthwhile experience. We even saw St. Peter's Church and the stunning Gross Munster Church.

Amongst some very good dining places, we found an Indian restaurant for an enjoyable dinner. Zurich is also famous for its chocolate, and Sahiba and I found a few that just dissolved in the mouth.

By the end of the day, I felt tired but Sahiba was full of energy. It meant that she had improved quite a lot. The next day, we took a boat ride in Lake Zurich. We also walked along the lake. Sahiba seemed to be loving it. We sat down in the small park Linderhof. It was very quiet.

Then we saw the place where Albert Einstein had stayed in the latter part of his life. I told Sahiba all about it. He had studied in ETH—a prestigious technical university—and had later come to teach here. He had developed his famous theory of relativity here. It was the revolutionary rest mass energy equation: $E = MC^2$.

'Imagine, Sahiba. It differed from Newtonian theory where mass is supposed to be constant. It was in 1905, and he was just 26!'

She laughed at my excitement. The next morning, we reached the railway station to catch the 5.30 a.m. train to Lucerne.

## VII
### Lucerne

Lucerne is supposed to be the gateway to the Alps. We were advised to go to Lucerne first, but I had been adamant that we stay in Zurich for a day since Lucerne was less than an hour away. Our hotel, only two blocks away from the railway station, was right next to Lake Lucerne. Sahiba was already tired after the day-long excursion in Zurich. So, we picked up something light to eat from the restaurant and ate in the glinting sunshine from the room as we relaxed.

Not far away from the hotel, we heard about a musical programme. But we were still soaking up *The Sound of Music*; we also had a crowded itinerary next day. We just stayed put in the hotel.

Lucerne was very compact and easy to move about. River Reuss flows out of the Lake Lucerne. The city is blessed with medieval core, elegant historic buildings and beautiful Alpine atmosphere. We took a boat ride in the lake giving panoramic view of luxurious villas, Alpine peaks and hilly landscape. The lake is known as the 'lake of four Cantons'.

Then we took a trip around Mount Rigi in a cable and saw the beautiful cruise towards Meggenhorn castle. The guide told us that it is known as the 'Queen of Mountains'. We saw the thirteen lakes and took in the spectacular views of the snow-capped Swiss Alps. We were completely overwhelmed by the scene.

The next day, we took a trip to Mount Pilatus in a cable. This trip took us over 2,100 metres high to see the unforgettable landmark of Lucerne. We took the cable way from Kriens to Frakmuntegg, and another cable car took us to the summit, also known as 'Dragon Mountain'. Then we descended from there by taking a cogwheel train with a steep gradient—it was quite scary. Sahiba held on to me in fear. On our way back, we also saw the Chapel Bridge that ran diagonally across the River Reuss.

On the last day of our stay at Lucerne, we visited Jungfraujoch—the top of Europe. It was really thrilling to reach the highest railroad station and this time, we were not as afraid as we were when we took the cogwheel train to Jungfraujoch. We enjoyed passing through the mountain pass of Kleene Scheidegg, right beneath the famous Eiger north face. It was a tiring nine-and-a-half-hour excursion. We returned to our hotel feeling quite exhausted.

After a bit of rest, I asked Sahiba how she was feeling.

'Barun, we have climbed so many mountains physically now. We have also forded so many streams. We cannot complain, you know. After all, we were chasing our dreams.'

I laughed at her references.

'Our dreams? I don't have any dreams. And, I thought you had found your dream already, Sahiba.'

'I wonder... Do you mean that I have reached my dream of acquiring a professional qualification? I have. But is that all?'

'No, no. I never meant it to be the end of all dreams. Beyond this, everything is about your personal life. You will surely find a prince charming. Shruti has. Why not you? You are most comely. It is just a matter of time, Sahiba.'

'Matter of time... Everything in our lives is related to time. But the question is larger. What am I looking for? I don't think about it. Shruti depended upon her parents to find the answer. Either I go solo, or you again become my navigator.'

'Look, I have no experience in this area. I cannot possibly be a guide to you in this matter. I think you have to follow the rainbow. Do you know, what a rainbow meant? It is a matter of your heart. What is dear to you? What would you like to love? In the song, Maria looked into the eyes of Captain and said that she knew what she was searching for. You have to depend upon a feeling like that. A rainbow will take you from one plane to another, Sahiba.'

Sahiba smiled lazily and said, 'The heart is the queerest thing. But I will tell you. I have yet to climb a few more mountains, I suppose. Yes, I agree that the rainbow perhaps transports us from one mountain to another.'

I sensed a danger in pursuing the matter of the heart. So, I changed the subject. I told her that we had to leave Lucerne the next day to go to Geneva. We were going to be there for only a day and had to return to Delhi from there.

I said, 'Sleep, my dear. Let your heart rest a bit.'

## VIII
### Geneva

The Swiss Railways were very comfortable. We covered a distance of about 190 km in less than three hours and reached before noon. We checked into our hotel and I told Sahiba that we would not climb any more mountains now.

We took a cruise around Lake Geneva and saw the water fountain, Jet d'Eau, reaching 140 feet high. The cruise was very soothing and relaxing. Then we went to see the St. Peter's Cathedral. Sahiba always enjoyed looking at churches. We could have gone to the International Palace of nations, where all the UN offices were located, but I decided against it at the last moment.

It was also interesting to see the Reformation wall. Geneva has always been a city of thinkers. The wall held memorials in recognition of theologians like John Calvin. Against the wall stands Reformation Monument in the recognition of thinkers like John Calvin and John Knox. I told Sahiba that they were all prominent leaders of the Protestant Reformation.

We also saw the famous flower clock. In the evening, we just walked alongside the lake and found an Indian restaurant to end our day with a delightful dinner. We returned to our hotel early to rest for our morning flight to Delhi.

Sahiba came up to me and said, 'What a lovely trip, Barun. I am so grateful that I can feel well again. I'm sure it has also given you a much-deserved break. I cannot thank you enough.' Then, she kissed my forehead.

Sometimes, I felt sorry for her. I knew that this trip had been good for her but she was still struggling within. But that was life. I asked her if she wanted to pack. She said that she did not have much of packing to do.

Then, I sat down and asked her to also sit down beside me. She sat down on the floor, still holding my hand. She said, 'Once, we are back in Delhi, everything will go on as usual. I will also have to pull myself up and get back to my job. After all, every good thing comes to an end, Barun. I will never have my fill of you.'

'Well, I am glad I could bring you here on this trip. I could see your spirits soaring. It was good after the sickness. I think you must have discovered a thing or two away from your original surroundings.'

'Most certainly, Barun. I am just marvelling at what I have found. I have got to tell you. I don't think I can wait any longer. I must tell you tonight,' Sahiba said, almost in a whisper.

*Seven*

# Sahiba Follows the Rainbow

I looked into her eyes and saw the beauty of the many lakes we had seen. It seemed that the captivating view of the Lake Geneva in the night was opening windows which were shut till now. Sahiba looked at me intently, seemingly struggling to find the right words. She still looked like a princess to me, one who had escaped and was trying to find a new world for herself.

She began to speak. 'Barun, you told me the other day to follow the rainbow, to follow my heart. I am now convinced that it has to be you, Barun. No one else. I have been struggling a lot. But I find that it is in vain. I have to reach my dream. I love you, Barun. I am honest.'

I was stunned and left speechless.

'Are you mad? Do you know what you are saying? I am over fifty and I have never been married, never even thought of marrying. It is a problem.'

She watched my outburst. 'It is unthinkable,' I continued. 'You are not in your senses. I can never marry. How can I marry you, a girl half my age? I have held up a certain degree of purity, and have never looked at you that way. You're an innocent child of Maya, a girl who needs support.'

'Yes, that is true. I still need support. How can I find anyone else?'

I shook my head.

'Age is only a number,' she continued. 'I don't know how you could lose your purity if you were to marry me. It is very clear, Barun. This is not a longing for the body. You have already seen this. We have stayed together in one room. It is a union of souls. What difference does it make if your soul is in a body older than mine? Souls are immortal. They do not age. I will not ask you why you are a bachelor or why you have not married before. There must be a reason. But unless you have taken a religious vow, it will make no difference if you marry now. Who is going to ask you why you have married someone so young? This has no relevance in the world we live.'

I was swept away by her incisive logic. Where had she learnt about the body and the soul? She was now talking in terms of soul consciousness. It was altogether a different plane.

I asked her, 'Have you seen *Charulata*? The film?'

She shook her head.

'It is a famous film where the heroine is married to an old man. She was just thirteen when she married and her husband was over forty—more than three times her age. Her husband was busy with his business all the time and the girl grows up into a lovely woman. She needed attention from her husband as a man, which he was unable to provide. And then she has an extra-marital affair. That becomes a problem.'

Sahiba smiled, 'I am not thirteen years old. You are not three times older than me. Age wise, both of us are going to be older in time. In the movie, the girl did not even know what a marriage was, she was a child. Here, you and I know what we are going to do. Can you compare me to the girl in the film, Barun?'

I was very upset and could not reply. I just looked into her eyes. I had been a bachelor for so many years and now, suddenly, someone very close to me had shaken me up. I tried to get a grip over the situation when Sahiba spoke very softly, 'In my great grandmother's story, you remember how she felt—someone had touched her bare body, she knew she was helpless. When she recovered, she realized that she could not marry anyone else. And she convinced Sham Sher Singh, her man servant, to marry her. There was no other option.

In my case, my soul has been stirred by your kindness and your humanity. You have given me support. While I was sick, I was still a village girl. I did not know whom I could trust. I now have an impression on my soul. Where can I go with that in my heart? I cannot go anywhere else. My heart won't obey me. You can understand where you and I stand'

She said with tears in her eyes.

'I know where I stand now,' I said. 'I can only say that you and I have been beautifully set up by Sadhana and Nick.'

She said, 'God bless them for what they did. I can't say it was by design. But with hindsight, one can say that they thought that this relationship should have turned towards a more logical ending.'

I turned away and said, 'Such decisions cannot be taken in a huff, Sahiba. So, get up and sleep. We are returning to Delhi tomorrow.'

I got up and went to bed, angry with myself. Sahiba followed me quietly.

## II
## Back to Delhi

We got up in the morning and had tea together, but we hardly spoke to each other. I noticed that she had not slept well. Sleep had eluded me as well.

We were at the airport in time for our flight at 12.30 p.m., which was scheduled to land around midnight. Our seat in business class was again good and we were comfortably seated. This time, Sahiba knew how to fasten her seatbelt and did not need much assistance. Soon after the take-off, they provided some lunch. After that, I thought we could catch up on some sleep. As she relaxed in her seat, I said with a smile, 'You can use my shoulders, if you wish.'

'May I? Thank you very much, Barun. I would love to… but not if you are angry,' she said.

'I am not angry with you. If I have to be angry, I have to be furious with myself.' I smiled and pulled her head towards me.

'I'm glad. I'll apologize if you are angry. But when you are following a rainbow, one can't be angry.'

Then she closed her eyes. I looked intently at her innocent face. I felt that I should caress her to help her sleep, but I held back. But as I looked at her calm and innocent face, I too closed my eyes. I did not know when I fell into a deep sleep.

I got up when cabin lights were put on and tea was being served. I found that Sahiba was already up. When I woke up, she smiled. 'It is so good to see you sleeping, Barun. I also slept a lot. What time are we reaching Delhi?'

'Another four hours.'

We landed in time and were out with our baggage. Sahiba said that I could drop her off at her apartment.

'Why are you going to wake up the whole household? Please come to my place. You can go back after a day or two, or as you wish.'

'But your house has been locked up for so many days. It will be inconvenient, won't it?'

'You are forgetting the good and efficient Sadhana, my dear. She must have already come and spruced up the house. If I am not too mistaken, she must have left some dinner for us on the table as well. If you don't come, she will keep asking me about it. So many good reasons to come along. And, I too would like you to come. Otherwise, I will think you are angry.'

'For this reason, I must come with you, Barun. I had forgotten about Didimoni. She is such a nice person. My trip would not be complete without seeing and saying goodbye to her.'

We were home in half an hour. As predicted, the house was neatly done up. There was some dinner also kept on the table. It was welcoming to see some flowers in the drawing room.

'I think Sadhana surpasses my expectations. She would never keep flowers for me alone. It must be specially be for you, Sahiba. Will you like to eat something? Let's see what has she put up. I'm not hungry but if I don't take anything, she might be offended.'

'I must thank Didimoni. I don't mind some rice and dal. And look, Barun, there is some kesar payas for you.'

We found the home-cooked food too good to resist and ate heartily. We then went back to our rooms and slept.

We got up in time to find that Sadhana had arrived. Sahiba hugged her.

Sadhana said, 'I am glad to see you, Bibi. The colour has returned to your face. That means the trip has done you a world of good, Bibi.'

Sadhana smiled warmly.

I greeted her as well. 'How was your trip, Sadhana? Is everything fine? When did you come back? You know I was telling Sahiba that you must have returned and must have kept something to eat also. But I was quite surprised to see flowers in the house. Not for me, I suppose?'

'I came back the day before. Everything was fine. It was

good that I could go. Thanks to you, Babu. I kept something to eat in case you wanted it. And these flowers, I thought Bibi would be happy to see them.'

'So, here you are Sahiba. You know, Sadhana, she insisted that she go back to her apartment in middle of the night. I brought her here for you and told her that if you did not come, I would have to do a lot of explaining to Sadhana. Then, I told her that if she wasn't angry with me, she should come.'

Holding on to Sahiba, Sadhana said, 'It is so good that you came here, Bibi. How else could I have seen the colour back on your face, first thing in the morning? And Babu, how can Bibi ever be angry with you?'

As she said this, Sahiba blushed and hid her face in her bosom.

'Okay, okay. What are you going to give us for breakfast? By the way, the payas was very good, Sadhana.'

Sahiba said, 'Didimoni, we got to eat Indian food at so many places. But Barun is crazy about your homemade dishes. What would you like to have, Barun?'

I waved my hands, 'Beggars can't be choosers. Can they?'

Sahiba knew that I liked parathas for breakfast and made a few. I then told Sahiba that she could sleep a while to ward of the jet lag. She just shook her head. 'I would like to speak to Shruti. She must have been expecting me at night. I also want to know how she has been.'

Then she added, 'Since you are going back to your office on Monday after the weekend, I must also join my new office.'

## III
### Sahiba's Dream

I slept for a while as Sahiba was busy with her phone calls. Then, I saw her intensely gossiping with Sadhana, telling her all about the trip. I left them alone.

In the evening, I called Nick and asked him about work. He was very chirpy as he picked up the phone. He greeted me, saying, 'How have the two-some enjoyed the trip? When did you get back?'

'Two-some! What do you mean, Nick?' I retorted.

'Sorry. I meant the two of you.'

'Not the same thing, Nick. But thank you for suggesting the trip and also for the arrangements you made. It went well. It seems like Sahiba has gained a lot from the change in air.'

'Oh, I am so glad. Everything is fine here. We are going to have the annual meeting of the board in a month and a half and you know how crazy everything is then. I don't even have the benefit of your presence. I wonder if you can join me here, at least ten days before the meeting is scheduled to start? It will be of great help. You can be here for a month or so. Sahiba can also travel with you. It will be very nice to have both of you together,' Nick said.

'That should not be a problem. I can plan accordingly. I don't know about, Sahiba. She told me that she wanted to join her new job the coming week.'

Nick said he understood and after a few pleasantries, we hung up. Sadhana then suggested that she would prepare the dinner early so that we could eat and sleep early. She said that her brother was coming to meet her as well.

Sahiba said, 'Don't worry, Didimoni. I will see about dinner. It will be a good idea to sleep early.'

That made Sadhana very happy and she left soon after. Sahiba cooked and we quickly finished our dinner early as Sadhana had suggested.

I was quiet at the dinner table. Sahiba spoke about Shruti and told me that they sounded happy.

She asked, 'Have you spoken to Nick? I also wanted to

thank him for his help with the trip.'

I just nodded.

We finished our dinner. Sahiba set everything right in the kitchen and then she joined me in the living room.

'Care for any coffee, Barun?' she asked.

'We have been commanded to sleep early; the coffee will spoil it. Won't it? It's all the same. I find everyone conniving against us. Of all persons, Sadhana put up some flowers. Nick asks about the "two-some". Then, Sadhana cleverly leaves us alone. Can't you see their explicit design?' I asked her in exasperation.

She laughed and said again, 'God bless them, Barun.'

'That means you have not given up. So, let us have the coffee, at least.'

She went and brought the coffee immediately. She handed me my cup and sat down on the carpet again with hers. I thanked her.

'You are welcome. You know, Barun. You said sometime back that beggars can't be choosers. But truly speaking, I am the beggar here. I cannot choose what I want. So, there is no question of giving up. I shall have to accept what I get in return from you. I don't want you to marry me out of pity or compassion. You have already done so much for me and for all of us,' she said with a great deal of humility.

'There is no question of marrying you out of pity. It would be preposterous. I am battling with myself.'

'Why?'

'Well, I was the only child of my mother, who loved me so much. When I grew up and became marriageable, I saw how wives dealt with their mother-in-law. It was all right for a mother to be possessive of her son. It was also all right for the wife to be possessive of her husband. This was a conflicting situation, which could not be avoided.

## Sahiba Follows the Rainbow

I chose not to marry because I did not want to risk that kind of conflict. I found that the service was demanding and it was better to be single. I had to fend only for myself. My mother always insisted or pleaded with me to get a daughter-in-law for her. But I knew what she was asking for. It was only going to be trouble. Then it became a habit. After my mother's death, I thought that it was my mother who wanted a daughter-in-law. Now, she was no more. Why should I marry then? As the years have passed, I don't want to marry. I don't think I need to marry.'

'Our marriage won't be like that. I respect your sentiments, Barun. Unfortunately, it is not possible to have your mother here to judge. Age cannot determine eligibility for marriage. So, relating age to eligibility is actually a myth. In this country, we may sometimes link it to age. But outside this country, no one cares. I have mentioned that.

Both of us are adults. We fully understand what we are committing to. We know what plane of consciousness we are referring to. Things like soul-searching may not be easily appreciated or understood by many.

But that cannot be helped. Some people live together as a couple, instead of being formally married. But morality apart, the idea is ridiculous. It is absurd to me, irrespective of religious beliefs or social norms,' Sahiba said.

The combination of her innocence and sincerity was lethal. I searched for a reason to decline her offer. I found myself defenseless. Was I becoming a mama's boy? I looked towards Sahiba in need of some help. But she had fixed her gaze on me in seriousness.

I said, 'There are two basic obstacles in my way. Number one: why should I marry now, if I did not marry so far? Number two: why should I marry you, when you are so much younger and when I have looked after you as Maya's daughter?

Basically, the question remains, what will people think about a union like this? They may not say anything to our face but that question will always loom large. Will a union with such a large age-differential be sustainable in the long run? It is not possible to do away with the physiological compatibility needed to sustain a relationship over a long period. Finally, what is the compulsion to marry?'

'The answers are very simple. If you never do the things you are unaccustomed to, perhaps you should never get married. I know that is not true. Moreover, being bound by force of habit or by dogma is the prerogative of a donkey. Don't you see that?'

I laughed and she continued.

'Secondly, in marriage, age is a mere number. There is no limit set on it in any society, not for adults. Some people might think what would be the desirable age. But that is without any justification. What is the good rationale for that? I believe and you will also agree with me that only love sustains a relationship. We are talking about souls in search of each other. Then why are physiological needs a factor for compatibility?

'There is no compulsion either. It would have been something to talk about if you were marrying me for my beauty or I was marrying you for your money or wealth. I am not a beauty to launch a thousand ships like Helen of Troy. You also do not have that kind of wealth. Both these questions are meaningless. You know this and have seen this. A correct question perhaps would be what would this marriage achieve?'

'And if we think about what people will think, it is difficult to know the answer. Don't you see that we are simply erecting a wall around us? A wall of norms—what should or should not be acceptable? Mother Reverend said that we should not erect walls that will prevent freedom. These walls are, in any case, made of our imagination. We suppose they would be like this. But even if they are there, it is meaningless.'

I did not answer. I was already amazed by her incisive arguments and preferred to listen to her.

She said, 'We are fond of each other. I look towards you as my liberator or benefactor. You see me as a result of what good education can do. Not simply that.

After my mother's death, you have always borne some kind of responsibility. It is obvious if you think about the way you have looked after me while I was sick. Had Maya been here, she would have never thought beyond you in terms of my husband, I know. Even if we are not married, you won't ignore me. So, this marriage can bring two people to a common platform. That is what this marriage would achieve.

So far whatever you have done is with passion—whether for the bridge or for the people you have helped to gain respectability in society. This marriage can now provide passion in your life. This passion has been missing in your personal life. This is what this marriage will achieve. You will surely agree with me, Barun.'

'I know Sahiba, I am caught in a deluge, a vortex of emotions. It is sucking me in. I don't know to swim. I do not know whom to look up to bail me out. I don't know, if anything, will remain of Barun after I sink into it. You know that Barun has had a public profile. How will people see me now?'

Sahiba touched my shoulders and said, 'Barun, you can clearly see that this deluge, as you call it, is not my creation. I am myself being sucked into this vortex. How did this all begin?

Your love and benevolence for the poor. It has worked like a spark. I was charged to seek a fortune for myself. On its course, the Vidhata brought us together to revive the memory of our past. God has created a situation where I am placed once again in your care. Your acts of benevolence towards a person who had lost everything is bound to stir the soul.

I had lost my name, home, mother—almost everything. When souls are stirred, ripples of emotions are bound to be released. That is why I say I am no Helen of Troy. Your profile remains intact, Barun. Doesn't Nick call you a good Samaritan? I am lost in your goodness.'

I shook my head and held her hands and said, 'For me, you are Helen of Troy, you've launched a thousand ships in my heart. Let my princess have her way.'

Sahiba gushed in joy and hugged me. 'Thank you, Barun. Thank you.'

Then she suddenly turned away, saying, 'Thank God! If I am the Helen of Troy, you are the richest person on this planet, Barun. The richness of your heart is compelling me. But wait here for a moment.'

She disappeared into her room and seemed to take a while.

I wondered what she was up to. But she came back in a new sari. She was dressed in all her jewellery. She came up to me and touched my feet. I protested and took her into my arms. Then she looked at me with tears in her eyes. 'I love you, Barun.'

There could not be a greater demonstration of love between two people. Her joy and ecstasy were infectious. She took a step back and started singing the famous number from *The Sound of Music*:

*'There must have been in my youth or childhood,*
*I must have done something good.*

*For you are loving me, standing there,*
*Whether or not, you should,*
*Somewhere in my youth or childhood,*
*I must have done something good.*
*Nothing comes from nothing,*
*Nothing ever could.*
*So, you stand here and loving me,*
*I must have done something good."*

I said, 'In the movie, the Captain asked Maria if she had found her dream. Have you, Sahiba?'

Sahiba nodded and said, 'Yes, I know I have, Barun. I told you that I would tell you when I do. So, here I am, after having climbed so many mountains, after fording streams and following rainbows.'

I said, 'In the movie, Captain Von—'.

She stopped me and kissed me for the first time. It was a moment of fulfilment. She again looked at me, 'Barun, I can't thank you enough. I am so happy. I want to tell everybody.'

She said, 'I will tell Didimoni first thing in the morning. Would you like to tell Nick? Both have been the chief collaborators. They will be happy to know that they have succeeded.'

'I have to tell Nick, of course. Only a couple of hours ago, I was admonishing him for calling us a two-some. Yes, he asked me to come to the US for a month to assist him in the annual board meeting. He has also invited you. If we are to be married, both of us can go together. It can be our honeymoon.'

She laughed and agreed.

'But before that,' I said, 'I must thank you for dressing so quickly for me. I find you have hardly any jewellery on you. It does not become of a bride to be, my dear.'

'I have you as my brightest jewel. What other jewellery do I need?'

'Oh, Barun. Yes, it would be wonderful to go to US. I want to show Nick, what I have got.' She laughed like a child. Then, she continued, 'And I want to beat Shruti. Can't we, Barun?'

'You have beaten everybody, including me. You told me once that you were a sharp shooter, just like your mother or your great grandmother. I did not know that I was on your radar.'

'Oh, Barun, I never thought of you like that. But when I came close to you, I was lost to you. Today, I feel like I am on top of the world. I think my mother was very far-sighted. Otherwise, why did she put my surname as Deb? It will be so exciting to be the wife of Dr Barun De.'

## IV
### Wedding bells for Sahiba

'First things first. Now how do you become my wife and I your husband? Do we have to announce in the newspaper?' I joked.

'That is very simple. I don't have any relations, nor do you. We don't need to seek any permissions. Now, the wedding can be either according to Hindu religious customs or we can have a church wedding. Choice is yours.'

'I am no longer a Hindu in the usual sense now. What I have learnt is that Hinduism is no religion as such. Who has established it? Nobody knows. People talk of Shankaracharya, but he only reestablished it. Actually, our Sanatan Dharma is just about being good to one another. It is a message of kindness, brotherhood and well-being. Yes, I believe in this broad religion of universal brotherhood. That being the case,

Hindu customs are no longer an option. If you like, we can go to a church. It could be a wedding like Maria's.'

'I am obsessed with the image of that wedding. I'd love it. Barun, the best place to go to will be our St. Joseph's Convent in Darjeeling. Mother Grace will surely be happy to marry us in the church. It will be fantastic. I can go to Darjeeling and fix everything up.'

'A bride arranging her own wedding? That does not sound too well. You can speak to Mother Grace and ask if she can host our marriage there. After that, whatever arrangements are required we will arrange from here. Okay?'

'I will try to speak to the Mother tomorrow. It happens to be a Sunday. But she should be free by the afternoon. When do you wish to call Nick?'

'I shall talk to him on Monday. By that time, I suppose you will be in a better position to say what you are going to do. It is really too easy if you have no relatives to call or think about for such an occasion. Well, one can lament the lack. But I think it is much easier and comfortable that way.'

'You are right. That is why I value Didimoni so much. She is so affectionate and caring.'

I said that it was time to sleep otherwise she would not be in a position to do anything the next day.

She laughed and said, 'How can I sleep now? I am too excited.'

I patted her and said, 'Too much excitement is injurious for health. So, avoid it my dear. You should look normal when you face Sadhana, or she'll be outraged.'

I guided her to her room. She would not let me go. I said, 'Sleep, baby, sleep.'

I came back to my room and lay down on the bed. I realized how a storm had arrived and changed everything in my life. I felt like I had moved askance. But my heart effused love for Sahiba, who cared for me.

It was impossible to spurn the hand offered to me. It was based on trust. Even god could not refuse it.

But my heart was beating in an old body. The body could age, but wasn't the heart ageless? I once again thought whether what I had agreed was out of compassion or pity? I realized that the difference between love and compassion was thin. One cannot help but love a person who is alone, friendless, without any relative in the world. If god also thought the same way, all those who needed him would be left alone. Sahiba was so devoted. I could not but accept her. To leave her alone would have been unjust.

I got up in time in the morning. I thanked god that he had given me the courage and insight to act in the way I had done. It was now my responsibility to restrain myself with honour.

I came out to find Sadhana putting our tea out and waiting for us. In a while, Sahiba also came out, beaming and colourful. She went straight to Sadhana and pulled her out of the kitchen. She then held her in her arms and said, 'Didimoni, believe it or not. Barun and I have decided to marry.' Then she bent down and touched her feet.

Sadhana was totally taken aback and embarrassed. She pulled Sahiba up with love and in surprise. 'This is the most auspicious news of the day. I am so happy for Babu. You will be the happiest couple, I am sure.'

Then, she walked to me and said, 'Babu, make Bibi happiest. You have done so much. But you should make her the happiest person. And look, on this day too she is not wearing any jewellery. She should have at least a bracelet, a chain and some earrings. And a mangal sutra. Maybe ... an anklet? Babu, let us dress up the bahu properly.'

'Come on, Didimoni. I have never put on so much

jewellery in my life. I will look ridiculous,' Sahiba argued.

Sadhana tenderly touched both her cheeks, 'Oh, it is so beautiful. This is an occasion of a lifetime, Bahu Ma. Had Babu's mother been here, she wouldn't have listened to you. With the grace of god, you get married only once. In our society, ornaments are considered a sign of suhag, so please. '

Sahiba looked towards me for some help.

I thought about it and said, 'I too talked about this. A bahu has to wear proper ornaments. So, we'll go get some after you finish talking to Mother Grace. And thank you, Sadhana, for blessing Sahiba as the bahu of the house.'

Sadhana just smiled appreciatively and said, 'You sit down. I'll get more tea.'

Sahiba looked at me very lovingly indeed. Her eyes were moist. Much like me, she too had not received the affectionate touch of an elderly woman for a long time.

She said, 'Maya would have been so happy, Barun. I now realize that if you had not come into our lives, I would have been destined to wed the son of the blacksmith in all probability. I am now going to be the wife of the most handsome and eligible man, a man who has turned me around. Now, I have a mother-like figure who even though has very few physical possessions in the world wants me to be decked up like a real princess. Barun, you can't imagine what you have done. I can't thank you enough, my dear.'

After putting down the tea tray, Sadhana sat down on the carpet. 'Babu, I must thank you. Bibi is going to be a wonderful wife. I am so excited. You have to make so many arrangements for the wedding.'

'Thank you, Sadhana. Sahiba wants a church wedding. She is going to talk to her Mother in Darjeeling. Then, we will decide what to do. Nick has asked me to come to the US next month. If we're married by then, we can go together.

In any case, we want it to be a rather simple affair.'

'That is fine. I have seen church marriages. Brides are attired in beautiful gowns. You have to get a gown, Bibi,' Sadhana said.

'No gown for me. I have seen brides wearing saris too. I would like to wear a sari,' Sahiba said.

'You first have to talk to Mother Grace. And, don't forget that you are a princess. It has to look regal. Remember how gorgeous Maria looked in her wedding gown. You can discuss this also with Mother. In the end, this is going to be your choice. You are the bride. After you finish talking to Mother Grace, we can go out to see what jewellery you need.'

She was very excited. She left to call Mother.

Mother was elated to hear about the marriage and told her that the church was Sahiba's home. 'We will arrange everything for the wedding. You will go as a bride from your home. We also have a beautiful gown, which you can put on. It will look very nice and appropriate for a daughter of this church.'

Sahiba agreed.

'The wedding can take place ten days from now, if you are ready. Please confirm, if it suits you.'

Sahiba asked me and I told her we could do as the Mother said. Everything was now resolved.

Sahiba confirmed it with Mother Grace. We then decided that we would fly to Bagdogra and book some rooms in a hotel in Darjeeling. Sadhana was delighted to hear this. She said that she would stay back and keep this house in order to welcome the newly-weds. Sahiba said that Shruti would have to join her, even if her fiancé might not be able to go. So, we would be a party of three.

We then went to a store to look at jewellery. Sahiba was hesitant and finally said that she would like to wear the necklace her mother had given her. I thought it was a good idea; it had royal charm. Then Sahiba picked out a pair of bracelets, a thin chain and a pair of earrings. She said that she would put on a mangal sutra, just as my mother would have liked her to wear.

As we returned for lunch, Sahiba told me that she must go back to her apartment. I was a bit surprised.

She said, 'It is now only proper for me to come here only after we are formally married. As a Bahu Ma.'

'Oh, do you mean that living here now is like living in sin?' I said teasingly.

'I have never sinned. You know that. I am sure even Didimoni would like it.'

'Alright, will you come here before we go to Darjeeling?' I asked.

'No, I will join you at the airport. I am not coming here. Not before the wedding,' Sahiba said.

'Then collect all that you want to carry with you. Now I can meet only after the wedding.'

'Oh, come on, Barun. How can I do without meeting you all this while? You are permitted to flirt with me outside this house,' she said with a wink and put her head on my chest. Then, with some mischief, she said, 'What is this? Your heart is not beating as fast as mine.'

'That I will have to find out if it does. Anyway, do you expect me to run and chase you around the trees like we're in a Bollywood film? You have already climbed many mountains, Sahiba. I have yet to do so. But the ten days will feel too long. You will be in Vasant Kunj and I will be here alone. You will have your friend for company. What do I do here alone without you?'

'We will meet. We can talk. Learn to live without me. I want to see how you conduct yourself.'

'Am I being tested? Well, meeting elsewhere sounds exciting. I am sure Sadhana will find out and be amused.'

Sahiba was gone by the evening, after telling Sadhana that she was going away. Sadhana had nodded but said nothing. That meant that Sahiba was correct. Sadhana appreciated it as it was proper.

I didn't understand it. Propriety belonged to the domain of the world of logic or accepted social behavior. In matters of the heart, it had hardly any place.

I spoke to Nick in the morning. He was elated to hear about the wedding.

'This is the best piece of news I have heard after a long, long time, Barun. I would have been very happy to join the wedding. But you know that with this meeting coming up, I can't do that. But Edna and I will welcome both of you here. It will be so good to see the two-some. So, let me know your detailed itinerary so that I can take care of everything.'

'I will. Thank you, Nick.'

'And, congratulations to Sahiba and you. May god bless both of you.'

*Eight*

# Sahiba Weds

I am Shruti Shirodkar, Sahiba's friend and roommate. We live in an apartment in Vasant Kunj together. We have been friends for more than four years.

I remember Sahiba as a girl from Darjeeling. She was staying at the YWCA and looking for a job, which could enable her to complete business management programme. An event management company, where I worked as well, offered Sahiba a job. I was asked to help her adjust into my team and train her in the management of events. We had to manage several types of events.

Sahiba had to manage seminars and symposiums, big budget items. I remember that she was quite shy when she had first come to me. She did not know anything about event management and had never attended a major seminar before.

I appreciated her simplicity and honesty, and in no time we became good friends. When she had to vacate her room at the YWCA, I offered that she stays with me. She readily agreed. Since then, we have been always together. She is a little older than me and behaved a lot like an elder sister, which I appreciated.

Soon she got admitted into a business management programme and since then she has been so disciplined. She did well. We both were similar, even though our upbringing differed. I come from a good family in Nagpur, and she was from a convent, but we agreed upon many things. So, we really had a good time together.

She was very happy when I was recently engaged. I really did not know much about her background. I only knew that she was a tribal woman from St. Joseph's Convent in Darjeeling. Once she met Barun at the seminar, I heard about her life. Barun told her many things about herself.

After that, she told me that she actually belonged to a tribal family from Bagaha in Bihar. Many years ago, Barun had been there as the chief engineer to construct a bridge on the Gandak River. With his help, Maya, her mother and also many villagers were able to improve their economic status. Taking his advice, Maya had sent Sahiba to Darjeeling to receive an education. It was a surprise to learn that Sahiba belonged to a royal family in Rajasthan, which Barun told her. Apparently, her great grandmother was a princess who escaped from her state to save her honour.

I loved Sahiba. She too was a real crusader. Not only her, but her ancestor had also shown great courage and grit to run all the way to the Bagaha forest to save her honour. Our respect for Sahiba grew so much.

While I was away for my engagement, Sahiba had fallen sick. Barun looked after her so dearly.

Barun is much older than Sahiba. To me, he seemed like a respected professional and a benevolent man. I had noticed a strong attraction between the two despite the gap in age.

Recently, Barun took Sahiba to Austria on a trip. That had done her good and she recovered quickly. It had also brought about some dramatic changes in their relationship. A new relationship blossoming between them had the fragrance of a pure and sublime love. The dignity and maryada were always writ large in whatever they did together.

## II
## Sahiba Returns

Sahiba called me on Sunday in the morning. She asked if I was awake, and since I had woken up she continued to speak. She said, 'Shruti, listen. I am getting married.'

I laughed and said, 'I am not surprised, Sahiba. I was waiting for this news. Congratulations. I am so happy for you. I am dying to know the details. When do I see you?'

'Strange girl. You are not even asking whom I am getting married to. I shall come back to you in the evening.'

'That is no secret and there are no prizes for guessing. We all knew where the two of you were headed. I look forward to seeing you.'

Sahiba laughed in an embarrassed tone as I teased her. Later in the evening, Sahiba arrived and embraced me. We sat down at the table.

I said, 'I wanted to congratulate Barun. But I thought I would do that when we meet next.'

'Oh, Shruti, it has been so exciting. Don't talk about Barun. He was so reluctant. He looked like a confused small boy. I had to practically convince him that this was the best thing to do. He kept asking me why he should be married, if he hadn't married yet. I said, "Baba you have been doing so many things you have never done before." Then, he finally blinked like a poor boy.'

Sahiba then went on to show me the jewellery she had bought for the wedding—some beautiful pieces. She told me that the wedding had been fixed and was to happen in ten days. I was delighted. 'That is really fast. You beat me here, darling.'

'Mother Grace told me that she would make all the arrangements for me to be married there. She suggested this schedule and Barun agreed to it. He has to go to Washington after, so it suits him. Now both of us will go together to Washington—a sort of honeymoon, you know? Nick has invited us. Now there is so little time left. I have told Barun that you are also coming to Darjeeling.'

'That is fine. I shall certainly come with you. Manish may not be able to come. Poor fellow is always busy.'

Sahiba clapped in glee.

I continued. 'I have not seen a Christian wedding so far. It will be wonderful to see you in a wedding gown.'

'I wanted to wear a sari for the wedding. But Mother says that I am going to be married at a church, so a gown will be proper. She says that she has a gown. Barun says that I should look like a princess so, I have agreed. Oh, Shruti. I am so happy. You know, Mother still says that I belong to the church.'

I smiled at her kindly.

'And look Shruti, I told Didimoni that we were to be married. She too was happy. She started calling me Bahu Ma. After that I realized that I should no longer stay in that house. I should now only go there as his wife. So, I've come to you.'

'Didimoni is really very affectionate Sahiba. I just feel sorry for Barun who has been left alone in the house. You know he has always been with you since you were sick.'

'Yes, I understand. He was saying the same thing. But I told him that we could meet outside the house. I told him that he could flirt with me before the marriage.'

I laughed and said that it was a good plan. Sahiba had to get a few things for herself. I said that we could do so in the afternoon. I would get back from the office and then we would go out.

Sahiba called me up around two o' clock to say that

Barun had called. He wanted to meet her in the afternoon and our plans had to be deferred.

I came back to my apartment by 5.30 p.m. After a while, both of them turned up. Sahiba was looking a bit apologetic and Barun seemed a bit embarrassed. I congratulated Barun first. He grinned and thanked me. Then I asked them, 'May I ask you guys something? What were you up to? It looks like Barun also didn't go to the office.'

Barun spoke in a huff.

'Now don't ask me, Shruti. I don't know what your friend was up to. She called me at two o' clock saying that she has two cinema tickets and that she was waiting for me at the entrance. Before I could say anything, she hung up. Luckily, I was free. I sent my driver home. I told him that I would come on my own. The fellow would have seen us together. He would have carried tales to Sadhana. When I reached the hall, I found her waiting in a beautiful dress and black sunglasses.'

Shruti said, 'Oh my, Sahiba. You're quite clever. You told me that Barun called you. Barun, only now do I notice this side of her. She used to be such a nice girl. Is it because she has been in your company, Barun?'

They laughed along with me. Then, I asked Sahiba how the movie was. She smiled and said, 'I don't know.'

'What do you mean, I don't know?'

Barun said, 'Frankly, I never saw the film. When I reached, she said that the show had started and we needed to hurry. We went inside and sat down and tried to make sense of the plot. Sahiba sat down and put her head comfortably on my shoulder and said that she was feeling very sleepy. She then slept off.'

I laughed at Sahiba.

Sahiba said, 'What can I do? I knew Barun would not

have slept last night either. So, I had to pull him out of the office. He also slept comfortably. I think people do not mind sleeping in the auditorium, particularly during an afternoon show. We came out and had some popcorn. He had left his car, very wisely. We took an auto and we are now at your service. Hopefully, we can have some tea.'

Both of them were grinning and looking at me lovingly. It was such a beautiful picture.

I said, 'Sahiba, weren't you the one flirting?'

She laughed. 'You don't mean that. I have done Barun a beautiful service. Barun, you must appreciate me.'

'All the way, my dear. I have never flirted in my life. I am an engineer, you know. You have given me my first lesson in flirting. I needed it very badly,' Barun said.

The couple looked so cute and innocent. I knew that Sahiba had never flirted in her life before, even though she was so beautiful. Barun was actually such a serious-looking person, and I imagined he had never been exposed to this kind of relationship. Both of them were trying to be good to each other in such a comical way. But their true love was apparent.

I said, 'For god's sake, both of you remain like you have been all along. It is wonderful to see my friend so happy after a long time. Sahiba now can be a princess, like her mother wanted. Now, Sahiba, tell me when do you want to go shopping?'

Sahiba glared at me, then turned to Barun.

Barun laughed and said that he could come along or send the car.

She said, 'Thanks. No male help needed. The driver will go and tell everyone everything. I can go alone. This time, make no mistake, Shruti. I am definitely coming.'

## III
## A Darjeeling Wedding

We discussed our travel plans for Darjeeling. Barun told us that the flight was around 10 a.m. and we would be in Bagdogra by 12.00 p.m.

He said, 'I have arranged for a car, which will pick us up from the airport. We should arrive in Darjeeling by the evening. I have also booked two rooms in a hotel. One for Shruti and the other for us. We'll have a pre-wedding ceremony the next day, and the wedding the day after that. We leave the following day to catch a flight back to Delhi.'

Sahiba said, 'I have talked to Sister Jane too. They are all working out all the details. Sister Jane has said that they would have to do a ceremony prior to the wedding. The wedding takes place normally around twelve o' clock, followed by a customary lunch at the church.'

I said excitedly, 'I haven't seen a Christian wedding before. I am looking forward to it. Also, Sahiba you need to buy a few dresses. There are so many ceremonies. You can check with Sister Jane. There is still time so we can organize it. It has to be special, Sahiba.'

Sahiba blushed and agreed.

Barun said, 'I'll come to pick you both up from here in the morning. I think we ought to donate something to the church as well. They are going to undertake all these expenses for this wedding.'

Both of us nodded in agreement.

Sister Jane subsequently informed Sahiba about the programme. First, they would have a traditional mehndi, followed by a bridal shower. The convent had organized a musical evening also.

We made all the arrangements accordingly and left in

time. Our flight from Delhi landed at Bagdogra. We were at St. Joseph's Convent by late afternoon. As we were getting out, Sahiba said, 'It's so strange to be here as an adult. I came here as a child with Sister Jane.'

Sister Jane welcomed us and hugged Sahiba with warmth. She said, 'Sahiba, you are the daughter of this convent. You have to stay with us. You can go with Barun only after you are married. Shruti can go back to the hotel. The two of you should be for mehndi here by ten o' clock tomorrow.'

We nodded.

'Then we'll do the mehndi. Then, the bridal shower. Barun, please join in these ceremonies. We have arranged an evening of music here. We hope Sahiba will sing. If you join too, that will be great.'

Barun and I left for the hotel. The room he had booked was very comfortable. Barun took a lot of care of me and we talked a lot over a quiet dinner. Barun asked while I was entering my room, 'I hope you are not scared to be alone in a hotel room? Sahiba is very scared.'

I laughed and said, 'Don't worry, Barun. No such problem with me. I wonder why Sahiba finds it so scary. Right now, she had company. They must be reliving her school days in the convent. But the experience must be very different this time around.'

'Yes,' said Barun. 'She is now being treated as a bride.'

We wished each other good night and slept well to be in time for the ceremony.

It was a small function. Sahiba was sitting on a chair in a sari while some mehndi was being applied on her hands and feet. Sahiba had also invited some friends from school and college who had joined in. Sahiba excitedly spoke to her old friends.

We were greeted warmly. I sat down with the group and

treated myself to some mehndi.

Barun came closer to Sahiba to watch the fun. Sahiba introduced him to her friends. Then she told me, 'Shruti, I had a wonderful time last night. I went all over the place. I'd never imagined that I would come here as a bride. God has been really kind.'

I smiled and hugged her carefully, trying no to disturb the mehndi on her hands. After the ceremony, Sahiba went to wash up and was soon ready for the bridal shower.

She put on some of the jewellery for the occasion. Mother Grace came to the function as well and started with her blessings and gave the couple a small gift. Mother spoke with Barun warmly. She congratulated him and said, 'Sahiba had come to the Lord's house as a small child. I learnt that her mother had sent her away on your advice. Today, my heart is full with joy to see how that girl has blossomed into a lovely lady who is choosing to wed her own mentor. The Lord is truly great. Inscrutable are his ways!'

Barun agreed with the Mother. 'Yes, I had gone to construct the bridge on Gandak more than two decades ago. Meeting Sahiba after two decades was lucky.'

It was a solemn occasion. I was overjoyed to see the bride being blessed by her old friends and sisters. There were many gifts for her, but a small gift from Sister Georgia brought tears of joy to her eyes. She was given a set—a comb and a ribbon—she had used as a small child in the convent.

This was followed by a good lunch. After the lunch, Barun and I returned to the hotel. We rested for a while. Then we left for the convent again.

Sahiba was looking exquisite in her blue-coloured lehenga. She was wearing the royal necklace and looked like a princess. Barun too was handsome in his black suit. He was wearing the same tie that Sahiba had given him.

I went up to Sahiba and kissed her.

Then we all listened to musical presentations from the many people at the convent. Sahiba also joined them in the choir.

Barun walked to the stage and was applauded. He then sang, 'Pal pal dil ke paas, tum rehti ho' and Sahiba played the piano. It was a touching scene. As she played, tears rolled down her eyes.

The second song was a duet, a Rabindra sangeet they had both practiced called 'Purano sei diner kotha.'

Sahiba played expertly on the piano as they sang the melodious number. It made me think of two children who had been separated and were now joined in union. As they finished the number, Barun walked to Sahiba, knelt down and kissed her hands. There was a standing ovation as both of them stood before the church with folded hands seeking their blessings.

They walked out, hand in hand, to attend dinner.

## IV
### The Solemn Wedding

The day had arrived for the wedding. Barun and I were ready. Barun looked very elegant in his pastel-coloured prince suit. I had put on a lehenga I had bought especially for the occasion. We reached the church in time and were welcomed in.

I went to meet Sahiba who was almost ready and waiting for the signal to move. She was wearing a beautiful white wedding gown. I gave her a bouquet of flower. She gave me a long hug and whispered into my ears, 'Shruti, I am nervous. Now, the D-day has arrived. May god help me dear. How is Barun?'

I patted her and whispered, 'Everything is going to be

fine. I have left Barun at the altar. I can tell you that he is looking very dashing and equally nervous. Sahiba, you yourself look gorgeous.'

Mother Grace then blessed Sahiba as she bowed down before her. Sister Jane was the master of the ceremony. With the ceremonial music in the background, Sahiba walked down the aisle. Sister Jane and I accompanied her on the flanks. She walked with royal grace, looking every bit the princess. Had her mother, Maya, been here, she would have felt so proud. After all, the sacrifices she had made for her daughter had borne fruit.

She reached the altar where Barun came forward to hold her hand. They then moved towards the priest, who congratulated them. The marriage rituals were simple. The priest first asked them for their consent to marry. Then, he read out some verses from the Bible, a homily.

He said, "For Husbands, this means you love your wife just as Christ loved the Church. He gave up his life for her. Therefore, a man should leave his father and mother and hold fast to his wife and they shall become one flesh."

This was followed by the vows, which each one of them had to take.

'I take you to be my wife/husband to have and to
hold
from this day forward
for better, for worse,
for richer, for poorer,
in sickness and in health,
to love and to cherish,
till death do us apart,
according to God's holy law;
and this is my solemn vow.'

Thereafter, the priest declared them husband and wife. Both of them bowed before the priest to receive his blessings. There was a customary kiss, which husband did and wife blushed. Barun and Sahiba performed it with grace. Then they signed the register.

After that, they moved hand-in-hand towards us.

Mother Grace was the first to congratulate and bless the couple, followed by many others. I ran up to them with open arms and hugged them both. It was a fantastic and memorable occasion.

We then headed for a customary lunch. The occasion was festive. After the lunch, both of them went up to the Mother to thank her for everything she had done. Barun had brought a cheque for the church as donation on the occasion, which was accepted gracefully.

Sister Jane had packed Sahiba's luggage already. She promised to see them in the morning before they left for the airport. The three of us returned to the hotel together. It was so good to see them sitting down cozily for dinner. I left them alone to a candle-lit dinner.

After they spent the night together, we saw each other for breakfast. Sahiba blushed in her beautiful new sari. I asked her with a wink, 'Lovely Sahiba?'

She just laughed and said, 'Don't worry, you will know shortly.'

We left for the airport in time and reached conveniently. Our flight to Delhi was on time. While sitting in the lounge, I told Sahiba, 'I had not seen a Christian wedding before. It is so compact. Everything was over in thirty minutes flat. In our case, the wedding goes on for almost the whole night.'

Sahiba said, 'In our village too it ends within an hour. The bride remains in the village and the groom moves there. In your case, tell everyone that it should be over in an hour or two.'

'As if they are going to ask me before it! I wish I too could have a Christian wedding. The vows sound so comforting,' I said laughing.

We boarded the flight. We would soon be in Delhi. The couple would go to their home, where Sadhana would be waiting to welcome them. I thought that had Barun's mother been there, she would have been so happy. During all this time, Barun had remained silent. He glanced at Sahiba, his wife, occasionally. On the flight, Sahiba dutifully put her head on his shoulders and was fast asleep. Barun looked towards me and just smiled.

The flight landed in time and soon, we were out of the airport. Bahadur had brought his car, and it was decked with flowers. Sahiba put her hands on her mouth in pleasant surprise. I also accompanied them.

Sahiba would now return to the house as a wife and the mistress of the house. May god bless her and her home.

*Nine*

# Sahiba, Bahu Ma

I am Sadhana. I work as a housekeeper at Dr Barun's home. I belong to a village near Ranaghat in West Bengal. I have an aunt, the sister of my late father, in the village. I have a younger brother who now works in Bangalore. We were very small when we lost both of our parents. We had received some education in a nearby school. I was married off, but soon separated from my husband because of sheer incompatibility. I never married again.

With the help of some relatives, I moved over to Delhi and started working as a housemaid. My first landlady taught me some English. Then, I worked in the embassy. Due to my honesty and sincerity, I earned good credentials.

I took up the job with Dr Barun when he came from the US. My experience of working with people from the embassy had proved to be good so far. Soon, Barun Sir, whom I called Babu started reposing a lot of confidence in me. I called him Babu because he also belonged to West Bengal. He was a bachelor and was easy to work with. Things were going on fine.

Babu introduced me to Sahiba Bibi. Sahiba unfortunately fell sick with typhoid. She was hospitalized. She was cured, but she required attention and so, Babu brought her home. I came to know that Babu knew her mother. Babu has always been kind and considerate.

In time, Sahiba finally recovered. Bibi was a very kind person herself and very respectful in the way she treated me. She called me Didimoni.

While I saw them interact, I quickly realized they both liked each other despite the difference in the age. I really wanted them to be married as they would make a wonderful couple.

I knew that a change of air would work wonders for typhoid patients and I suggested that Babu take Sahiba somewhere. Babu's boss suggested a trip abroad. He felt that Babu too needed a break. Thus, both of them went to Austria.

Simultaneously, I learnt that my aunt was not keeping well in the village. I too went and visited her in the interim. In the village I saw that my aunt needed attention. I promised her that I would give up my job and return to look after her. I wanted to discuss this with Babu after they returned from the vacation.

When they returned I saw that they were both in high spirits. Bibi announced that they had decided to marry. I was totally surprised and overjoyed. I was sure Sahiba would make Babu very happy. Then, I also thought of Babu. His mother would have been very happy to see her son married. I too was glad that Sahiba would be the Bahu Ma of the family.

They left to be married in Darjeeling. I stayed home to make all the arrangements to receive the newly-weds according to the customs of a Bengali family. Bibi deserved a befitting welcome.

They were finally arriving this evening. I had already prepared dinner. Bahadur had helped me arrange the house with flowers and some balloons. I had prepared a rangoli at the doorstep. I had also kept a small pitcher or kalash full with water. Buntings of mango leaves were put on. Bahadur too went and got the car adorned with flowers.

## II
## Bahu Ma Arrives

Bahadur called as they were entering the block. I was wearing a good sari in the traditional Bengali style. As the couple came up using the lift, I stood in the doorway and blew the conch shell to welcome them.

It was such a lovely sight. Sahiba crossed the threshold of the house by pushing the pitcher with her feet. In our tradition, it indicated that she would never leave the house till her death. It also signified that she had brought honour and prosperity to the house.

I had also lit an arti for her and put aside some sindoor (vermillion). I asked Babu to apply it as it is the sign of suhag for a married woman. Then Sahiba was finally in the living room. She touched my feet. I picked her up and blessed her.

I said, 'Oh beautiful, stay beautiful.'

Then, I made her eat some Suhag curd as a good omen. I told Babu to give her the mangal sutra to wear. Babu came and hugged me saying, 'Sadhana, you have fulfilled the role of my late mother. I am so grateful.'

I knew he was silently weeping and remembering his mother.

Then, I also welcomed Shruti and told her, 'It is your turn now, Mishi Ma.'

I had kept their favourite tea ready. Bahu Ma was sitting beside Babu. They were a lovely two-some. I prayed to god that they remained happy forever.

Babu said, 'Sadhana, I have been missing this tea. Thank you.'

Then, I told them that dinner was almost ready. Bahu Ma said 'Didimoni, I am coming to the kitchen to help you. Just let me change. Shruti, you will have dinner here before you go.'

I told Bibi with a smile, 'You can't enter the kitchen unless a ceremony is first performed. From now onwards, you are a griha lakhsmi, you know. So please change and come. We will also have the ceremony while Shruti Ma is around.'

Sahiba raised her hands in exasperation and started going to her old room. I stopped her and told her with a smile, 'Bahu Ma, that is no longer your room. Now go to Babu's room.'

She blushed and went there instead. She returned after a while in fresh clothes. She stood before the kitchen door and said, 'I am here, Didimoni.'

I washed her feet and sprinkled dry rice on her head. Then she was allowed to come inside the kitchen. Everything was kept ready to cook kesar payas, which she did with utmost devotion. Then, she first offered it to Babu, followed by Shruti and me. I had kept a thousand rupee note as shagun, which I placed in her hands. She was so touched.

Babu asked whether he had to pay Sahiba as well. I said, 'No, it is my prerogative today, Babu. I now belong to Bahu Ma.'

Dinner was arranged and we all ate heartily. Bahadur dropped Shruti off. Then, Babu came to me. His voice was full of emotion. Sahiba Bibi was also by his side. 'Sadhana, I don't have words to thank you. I shall also not thank you. You have today fulfilled what my mother would have done. Your gesture of blessing Sahiba with your own money has today dismantled the wall between mother and housekeeper. I now touch your feet. Please, forgive me.'

I smiled and hugged them both, then sent them both to bed.

In the morning, I expected them to be late but Sahiba was already up and ready after a shower. She came and greeted me. 'Didimoni, I am here. Shall I prepare the tea?'

I was so happy to see her in the kitchen. As per traditions, the Bahu was always ready in the morning to help with whatever was required in the kitchen. I held her lovely face in both of my hands and said, 'I am so happy to see you, Bahu Ma. I don't know where you learnt the correct manners. But I am overwhelmed. Now, don't you worry. Tea is already done. So, go and sit down with Babu. Now, when you return from the US, maybe you can do more. Please enjoy for now, Bahu Ma.'

'No, No. I start now. I have to learn a great deal from you, Didimoni. You know I've grown up in a village, but at the convent I learnt many things. I watched Bengali movies and read some books about how a daughter-in-law should conduct herself. I told Barun in the morning that this home is a temple. I have many things to learn now. I have to prove myself a worthy Bahu,' she said and hugged me.

She insisted on carrying out the tea tray herself. I accompanied her and told Babu, 'She is a perfect Bahu Ma. She has already announced her intention to make me redundant very soon.'

Sahiba Bibi smiled and started placing the cups as I watched. Then she said, 'Who can make you redundant Didimoni? You are going to be central to our home. You have worked so hard all your life. Now, it is my duty to make you a bit comfortable. That is what we will do.'

'In our village, when the Bahu Ma arrives, the mother-in-law normally leaves the house for a teerthayaatra. So, now when you come back, let me go away,' I said.

Barun looked hard at me and said, 'Sadhana, you are not going anywhere. Not as long as I am here. That is certain. You may go out for some time but you will stay here only.'

I said politely, 'Babu you have been very magnanimous and kind to me. There would have been no question of leaving. But you know, Babu, I have some responsibilities.

I had gone to my village when you were abroad. I found that my aunt is not keeping well. You know that she has raised me and looked after me and my brother in all possible ways after we lost both our parents. I told my aunt that she should not worry anymore. I told her that I would come back and look after her. Babu, she was so happy that she started crying when she heard that.

I had thought that I would tell you. But as soon as you came from Austria, the marriage was settled. So, there was no question of me going. Now, you will be gone to US for a month. I can go home and be with my aunt. I can reassure her that I would come back soon.

Babu, she is alone in this world. If I can't be with her, the heavens will curse me. She has become like a child in her old age. I will come back for a week to organize everything here. I shall also arrange a good replacement in my place. I shall then handover the entire household to Bahu Ma. She is so good that I am fully confident now that this house has the best landlady.'

Everyone was stunned. Bahu Ma came and put her arms around me.

'Didimoni, don't worry at all. If you think that you need to go now, you should certainly go. We deeply appreciate your sentiments about your aunt. My respect for you is already sky-high. I know that the elderly need the caring hands of children. Children too can redeem themselves that way. I understand these obligations.

So, Didimoni, you have to decide. From our side, it will be our humble contribution. Whatever money you might want today or you may need tomorrow, you have to just tell me. Barun and I are indebted to you. Both of us do not have parents. You have fulfilled that void.'

Barun also came along and put his arms around me and said, 'Sahiba has already assured you. We will do whatever possible to help you serve your aunt.'

It was overwhelming for me. I was overjoyed to receive their love, respect and kindness. I felt blessed by god. I found that I was weeping, but my tears were of joy. They were supposed to be leaving for US in four days. Babu had made all arrangements for me to leave for my village. They left me with enough money as well.

In those four days, the new couple made the house full with joy and festivity. Babu told me all about the wedding and the songs that they had sung. Bibi even sang a few lines of a Rabindra Sangeet for me. I once again blessed them. Their melodious voice and the emotions that it carried made the rendering unforgettable.

We were now at the end of our time together. Their flight was around midnight and they left for the airport by 9 p.m. I had promised them that I would come back two days in advance to keep the house in order.

Bahadur then dropped them off at the airport.

After they were gone, the house looked so empty. Bahu Ma had left her mark everywhere. In a short time, she had endeared herself to us.

I made some calls and arranged a replacement for them—my cousin who was quite reliable. Bahadur also knew her. I left the next day. I did not know then that I would never return.

## Ten

# Adieu

I am Nicholas Carlton—call me Nick. I work at the World Bank. I am married to my lovely Edna.

I can say that it was a masterstroke to have Dr Barun De as a technical expert at the World Bank. He was here for a railway project in India. He has a wide range of experience and has carried out some major projects in India.

He is also very innovative. If you give him a problem to solve, he is sure to find a workable solution. He often said that he had been in-charge of some difficult projects in India, which always had problems and it had become necessary to find solutions. He said that one had to seek help from people at the top. But at the end of the day, it was always one's own ball to throw. There was no point complaining or lamenting about the issue.

He would say, 'I had a dubious reputation of begging, borrowing or stealing to resolve a problem. I can go to any extent and will leave no stone unturned. I managed this because I believed that I was being paid to resolve an issue. If someone could help, it is fine. Otherwise, I am on my own.'

He is a person of impeccable integrity. No one could dare point a finger against him in matters of transparency or honesty.

He always believed that as a public servant, he was open to scrutiny. So, he would ask himself whether he could defend his action against a critic. He believed and said, 'In case I felt that I could not explain or defend myself, I would revisit the decision.'

Thus, out of intense introspection, his decisions were never questioned. In the course of this, he admitted that he had often earned the ire of his superiors. He had to pay a heavy price for his principles.

In the bank, however, these were the stellar qualities and attributes we cherished. Barun had become an instant favourite of all. He is a warm-hearted person. His concern for the poor or have-nots was well known. He was a bachelor and truly uncomplicated, and took his responsibilities very seriously. He also expected others to do the same. I like him as a person as well. Although I was his senior and boss at the bank, I knew that he was much older than me. He has vast knowledge about all engineering subjects. So, it is difficult to boss over such a person.

To be very fair to him, he was always very conscious of my superior position. As a result, he never gave me the chance to be anything but pleasantly humble.

Barun basically loves people. He always responded. At office, one could see him chatting with a junior or even a probationary executive. He would not only ask how he or she was doing but would also help if they needed it.

Later on, I came to know of how he had dealt with some dreaded dacoits in a project he was in-charge of. He could sit down with them to talk and explain how they could earn honest money. He was a straight and honest person, fearless and courageous. They believed in him and reposed their full confidence in him. Thus, Barun was successful in winning them over. They gave up their arms and joined the project as a stakeholder, working as ordinary contractors. Nobody had ever believed that these dreaded elements could ever be won over. But with the help of some committed engineers, he had succeeded in bringing peace and harmony to the area.

He had also changed the lifestyle of the people living in a village located in the dense forest in the foothills of the Himalayas. He had encouraged them to learn skills to work in the project. Thus, they started earning good money. They had never seen or dealt with money and were amazed to see what they could buy with money in their hands.

Barun also urged them to send their children to school to receive education. The present story, which I am now associated with, is the outcome of such useful advice. Sahiba's mother had followed his advice with great diligence. Sahiba was sent in a clandestine manner to Darjeeling for proper education at the convent.

Sahiba, I learnt later, actually belonged to a royal state in Rajasthan, where her great grandmother was the princess. On being persecuted by a local chieftain, she was forced to escape from their state in a daring and courageous move to save her honour. That was two hundred years and four generations ago. That was a big twist in the history of their family.

Barun met Sahiba by chance when we went to attend a seminar in Delhi. He introduced her to me and said that he was meeting her after two decades. Sahiba had still remembered him. She was beautiful and very impressive. She was completing a business management programme in Delhi.

## II

Barun had gone back to the Delhi office on a transfer. Sahiba had gone to visit Assam. She returned to Delhi soon after Barun had joined in Delhi. Unfortunately, she was sick with typhoid. She was alone then and Barun took her to a hospital.

She soon recovered a little but needed help. Barun brought her to his home as she was convalescing. I had visited them when I was in Delhi.

It was quite obvious that their relationship was blossoming. I was not sure if Barun was aware of this. We used to call him a good Samaritan as he always helped people.

I advised that he take Sahiba to Europe. I felt that the change would do Barun some good as well. They had returned quite happy after the trip. After two days, Barun had told me that they had decided to marry. I was delighted. Had I not been busy with the upcoming board's annual meeting, I would have certainly attended the wedding.

I had asked Barun to join me in the Washington office to help me out with the meeting. After he told me about his marriage, I invited them to spend some time here for their honeymoon. My wife and I also invited them to spend some time with us after that. Barun could then help me out for the meeting in our Washington office.

They accordingly visited LA and San Francisco first. After spending a week there, they came down to Washington. Edna and I went to the airport to receive the couple. I was so happy to see them as a married couple. They were put up in a hotel. When we were busy at the office, Sahiba would go down to meet Edna. They would also often go to shop. Edna said that Sahiba was a warm person and she loved meeting her. They became good friends in no time.

I personally liked the innate innocence on her face. Her eyes seemed to be smiling all the time.

Edna tells me that Sahiba talks about Barun all the time. Sahiba once said, 'Edna, I feel that I am so lucky to have found Barun. He had caused change in the way we used to live in the primitive village of obscurity. Also, the dacoits, who were Rakhi brothers of my mother, had helped me escape to the St. Joseph's Convent. Today, it is a dream come true when he touches me because he taught us to dream.

When we were in Europe, we were on *The Sound of Music* tour. The picture of Abbey reminded me of my days spent at the church. I suddenly realized that I was climbing mountains. I had to ford the streams. I had to follow the rainbows till I found my dream. Then, I gradually realized that I had found my dream.

You know Edna, my great grandmother, the princess Sahiba had to escape with her man servant Sham Sher Singh to save her honour. In the forest, where they had taken refuge, she was struck with deadly malaria. This disease causes very high fever in the patient. Apart from some herbal medicine, the patient has to be bathed frequently to keep the body cool. This fellow had nursed her and saved her from certain death. The princess had told Sham Sher Singh that no person other than one, whom she would marry, could have touched her bare body. She felt that she was no longer pure. So, she had offered herself to Sham Sher Singh for marriage.

I now felt for the first time that Barun has stirred my soul with his benevolence and kindness. There couldn't be anyone else in my life to whom I could now belong. The question was not there of our two bodies but it was the relationship of inner self, between the two ageless souls. I cannot describe my joy now as I hold my dream in my hands.'

Having seen them together, I wish to salute their love. It was a story of intense love to which I wished to salute. That is why nobody could have seen any visible demonstration of their love.

It has been almost a month since their dream presence lifted our spirits. I had known Barun rather well. But I had never observed the depth of sensitivity which he exhibits in the way he loved Sahiba. This was a facet of his personality

I had not seen so far. Even though he was a bachelor, he loved life. No one could say that his former life was drab or dry. But today, he sparkled with divine joy. The innermost soul which stirred and touched Sahiba was truly divine.

I even heard Sahiba and Barun sing the beautiful number from *The Sound of Music* together.

*"Nothing comes from nothing,*
*Nothing ever could,*
*So, you stand here and loving me,*
*I must have done something good."*

I had no true understanding of divinity so far. But seeing both of them, it was quite apparent that their love was pure. It did not involve their bodies. Their love was at the level of the inner self or soul that brought inner bliss.

The love, coming out of that bliss, was glowing all the time on their faces. It is said that such people created an ambience all round them, and it left an air of well-being and love for all. It was quite evident seeing them together how the glow or radiance of benevolence of Barun had reached unscalable heights and how Sahiba, under its glow had emerged from obscurity and blossomed into a fine and shining example of god's will and his indulgence. Frankly speaking, I had never witnessed such a beautiful relationship in my life and my understanding hitherto was not good enough to feel and appreciate the divinity it emitted.

Just a day before they were scheduled to depart, Sahiba told Barun that Didimoni would stay to take care of her aunt.

Edna had not seen Taj Mahal before and wanted to.

Barun immediately invited us and said that he would organize a visit whenever she came to Delhi.

'People say that Taj looks best during a full moon night. We can all go together. Sahiba has also not seen it. After all, it is supposed to be a symbol of love.'

## III

They were in Delhi for the next three years. They lived happily together.

I too visited Delhi with Edna. We all went to Agra to see the Taj. Our plan was to spend a night at Agra to see the Taj Mahal on a full moon night.

The view of the Taj Mahal was splendid. The white marble glowed as the moon beams reflected off it.

I said, 'It is great to see how an emperor built such an exquisite piece of art in memory of his beloved queen.'

Barun said, 'There are many views on this. Some say that by building this beautiful Taj Mahal, the emperor honoured all the lovers who had lost their beloved ones. Then, a famous poet has said that the emperor had actually insulted the poor lovers who could not afford to build a Taj Mahal.'

I laughed on hearing this.

'You know, Nick. Many beloveds ask their lovers to build a Taj Mahal in their memory.'

'What rubbish? I don't want to die for Barun to build a Taj Mahal for me,' Sahiba said laughingly. All of us laughed.

Then Barun said, 'You know, it is actually a grave. So many people won't keep its replica in their homes. It is said to bring bad omen. Another interesting thing. The emperor had the hands of all the craftsmen cut so that another Taj Mahal could never be built again. So, it won't happen, dear Sahiba.'

Edna and I laughed at their banter. They still behaved like newly-weds and it was warm and loving to be in their company.

While we were having dinner, Barun said, 'Nick, I often wonder what was the need to build such an expensive memorial. Did the emperor want to show off how much he loved her? Whatever for? The love is so personal. I am sure neither Sahiba, nor I will be telling everybody how much we loved each other. It is ridiculous. Who cares if he loved his queen so much? People today come to see Taj Mahal for its architectural beauty—not for the love!'

Edna and I looked towards him in awe and amazement. Sahiba looked away with an enigmatic smile. Barun often did this. He had the power to lift a discussion to a higher plane. It was not easy for common people to comprehend such lofty ideas. But I am sure Sahiba shared such lofty thoughts.

Anyway, I felt that both of them were perfect hosts. They made us really comfortable with their hospitality.

## IV

I had found a good and reliable aide in Barun. Thus, when his tenure with the bank was coming to a close, I told him that we would extend it further. He thanked me but said that he did not wish to continue. I was taken aback. He had never before given any indication that he wanted to quit.

I asked, 'I am sorry to hear that. But tell me, if you don't mind, what are you going to do now?'

He laughed on the phone and said, 'I will be climbing mountains.'

I did not understand, so I asked him, 'Climbing mountains? What do you mean?'

'Nick, I am going to Rishikesh in the Himalayas.'

'I am sorry, Barun but you can't be climbing the Himalayas at this age,' I persisted.

He laughed and said, 'No. No mountaineering of a physical kind, Nick. It is spiritual climbing. I have found that I am stagnating at this physical level. I have done what I could. But I must seek greater heights in spiritual understanding.

You remember, Sahiba had told me that I had stirred her soul. It meant our understanding and love could not be at the physical level. Sahiba has already climbed many mountains. She had told me that our meeting after two decades was ordained. God had brought us together to deliver a message.

I did not understand the import of that statement. If some message had to be given, it could not be that we were an ordinary husband and wife who live for procreation alone. The vow we took in our marriage to be one in flesh could not be true. As souls, both of us had a separate trajectory to follow. Both of us, that way, are unique. That must be the real message, I suppose.'

'I can't tell you, Nick. I don't know how many mountains I still have to climb, or how many streams I have to ford, or how many rainbows I have to follow before I reach where god wants me to be. God says both of you are not ordinary. Both of you have been extraordinary already. That means it has to be a further extension of our efforts to reach our dreams. It can't be an ordinary dream, Nick. I hope, you understand.'

I said, 'Barun, it is all beyond my comprehension. What is Sahiba going to do?'

Barun spoke very softly, 'We have discussed it together. I had told her if we have a child, we would be raising him or her. Then what about the message god wanted us to convey? That means we live the life of ordinary couple. She did not say anything. But she realized that she had to look further and beyond children alone.

'She said that for so long she has only received from others. She could not be bogged down and cling to her own life and family now. She says she is now content. She has everything. It is now time for her to go back and repay and help other children shape their futures. She says if she does not, she will be in eternal debt. She plans to go back to the St. Joseph's Convent and be a teacher at the school. She says she will help children dream and then help them realize their dreams.

'I had once told Sahiba that I didn't have a dream. But unless I climbed mountains, I shall never know what dreams can look like. So, we need to follow our separate trajectories. Nick, both of us do not have parents. So, Shiv Baba says he is the Supreme Father. I need not worry. So, we have no worries at all now. But I thank you and Edna. Both of you have been so good and kind to us. May god bless you.'

I was not clear as to what message they wanted to convey. It was certainly love, adventure, courage, trust, sacrifice and service to humanity—like the good Samaritans they were. But there must be more to it. Inscrutable are the ways through which god works.

So, I thought that we have to wait. We will soon discover more about their journey. I haven't heard anything from them since. For the first time I cried. I will remember their adieu for all time to come.